ROBERT MUSIL &
THE CULTURE OF VIENNA

Hannah Hickman

OPEN COURT PUBLISHING COMPANY
La Salle, Illinois

OPEN COURT and the above logo are registered in the U.S. Patent and Trademark Office.

Published by arrangement with Croom Helm, Ltd., Beckenham, Kent.

© 1984 by Hannah Hickman

First paperback printing 1991

Printed and bound in the United States of America.

Library of Congress Cataloging in Publication Data

Hickman, Hannah, 1928–
  Robert Musil and the culture of Vienna.

  "Published by arrangement with Croom Helm, Ltd.,
Beckenham, Kent"—T.p. verso.
  Bibliography: p.
  Includes index.
  1. Musil, Robert, 1880–1942. 2. Authors, Austrian—
20th century—Biography. 3. Vienna (Austria)—Intellectual
life. I. Title.
PT2625.U8Z735 1984   833'.912 [B]   84-5097
ISBN 0-87548-419-0
ISBN 0-8126-9156-3 (pbk.)

CONTENTS

ACKNOWLEDGEMENTS

The preparation of this book would not have been possible without help from many sources. At the University of Manchester, I was introduced to Musil's work by Professor Idris Parry, and encouraged in the earlier part of my research by Dr Raymond Furness. The late Mrs Eithne Kaiser of the Robert Musil Research Unit, University of Reading, provided essential help by making unpublished materials available to me. Professor Dr Karl Dinklage, Director of the Robert-Musil-Archiv, Klagenfurt, generously supported my work with three study visits, and by giving me books and photocopies of texts, including Musil's PhD thesis. Other help has come from Dr Josef Strutz of Klagenfurt. Professor Dr Marie-Louise Roth of the Arbeitsstelle für Robert-Musil-Forschung, University of Saarbrücken, and President of the International Robert Musil Society, has provided constant and positive encouragement. During a visit to the United States, Professor Herbert Lederer of the University of Connecticut, Mrs Janis Solomon of Connecticut College and Professor Wilhelm Braun of the University of Rochester were particularly helpful. Finally and most vitally, Mrs Eileen Grimes contrived to type a clear manuscript from a less than clear original.

I should like to acknowledge the help and support of all these and others; to express my very deep gratitude to Miss Nell Gill, whose generosity enabled me to undertake this research in the first place; to my family for constant interest, and to my husband for his constructive criticism, support and patience.

Note on Translations

Where English translations of works by Musil and other authors are available, they are listed. Translations in the text are sometimes quoted from these, but may be adapted. Other translations are my own.

For a list of abbreviations used, please turn to the Bibliography.

INTRODUCTION

Robert Musil (1880–1942), the Austrian novelist, achieved fame in Germany and Austria for a few years after 1930 and was then virtually forgotten until 1949, when an article in the *Times Literary Supplement* saluted him as the most important writer in German of his time.[1] From then on his works began to reappear in the original German, while English and French translations of his major novel soon followed; nevertheless, even in his own country he was not until recently widely known. Though now regarded as a writer, Musil was in fact a man of many parts. His great novel, *The Man without Qualities*, is a vast panorama of life in Vienna immediately before the outbreak of the First World War. Were this novel nothing but a portrait of a doomed society, it would still be remarkable for its brilliant observation and sure command of language, but it is much more than this. It represents nothing less than the attempt to chart the possible life of a truly Modern Man, one who has freed himself from all the constraints of society, religion and convention, has studied widely, thought deeply, and who seeks to fashion his life according to the logic of reason and of feeling at one and the same time.

Who or what was Musil? Scientist? Philosopher? Psychologist? Those who encounter him for the first time are by turns baffled and spellbound. It seems impossible at first reading to grasp the sweep of his mind, to follow the procession of characters in his *Comédie Humaine*, even to decipher his enigmatic chapter headings. Yet we sense in his great novel a wisdom and knowledge which make us curious to proceed, all the more so since it is at times exceedingly funny. It soon becomes apparent that here is a major writer. What else did he write? What help is to be gained from knowing the circumstances of his life? The present volume is intended as an introduction to Musil's work for the English-speaking reader. The English translation of *The Man without Qualities* has recently once again become available; his first novel and some of his stories have also been translated. A great deal has been written, mainly in German, on aspects of Musil's fiction and his two plays. *The Man without Qualities* in particular, huge and unfinished though it is, has a tantalising fascination for its readers; its underlying ideas

1

elude classification and so, indeed, does the author. Much of what he writes appears sane, matter-of-fact, logical, and yet he leads the reader to extreme situations and outrageous conclusions.

An attempt will be made in this book to trace the development of Musil's mind not only in his literary work, but also by reference to his notebooks, essays and other writings. His mind is truly creative in its constant endeavour to explore every possibility of interaction between themes, characters and situations. Yet it would be far from the truth to see all this activity as merely a kind of 'free play'. Not only is Musil keenly aware of the philosophical, scientific and psychological ideas of his time, but he abandoned a promising career in engineering in order to study these ideas at first hand. The intellectual basis of his work is evident, and the notebooks in particular bear witness to the way he grapples with thinkers and ideas; moreover, they show him as an acute observer of political events in the first half of the twentieth century. However, the notebooks provide only a foundation for his writing; if his work consisted of nothing more than a kind of *Encyclopedia of Twentieth-Century Thought*, it would have been forgotten long ago. The appeal of his finished work lies in the combination of the intellectual framework he constructs for himself with superb use of language, telling irony and the ability to create representative characters who move in a sometimes stately, sometimes frenetic dance within their world, aspects of which strike us as disconcertingly familiar.

In this study the literary works will therefore be considered in the context of his other writings and of his life, all quotations being given in English translation. The plan of the study is largely chronological, although the biographical sections take up a relatively small amount of space. Attention will also be paid to precursors and contemporaries whose influence Musil acknowledged, or who may be shown to have affinities with his thinking, for example Nietzsche, Emerson and Mach. It follows that in such a survey the fiction and two plays cannot be treated in as much detail as in a purely literary study; the bibliography gives indications for further reading. On the other hand it is hoped to suggest links with other disciplines, and to show, however tentatively, that Musil's work and thought have a contribution to make to present-day thinking comparable to the effect produced when Book I of the major novel appeared in 1930. The tensions between intellect and feeling, science and art, action and contemplation, which in one form or another appear in all his writings, are not confined to the lives of his fictional characters, but affect our own lives too. The appeal of his great novel lies at least partly in observing recognisable types of modern society, and in the depiction of situations strikingly similar to some we encounter today. The questions surrounding the relationship between individual and society, indeed the very existence of identifiable individuals in modern society concern us as much, if not more, than his readers half a century ago. The Austro-Hungarian empire with its ossified social and political systems and its inability to adapt to modern needs, bears some resemblance to the world in which we find ourselves. Musil's various Utopias and his attempts to work them out in the lives of his characters illuminate our own problems and challenge us to find effective solutions in our turn.

In an interview published in 1926 Musil was asked to sum up his intentions in writing *The Man without Qualities*. He replied: 'To provide help in understanding and coming to terms with the world', describing the novel as an attempt both to dissolve the existing world and suggest a possible new synthesis of its elements.[2]

Robert Musil was born on 6 November 1880 in Klagenfurt, capital of the Austrian province of Carinthia. His father, an engineer, later became professor of machine construction at the Technological University of Brünn (Brno). His mother's home was Linz; her father was one of the builders of the first European railway, between Linz and Budweis (České Budějovice), and one of its superintendents. Musil, an only child, was sent from the age of twelve to military boarding schools; the external action of his first novel, *Young Törless*, reflects this period. At seventeen, however, he left his second school and enrolled at the Military Academy of Technology in Vienna. From 1898 he studied machine construction at the Technological University, Brünn, in his father's department, and gained his degree in engineering in 1901. After a year of compulsory military service, Musil took up a position as assistant to the professor of engineering at the Technological University of Stuttgart.

This year in Stuttgart, 1902–3, proved to be a decisive one in the young man's life. The high hopes with which he had taken up the assistantship, lowest rung on the academic ladder, soon gave way to boredom and disillusionment. He began to feel with increasing force the one-sidedness of a view of life in which nothing was considered of any value except what could be measured and quantified. Although he had done well in his engineering studies, he became more and more convinced that other aspects of life, equally important, were being suppressed by the positivistic outlook of the older generation. Under the influence of Darwin and Nietzsche, Musil and his contemporaries could no longer share the confidence of their fathers in the ability of the intellect to explain the universe. While Darwin's 1859 *Origin of Species* had shocked believers by denying the divine creation of man, it also appeared to show that human beings could make few claims to distinction from, or superiority over, animals, a shattering blow to self-esteem which affected their sense of identity, and their faith in the powers of the intellect. Nietzsche had taught that over-emphasis on the intellect at the expense of the instincts was largely responsible for the ills of Western civilisation. Further, the increasingly mechanised and impersonal character of industrial processes and urban life seemed to many to deny previous optimism based on a belief in progress. At the same time, the novels of Dostoevsky, widely read in Germany and Austria, provided insight into minds under stress, and his analysis of the often unconscious processes leading to criminal actions revealed an aspect of human nature glossed over by earlier novelists. In a rather different way, Wagner was also engaged with the unconscious, by using long orchestral interludes in his operas to evoke in the audience emotions of which they would not normally be aware. All these influences combined to make the educated public acquainted with the idea of the unconscious and the problems associated with it.

The word *unbewusst* was first used in German in 1776. In English, the term 'unconscious' occurs as early as 1751.[3] From the eighteenth century onwards both philosophy and medicine became increasingly interested in this field, and discussion was furthered by the publication in 1868 of Eduard von Hartmann's *Philosophy of the Unconscious*, which was soon translated into French and English. Musil read the book as a young man and refers to it in the early notebooks; he is particularly interested in Hartmann's comments on the role of the unconscious in artistic creation. Bergson, who published his *Time and Free Will* in 1889, influenced French and other writers of the period; his remarks concerning the soul, the 'other life', are echoed in Maeterlinck's essays *The Treasure of the Poor*, which speak of 'another, inexpressible life'.[4] Musil knew these essays well, and chose a passage from one of them as the motto for *Young Törless*.

Although Musil's education up to the year 1901 had emphasised science and technology, he was well aware of the prevailing literary fashion in Vienna, where the poets known collectively as 'Young Vienna' were strongly influenced by French symbolism. The work of these poets, Schnitzler, Hofmannsthal and others, with its attention to the individual, his moods and sensations, has been called neo-Romantic. Some of Musil's earliest extant sketches attempt to follow the neo-Romantic mode, and a draft letter of 1903, written in Stuttgart, undertakes a systematic comparison between a poem of 1860 and one on the same theme of 1897, stressing the latter's greater sensitivity and ability to suggest unspoken overtones.[5] Many entries in the notebooks for these years show his active critical interest in literature, in the function of language, the psychology of the unconscious and related topics. These were questions that were in the air. The optimism of the nineteenth century, with its faith in the assured supremacy of man, was being challenged both in science and literature. In Austria-Hungary such tensions were felt perhaps more keenly than in any other European state: many of its citizens were uneasily aware that the empire, based on an outdated feudal system presided over by an aged emperor, could not endure against the active nationalism of its subject peoples and the demands of new social groups. Austria, Musil said later, could indeed be called 'a particularly significant example of the modern world'.[6]

Thus the frustrations of the political and social background, together with the disquieting realisation that life was anything but stable and permanent, that an unconscious life accompanied its external manifestations, but that language lacked the means to express it, all gave urgency to the attempts of those who were young in 1900 to find new ways of understanding existence. The young Wittgenstein grew up in Austria at the same period, and parallels between his *Tractatus Logico-Philosophicus* and Musil's first novel will be considered briefly in Chapter 2. When Freud's *The Interpretation of Dreams* was published in 1900, it caused widespread indignation by its open discussion of matters previously considered taboo in polite society. Nevertheless, Freud's approach to the study of sexual neuroses and their basis in the unconscious remained a scientific one, based on his clinical practice, while Wittgenstein composed the propositions of the *Tractatus* according to the strict rules of philosophical discourse, before saying of them on the final page: 'Anyone who understands me. . . must, so to speak, throw away the ladder after he has climbed up it.'[7] In a similar way Musil, in spite of external changes of emphasis during the course of his life, always remained true to the analytical methods of thought inherent in the nature of his mind, and reinforced by his early training. Looking back on this period he characterises the outlook of his generation as both 'morbid and technological'.[8] In spite of many, often conflicting currents of thought, these men saw themselves as members of a group, partly through opposition to the generation of their fathers, partly perhaps because the date 1900 seemed to herald a new beginning.

In the context of this ferment of new and contradictory ideas, Musil's disillusionment with his engineering post in Stuttgart grew ever deeper. The prospect of continuing his life in this career began to depress him profoundly, while at the same time he was grappling with all kinds of questions to which he was unable to find answers. So he began to write a novel incorporating some of his own problems in the problems of his characters, attempting to define them for himself by working them out in a fictional setting. *The Confusions of Young Törless*, to give it its full title, should therefore be seen against the wider background of doubt and transition, and in the perspective of the young Musil's growing awareness that he was at a turning-point in his life. The personal crisis of the author underlies the crisis of the protagonist. Problems which Musil had pursued in his reading and tentative earlier writings now assumed such importance that the direction of his entire existence was called into question: he had to clarify his ideas, and the writing of the novel provided the means of doing so. By November 1903 he had come to a decision: he gave up his post in Stuttgart and enrolled as a student once again, at the University of Berlin, to study philosophy, mathematics, physics and experimental psychology.

Notes

1. 'Empire in Time and Space', *TLS* no. 2491, 28 October 1949, pp. 689–90.
2. R. Musil, *Gesammelte Werke*, ed. A. Frisé, 2 vols., 1978, II, p. 942. Further references will be to GWI or GWII.
3. L. L. Whyte, *The Unconscious before Freud*, 1967, p. 66.
4. M. Maeterlinck, *Le Trésor des Humbles*, 1896, p. 164.
5. R. Musil, *Briefe 1901–42*, ed. A. Frisé with M. G. Hall, 2 vols., 1981, I, pp. 8–11. Further references will be to *Briefe* 1981.
6. R. Musil, *Der Mann ohne Eigenschaften*, GWI, p. 1905; *The Man without*

Qualities, trans. E. Kaiser and E. Wilkins, 3 vols., 1968. Further references to MwQ.

7. L. Wittgenstein, *Tractatus Logico-Philosophicus*, trans. D. F. Pears and B.F. McGuinness, 1974, p. 74.

8. R. Musil, *Tagebücher*, ed. A. Frisé, 2 vols., 1976, II, p. 1147. Further references to TBI or TBII.

1 DEVELOPMENT OF THE ANALYTICAL EYE: EARLY NOTEBOOKS AND INFLUENCES

During the course of Musil's first years in Berlin it is possible to discern two separate but related strands in his development. On the one hand lie his academic studies, culminating in 1908 in a doctoral thesis. On the other hand he was writing his first novel, published in 1906. Behind both these activities stand the notebooks, containing discussions, plans, sketches, and excerpts from books which interested him. Before turning to Musil's early novel it may be helpful to look at these notebooks, as they illuminate and complement all his other writing. This will also allow us to discuss his studies in Berlin, together with his thesis, and to consider the possible significance of these for his development as a writer.

Musil kept notebooks throughout his adult life; a few have not survived, and the earliest one of which the text is now available is no. 3, dating from about 1899, when he was nineteen. An abridged version of the notebooks was first published in 1955; in order to publish the volume at all, the editor had to omit large sections and particularly anything he recognised as a quotation. Yet the quotations are crucial if the reader is to gain a full understanding of the development of Musil's mind, and fortunately, a complete edition is now available. One of the most interesting sections of the notebooks for the early years is a series of sketches in no. 4 entitled *Monsieur le vivisecteur*. The title is significant: the term vivisection in the sense of psychological investigation was used by Nietzsche, Dostoevsky and Strindberg, whose work Musil knew. The original ambitious plan was for a whole book showing the figure M. le vivisecteur in the family, in society and so forth; on this first plan are found various titles as well as two important statements: 'To stylise is to see and teach others how to see', and: 'Paradoxes: let us for once turn everything back to front' (TB II, p. 813). Both these statements may be related to Musil's writing: the first shows his early awareness of the function of form, the second emphasises his fondness for paradox, a characteristic apparent in all his work.

The first complete piece bears the title 'Pages from the Night Book of M. le vivisecteur' (TB I, p. 1). The narrator looks out from his window at night: he sees nothing but white spaces and feels isolated, as if under a thick layer of ice, or like a mosquito imprisoned in rock crystal. He begins to analyse his own reaction, his reasons for preferring the night hours. Then, everything is clear, open, free of pretence and social obligations. At night, in contrast to the day, he can be honest with himself; he can act as his own historian or become the researcher observing himself as an organism under the microscope.

Another piece is entitled 'The Street' (TB I, p. 8). Here Musil engages in a kind of dialogue with himself. What is a street? Why, everyone knows that: straight, clear as daylight, it is there to enable people to move from one place to another. No, says M. le vivisecteur, a street may just as easily not be straight but crooked, with secret alleys, trap doors and subterranean passages, hidden dungeons and buried churches. How can others fail to be aware of this? Next, M. le vivisecteur analyses his own reactions, as in the first piece. If he sets himself a logical problem, his mind functions normally; but as soon as he turns to that strange part of his mind which functions not logically but by fits and starts, that which is called the life of the spirit, or the nerves, or by other names, then he is startled. This always happens whenever that incalculable part of himself begins to stir: like an untamed animal, it fills him with fear. After this, he remembers a dream. He had seen strange creatures, related to people met in the daytime, but oddly different, with certain aspects of their personality wholly dominant. He returns to the idea of himself as *vivisecteur*. He sees through things and through people: 'In all things you look beyond the external form in which they present themselves, and sense the mysterious processes of a secret life'.

These two pieces are remarkable in several ways. They probably date from 1900; indeed in the first one the author speaks of a January night and the beginning of the twentieth century, which could well be meant literally. This kind of writing is hardly what one would expect from a nineteen-year-old student of engineering. Admittedly, the cultural background, time and place are bound to influence the preoccupations of anyone trying his hand as a writer, but whereas some of Musil's earliest sketches unquestionably lean towards the literary 'decadence' then in vogue, the tone of the *vivisecteur* pieces is observant, clear and analytical. In fact, the two types of writing alternate in the early notebooks to such an extent that Musil's later polarity between 'exactitude' and 'the soul' is seen to be present from the outset. The second piece is particularly

striking in its juxtaposition of normal logical thinking and specu-
lations concerning the functioning of the unconscious, in its
dramatic presentation of the fact that these two aspects of the
human mind apparently can and do coexist without difficulty. The
first piece contains echoes of the widespread research into animal
psychology of those years; a few pages later the author lists works
in this field by three writers, the first being *Mental Evolution in
Animals*, by G. J. Romanes, a psychologist and friend of Darwin
(1883, German translation 1885). The other two titles mentioned
are of publications by K. Groos (1896) and K. Lange (1897), who
were concerned with the observation of animals at play and with
the possibility of basing a new evolutionary theory of aesthetics on
the results of such studies (TB I, p. 13). The link between the
unconscious and animals remains important for Musil in his first
novel, as will be demonstrated.

The approach of the author in these pieces gives the first clear
indication of an attitude of mind fundamental to Musil's thought.
It is an analytical approach: he studies himself and his own
reactions, other people and their behaviour; he compares,
considers, relates and contrasts, all for the sake of greater clarity
and insight. The same approach is characteristic of Törless, the
protagonist of the first novel, and of Ulrich, the Man without
Qualities. So one may well ask why, if Musil was so interested in
such studies, he did not take up an academic career concentrating
on research in psychology? Much later he wondered himself
whether he should have done so. The point to stress here is that the
vivisecteur pieces were probably written two and a half years before
he began any systematic study of psychology, and thus demonstrate
the vital importance of such questions to his way of thinking.

Another reason why these early pieces are significant is that they
provide evidence of the extent to which Musil as a young man was
influenced by Nietzsche. Most of the writers of his generation felt
Nietzsche's influence, two examples being Thomas Mann and
Hermann Hesse; indeed, Michael Hamburger speaks of Nietzsche's
'central and seminal relevance to all that has been thought and
experienced in the last hundred years'.[1] Nietzsche's incisive
language and independent views proved immensely attractive to
Musil, who read him first after leaving school and again four years
later. Some of the central imagery in his early writing may be
related to Nietzsche's work, as for instance the image of the
isolated explorer looking out over a wintry landscape which

recurs in the early novel and may be linked with Nietzsche's *The Genealogy of Morals*.[2] Even more important for Musil is Nietzsche's psychological awareness, as when he speaks of the relationship between feeling and intellect: 'rapid combinations of feelings and thoughts, which finally . . . come to be experienced no longer even as complexes, but as units . . . in fact they are rivers with a hundred sources and tributaries. Here too . . . the unity of the word does not guarantee the unity of the concept.'[3] This is a truth which strikes the young Musil with the force of revelation. In *Monsieur le vivisecteur* he writes: 'Yet all words have so many underlying meanings, double meanings, underlying feelings, double feelings, that it is best to keep away from them' (TB I, p. 2), and this realisation later overwhelms Törless at a dramatic moment in the first novel.

Thus even at this early stage Musil was very much concerned with perception of himself and the world around him. Another writer who exerted a strong influence in Austria at this period was the Belgian Maurice Maeterlinck. It is not possible to say definitely whether Musil had seen any of his plays at this time, but he certainly read Maeterlinck's two volumes of essays, *The Treasure of the Poor* (1896) and *Wisdom and Destiny* (1898), both translated into German before the turn of the century. Maeterlinck, one of the symbolist writers, explored in his first volume of essays the nature of 'the soul', 'the spirit' — in other words, the unconscious and its relationship to our conscious life. Linked with this is the relationship between feeling, intellect and language. The essays are speculative and sometimes repetitive; their value to the student of the history of ideas lies to a large extent in the way Maeterlinck interprets ancient and modern writers on these topics for the benefit of his readers. Two of the writers to whom Maeterlinck refers most frequently are Novalis, the German Romantic poet and scientist, and Emerson, whose influence in Europe was at this time considerable. Musil in his turn mentions Maeterlinck, Novalis and Emerson repeatedly, and it is possible to show close links between these writers and his first novel.

Emerson and Maeterlinck are mentioned together quite early in Notebook 4 (TB I, p. 17), and shortly after this follows a long section (pp. 27–35) which offers revealing insights into the young Musil's thinking at this critical stage. In May 1902 he began to read Nietzsche for the second time after an interval of some years and, recalling the reverent feelings kindled by the first encounter, remarked that this would enable him to take a fresh and critical view of his own life (p. 19). At the time of writing, during his year of compulsory military service, he felt empty and despondent. Further entries include discussion of novels by D'Annunzio and other contemporary novelists such as Wassermann and Potapenko; Musil feels the need to write, but can no longer blindly follow the fashion. Somehow he must come to terms with the phenomenon of literary decadence. Moreover, the conflict between the intellect and the senses was for him a real and personal one; in the notebook he reproaches himself for a year in which, as he puts it, sensuality only produced a sense of failure. This is the moment he chose to return to Nietzsche. Occasional references to various works by Nietzsche are followed from October 1902 by detailed excerpts and paraphrases from *The Case of Wagner* and *Twilight of the Idols* under the heading 'The concept of decadence'.[4] By this time Musil had taken up his post in Stuttgart and this was the year he began to write his first novel.

In the first section of his notes Musil is interested in Nietzsche's comments on decadence and its opposite, in music, in love and in literature. After this comes a second group of excerpts, arranged under alternating headings: 'Decadence' over negative statements, and 'Conduct of life' over positive ones. The term 'Conduct of life', written in English, is derived from Emerson; it was the title of his last book, published in 1860. That Musil was familiar with Emerson's ideas is also apparent from other entries in the notebooks. Emerson's works had been widely translated into German from 1857, and his popularity in German-speaking countries rose to new heights in the years around 1900. Translations of the *Essays* and *Representative Men* were available before 1900 in popular series such as *Reclam*, and from 1902, Eugen Diederichs in Jena began to publish new translations of Emerson's major works, including *Conduct of Life* in 1903.[5] In the context of Notebook 4 Musil places the heading 'Conduct of life' over those statements by Nietzsche which emphasise an optimistic attitude to life, as opposed to the others describing decadence. He marshals the evidence for his own debate with himself by arranging Nietzsche's thoughts around the questions which affect him personally.

Taking these notes in conjunction with a revealing letter of 1902,[6] it becomes clear that Musil's central concern at this stage is his own search for a balanced attitude to life as a foundation for his own future. This is also, as will be seen, the central concern of the protagonist in *Young Törless*. The temptation to veer from over-reliance on the intellect to the opposite extreme faces not only the fictional character, but the young author too, both in his personal life and in his attempts to become a writer. What Nietzsche has to say, under the name of Wagner, about German society in the late nineteenth century and, under the name of Socrates, about Athens in decline, appears to Musil as directly relevant to the solution of his own problems. With Nietzsche's aid he resolves to fight against his own weaknesses.

Musil finds, however, that the issues are baffling in their complexity. Like Nietzsche, he is forced to acknowledge that he is part of the age of decadence whether he accepts it or not: 'One-sided overvaluation of reason implies insecure relationships, lack of confidence in the instincts. A symptom of decadence' (Nietzsche, summarised by Musil).[7] This is one aspect of the age, embodied in his novel in the one-sided rationalism of the adults. On the other hand, 'Schopenhauer's "denial of the will to live" is the instinct of decadence itself'[8] — a mood of resignation also found in the novel. The young Musil finds himself in sympathy with Nietzsche's fearless, heroic attitude: '*Conduct of life*: We others, we immoralists, have on the contrary opened wide our hearts to every kind of understanding, comprehension, approval. We do not readily deny, we see it as an honour to affirm.'[9] A contrary view is, however, also quoted from Nietzsche, again under the heading from Emerson: 'All unreason, all baseness stems from the inability to resist an impulse.'[10]

In spite of Musil's admiration for Nietzsche's fearless analysis of human nature, he is not prepared to follow him without argument, and reproaches him for speaking only of possibilities, without showing a single one worked out in detail. In this he makes a critical distinction between philosophers and creative writers, which he later extends to Maeterlinck, Novalis and Emerson (TB I, pp. 19, 150). Musil proceeds, in the first novel, to do what in his view Nietzsche has failed to do, yet he follows Nietzsche's line of thought in important aspects of the inner action, as well as incorporating elements from Nietzsche in the characters and imagery. The protagonist is shown as a fearless 'seeker after truth', like Ulrich in the later major novel. The figure of the victim Basini, by contrast, characterised as one who cannot resist any impulse, is the obverse of the disciplined, sceptical thinker whom Nietzsche presents as the ideal. In *The Case of Wagner*, Wagner himself is presented as a hypocritical rattlesnake; this may be linked with the figure of Beineberg in Musil's novel, whose association with the snake image will be explored later.[11]

This whole section of Musil's Notebook 4, omitted from the 1955 edition, thus shows him taking stock of his own situation, using statements from Nietzsche with help from Emerson. In view of other evidence that Musil was well acquainted with Emerson's work, it is revealing to find the following passage in 'Fate', the first essay of *Conduct of Life*: 'The riddle of the age has for each a private solution. If one would study his own time, it must be by this method of taking up in turn each of the leading topics which belong to our scheme of human life, and by firmly stating all that is agreeable to experience on one, and doing the same justice to the opposing facts in the others, the true limitations will appear. Any excess of emphasis on one part would be corrected, and a just balance would be made'.[12] This is in fact the procedure adopted by Musil: following Emerson's advice, he places the heading 'Conduct of life', over those quotations from Nietzsche which emphasise the positive capacity of man to choose and act for himself, while the opposing statements are headed 'Decadence'. In passing, we may note that Nietzsche himself was influenced by Emerson far more than is generally realised. He refers to the American writer several times and numbers him among the four masters of prose of the nineteenth century; but the relationship was probably much deeper than his published comments would suggest. It has been shown that Nietzsche owned four volumes of Emerson and had access to others, and that six passages in his works can be identified with marginal comments in his own copies of Emerson.[13]

Thus Musil, reading both Nietzsche and Emerson at this early stage in his life, found certain ideas presented by both writers. For example, Nietzsche's emphasis on the will as a positive force may be related to his knowledge of Emerson's essay 'Fate': 'Forever wells up the impulse of choosing and acting in the soul . . . So far as a man thinks, he is free'.[14] Nevertheless, there are considerable differences in the methods of the two writers, one of which is that whereas Emerson's ideas are always qualified by, and balanced against, other equally important ideas, in Nietzsche's philosophy themes are developed to their extremes.[15] We shall see in Chapter 2 that both Nietzsche's and Emerson's influence may be traced in *Young Törless*; later, in *The Man without Qualities*, the author was to incorporate the search for balance and the tendency to extremes in two of the central characters, Ulrich and Clarisse.

*   *   *

In November 1903, when just twenty-three years old, Musil embarked on his second University course, reading philosophy, mainly logic, physics, mathematics and experimental psychology at the University of Berlin. The choice of philosophy and psychology as principal fields of study naturally follows the direction of Musil's reading over the preceding years. In all the authors he had read, one of his main interests had been problems associated with perception of the world, of the self, the frontier between the conscious and unconscious, and the relationship between reason and intuition. As was seen earlier, a widespread desire for knowledge in these fields existed in the latter half of the nineteenth century amongst writers, scientists and the educated public.

The study of psychology in German and Austrian universities at this time had not yet become separated from philosophy. Perception had been a central focus of research in experimental psychology since the publication of Wilhelm Wundt's *Contributions to the Theory of Sense Perception* (1858–62). In this Wundt maintains that all psychology begins with introspection.[16] The development of modern psychology in Germany and Austria is traced by E. G. Boring in his *History of Experimental Psychology* (1929). Carl Stumpf, Musil's professor in Berlin, was chiefly interested in the psychology of music and research in the perception of sounds; but he was also concerned with other aspects of psychology. Stumpf's predecessor at Berlin had set up a small laboratory, and under Stumpf this expanded into a large and important institute. The chair at the University of Berlin was considered the most distinguished appointment Germany had to offer, and although Wundt at Leipzig was regarded as the foremost psychologist, Stumpf's many and varied activities from the time of his appointment in 1894 established him as an independent force. As well as continuing his research into acoustics and the science of music, he was joint founder of the Berlin Society for Child Psychology (1900), and he set up with Erich von Hornbostel the gramophone archives for records of primitive music. In 1907–8 Stumpf was honoured by the rectorship of the university.[17]

Musil's Notebook 24 contains work notes and excerpts from articles and books relating to his studies in logic and experimental psychology; Notebooks 11 and 15, covering the same period, contain more discursive material, including notes on philosophical questions, discussions with fellow students and so on. Before we consider Musil's psychological studies in more detail, an attempt must be made to describe the context in which these took place. E. G. Boring points out that from 1874 onwards, the year which saw the publication of two important books by Wundt and Franz Brentano, there had existed two approaches to experimental psychology: 'These two books . . . while both supporting the empirical approach . . . represented opposing views of psychology. Each became, therefore, a starting point for a tendency in psychology, and the two tendencies are still with us to-day. Wundt represents the empiricism of the laboratory, Brentano the empiricism of philosophy.'[18] Wundt's psychology was primarily 'an introspective psychology of sensory elements that enter into associations and other combinations. Its data were habitually called the contents of consciousness, and, for want of a better name, Wundt's systematic position may be characterised as the psychology of content. In these terms, the fundamental dichotomy in Germany is formed by the distinction between *content* and *act*, a distinction that reflects the difference between Wundt and Brentano.'[19] The *act* as defined by Brentano is a psychical one, and he divides these into three fundamental classes, acts of *ideating* (sensing, imagining), acts of *judging* (such as acknowledging, rejecting, perceiving, recalling), and the psychic phenomena of *loving* and *hating* (such as feeling, wishing, resolving, intending, desiring).[20] In Stumpf's terminology these were called *functions*.

Stumpf was a pupil of Brentano, but in his later thinking tended to accommodate both act and content. During the period when Stumpf was becoming established in Berlin, Edmund Husserl published his *Logical Investigations* (1900 *et seq.*); this book, dedicated to Stumpf, represents the beginning of phenomenology, a discipline that deals with pure consciousness by a method of immanent inspection. Husserl's main interest was not psychology, but his views influenced the work of Stumpf as well as later researchers. In two papers published in 1907, Stumpf worked out a classification of experience, summarised by Boring as follows:[21]

1. First there are the *phenomena*, sensory and imaginal data like tones, colors and images, which constitute the subject-matter of *phenomenology* (not strictly the same as Husserl's use of

this term)

2. Then . . . the *psychical functions*, like perceiving, grouping, conceiving, desiring, willing
3. Stumpf's third class is the *relations* (within or between phenomena, e.g. relations of coexistence, of sequence, or of difference)
4. Finally . . . Stumpf created a special class for the immanent object of the functions, and called these objects *formations* (*Gebilde*)

Thus Stumpf brought phenomenology into psychology, and eventually his pupils began an experimental phenomenology that formed the basis for the new *Gestalt* psychology.[22] Some of these researchers were Musil's contemporaries in Berlin, and it will be seen that he himself was extremely interested in their ideas, both as a student and in later years.

In Musil's Notebook 24 (1904–5) he quotes and comments upon Husserl's *Logical Investigations*, beginning with Volume I, noting firstly a discussion of probability (Chapter 4) and then a longer section from Chapter 7 concerned with the laws of causality and of logic.[23] Husserl's Chapter 7 includes a paragraph, noted by Musil, on the distinction to be drawn between perceiving a red object, where the particular phenomenon 'red' and the act of perceiving are combined, and 'red' as a general species. The following section is also partly concerned with visual perception, this time of spatial relationships: the example used being the drawing of a parallele-piped, a figure bounded by six parallelograms, with opposite pairs identical and parallel. Such a figure may be perceived first as a flat area on the page, then in three dimensions as a 'hollow box'.[24] Another section of notes on Volume II of *Logical Investigations* relates to Husserl's polemics against the British philosopher David Hume, concerning the latter's theory of abstraction and the relationship between impressions and ideas; Musil disputes Husserl's interpretation of Hume.[25] The next two paragraphs on Husserl deal with the latter's discussion of an article by Friedrich Schumann, a member of staff of the Institute of Psychology in Berlin, known for his writings on visual space-perception. This is precisely the topic under discussion in these notes, the question being whether parts of a drawing, e.g. of a square figure, can be perceived independently of the rest of the figure. Although the word *Gestalt* does not occur here, it is clear that the ideas of *Gestalt* theory play a part in the argument.[26]

Later in Notebook 24 Musil annotates other parts of Husserl's book, for instance a section on the changing significance of words. Musil chooses the verb 'to secure' and investigates various objects which may be secured: peace; a balance; a screw nut, etc. After a long discussion, during which general and specific meanings of this and other examples are considered, the notes survey the formation of judgements.[27] This whole section is interesting in view of Musil's later work in *The Man without Qualities*, where on a number of occasions words are similarly examined with regard to all their possible uses and shades of meaning.[28] The last substantial entry from *Logical Investigations*, following immediately upon the one concerning words and judgement formation, returns to Volume I and discusses Husserl's statements on logical thinking. Musil attempts to work out the relationship with illogical thinking, the difference between logical and natural necessity, and so on. This concern with the distinction between logical and illogical thinking and the relationship between them was already evident in *M. le vivisecteur* and is found throughout Musil's creative work and his writings on aesthetics, forming one of the central themes of his *oeuvre*.

In another part of Notebook 24 Musil states a theory by Helmholtz relating to the psychology of colour vision, and proceeds to work out its implications.[29] A little later on he mentions Fechner's *Elements of Psychophysics*. Fechner was the founder of psychophysics, the science of the functional and quantitative relations between physical stimuli and sensory events;[30] Musil's notes discuss the correspondences between different levels of stimulus and the resultant sensations. Two entries in the notebook record sessions with the tachistoscope, an apparatus which allows a researcher to test the attention span of a subject by showing sequences of letters for short, exactly controlled periods. Another piece of apparatus commonly used for experiments in visual psychology, particularly in colour perception, is the chromatometer or colour wheel. Musil, encouraged by Friedrich Schumann, designed and constructed a colour wheel, in the first instance for use by his friend Johannes von Allesch, later to become assistant at the Institute in Berlin and Professor of Psychology at the University of Göttingen. Such colour wheels had been used in psychological laboratories for some time; Musil improved the design so as to permit greater efficiency during the course of an experiment, and published the following description at a later stage:[31]

> Two coloured discs, each of which is slit along one radius, are mounted on a motor-driven rotating axle in such a way that the coloured surfaces relate to each other in the desired ratio. The wheel is then set in motion, and as soon as the rotation speed is high enough, the eye perceives the intended colour mixture. The disadvantage of the older versions of this apparatus had been that they had to be stopped and re-set whenever it was desired to alter the proportions of the basic colours to each other. The new colour wheel however allows the experimenter to make changes during the course of rotation. This is achieved by mounting one of the coloured discs on the axle itself, the second one on a movable sheath placed around the axle. By adjusting a metal screw it is possible to change the position of the second disc in relation to the first during the course of rotation, and thus to produce every possible colour mixture obtainable from the two basic colours.

Musil's colour wheel was a great improvement on the one previously in use, since in contrast to the latter it was made entirely of metal, was equipped with numbered scales for exact setting and could be re-set during an experiment, as described. It was subsequently manufactured by the firm of Spindler and Hoyer in Göttingen and appears in their catalogues for the years 1908 and 1921.

Some other notes made by Musil at this time are based on an article by Stephan Witasek, a member of the Austrian school of psychology. The first Austrian laboratory for psychological studies was established in 1894 at the University of Graz by Alexius Meinong, a pupil of Brentano. Witasek studied with Meinong at Graz and remained there for the rest of his life. One of the most important concerns of these researchers was perception. Is perception to be thought of as nothing but a composite of sensations or elements, only distinguished in terms of quality? Problems of space-perception and temporal perception cannot be fully resolved by this method. Ernst Mach, in his *Analysis of Sensations* (1885), pointed out that form is in itself an experience independent of quality. 'You can change the colour or the size of a circle without changing its circularity, its shape in space; you can change by transposition the actual notes of a melody without changing the melody, its shape in time. Form is independently experienced; experience is sensation; therefore there are sensations of form.' After this, Christian von Ehrenfels, who had studied with Brentano and Meinong, published in 1890 a paper that created the concept of form-quality (*Gestaltqualität*). 'His problem was to answer the question as to whether form in space and time is a new quality or a combination of other qualities, and he decided in favour of the former answer.'[32]

The article by Witasek quoted and discussed by Musil concerns extensions of the doctrine of form-quality, and in particular the existence of complex perceptions.[33] As an example he gives the notes of a melody. If we analyse the content of a melody, we arrive at the components, i.e. the notes. In doing so, however, we lose a part of the content which cannot be isolated: the form-quality. Only when this is combined with the perceptions of the separate components may a complex perception be said to exist. Other entries deal with the question of imageless thought and refer to an article by Meinong in the same field.

During Musil's time as a student in Berlin, he came to know a number of men who later worked in *Gestalt* psychology. The 'new' school of this psychology was founded in 1912 by Max Wertheimer, Wolfgang Köhler and Kurt Koffka, all of whom had studied with Stumpf. Whereas the Austrian school sought to solve the dilemma of elementarism by finding a new element, i.e. form-quality, the Berlin school of *Gestalt* psychology denied the validity of assuming the existence of real elements. 'Its basal contention (was) that mental processes and behaviour cannot be analysed, since wholeness and organisation are features of such processes from the start.'[34] It began as a psychology of perception, but extended its investigations so as to cover learning and other aspects of the mental life. Musil knew Wertheimer, and later spoke highly of Köhler's book on static physical *Gestalten* (1920), which sought to extend *Gestalt* theory to biology and physics (GW II, p. 1085).

In addition to study notes, Musil's Notebook 24 contains some comments on literature and philosophy. In one entry however, in between comments on perception of various kinds, he applies the theory of wholes to creative writing and describes the process of attempting to formulate a thought: 'I am only partially conscious of the idea of the whole sentence, and the words come mechanically into my mouth and my consciousness. One may suppose that the unconscious intention is there, but the words often come of their own accord, and tentatively, often with corrections, the intention of the sentence unfolds in them and through them' (TB I, p. 123). Later in the notebooks and essays he considers the role of the unconscious in artistic creativity or in original thinking of any kind. Throughout his work numerous examples may be found of descriptions and imagery where the spatial relationships of the whole, the form-qualities, assume a symbolic significance as revealing as it is unexpected. The highly practical shape of a modern tram, for instance, is suddenly contrasted with the baroque contortions of the Plague Column in Vienna to emphasise the difficulty of whole-hearted allegiance either to the past or to the future.[35] A telescope is used to scrutinise isolated elements of a familiar street scene, with surprising results.[36] In an important essay on literature, dated 1931, the year after the publication of *The Man without Qualities*, Book I, Musil returns to the concept of *Gestalt*, relating it not only to form in art, but to skills and achievements of every kind, and particularly to language.[37]

*   *   *

Musil concluded his studies in Berlin with a doctoral thesis, *A Contribution to the Assessment of Mach's Theories* (1908). He first mentions Ernst Mach in 1902 while attempting to resolve the conflict within himself between the intellect and the senses, having come across his *Popular Scientific Lectures* (1896) just in time to remind him that the intellectual approach to life is, after all, of great importance: 'I never really doubted it' (TB I, p. 20).

Mach, who had contributed since the 1860s to early experimental work in psychology, particularly on perception, was a leading positivist thinker. His book *The Analysis of Sensations and the Relation of the Physical to the Psychical*, first published in 1885, attracted little notice at that time; between 1900 and 1902, however, it was published in three new editions which indicated widespread interest. Originally a physicist, Mach argues that things, bodies, materials cannot be perceived except through the complexes of colours, sounds etc. by which they strike the senses; analysis of the sensations received from the outside world is thus the only way to gain knowledge of phenomena. He sees all phenomena of the inner and outer world as consisting only of a small number of similar elements; the supposed entities, 'body' etc. are in his view only tools or concepts we invent to help us during the process of orientation. In the same way the self is only a concept invented as a tool for thinking purposes; in reality it has no separate existence: 'Once, on a clear summer's day in the open air, the world, together with my own self, appeared to me as a connected mass of sensations, only connected more densely in the self.'[38]

The fact that this work by Mach was so influential in the years after 1900 may be explained by a number of factors. In the first place his style is clear and vivid, and thus accessible to the non-specialist. Secondly, as we have seen, the relationship between body and mind, between reality and whatever might lie beyond it, had been investigated during the preceding decades by scientists, philosophers and psychologists, and highlighted by discoveries such as that of X-rays in 1895. At the same time, neo-Romantic and symbolist writing had explored the imprecise but nevertheless real area of moods and sensations, while impressionist and pointillist painters had concentrated upon the artist's subjective impression of the play of light and colours in the object of a painting. Hermann Bahr, the Viennese critic who had spent some years in France, called Mach's views 'the philosophy of impressionism'.[39] Hugo von Hofmannsthal, after attending some of Mach's lectures at the University of Vienna, found his self-confidence as a writer more and more undermined by the idea that reality, or what men had assumed to be reality, does not in fact exist. His growing despair and the resultant crisis are reflected in the essay known as the 'Chandos Letter'.[40]

Musil, concerned with problems of perception, at first found Mach's ideas attractive. As a trained engineer, and then a student in the Philosophical Faculty of the University of Berlin, he was particularly interested to examine Mach's claims that the empirical methods of the exact sciences were equally applicable to epistemology, the study of knowledge *per se*. In the text of his thesis Musil frequently refers to Mach's other works, *The History and Root of the Principle of Conservation of Energy* (1872), *The Principles of the Theory of Heat* (1900), *The Development of the Science of Mechanics* (1904) and *Knowledge and Error* (1905), as well as to the two books already mentioned. Musil's intention is firstly to set out Mach's fundamental beliefs relating to the theory of knowledge, and then to undertake a systematic examination of those beliefs from a philosophical point of view. Mach's ideas are summarised as follows:[41]

1. The task of the scientist is not to attempt an explanation of the world, but to seek knowledge by describing facts as minutely as possible.
2. The laws of causality do not, cannot exist, neither can concepts of 'things' or 'substances'.
3. The laws of nature do not imply necessity, but only relationships, and these are best expressed in terms of functional descriptions or equations.
4. Although science has thus given up its former objectives, it has now aquired a new one, for henceforth science should be regarded in the light of the theory of evolution. All its laws, concepts and theories then appear as economical aids to enable men to attain a satisfactory relationship with their environment.
5. Once this view is accepted, the difficult problem of the connection between psychic and physical aspects of life becomes irrelevant and may be disregarded.
6. This is made possible by recognition of the fact that the functional relationships which underlie the equations of science are in any case relationships between sensations or elements. These relationships and equations are found at all levels of existence, and to discover them is the new ideal of knowledge, derived from physics. Similarly, if psychology claims to follow the exact methods of science, it can only seek to establish such functional relationships, and its own concept of 'substance', i.e. the self or the soul, also becomes redundant.

   The given facts consist of elements in multiple relationships: some may be considered as part of physics, others as part of psychology; the distinction lies only in the method of observation and does not imply a dualistic division between body and mind.

Musil then proceeds to examine Mach's theories. It is not possible here to follow all his arguments in detail; however it may be stated at the outset that the question whether Mach's theories of knowledge are to be generally accepted is answered in the negative. Musil points to a number of contradictions in Mach's arguments. It might perhaps be said that his own references from Mach's works are selected with this purpose in mind; however, he unquestionably succeeds in showing that some of Mach's most ambitious statements are not supported by the stringent proofs which Mach himself demands. On the other hand, it is clear that Musil not only agrees with many of Mach's views, but is prepared to acknowledge that they represent leading ideas in contemporary scientific thought. The assertion that science, in the context of the theory of evolution, is to be regarded as a means of adaptation to the environment finds his full support (see Musil's thesis, pp. 13 ff.). The principle of economy lies in the fact that similar facts are grouped in the mind to form concepts, thus saving mental effort; this occurs in normal thinking, and, by extension, in scientific thinking. The procedure also implies continuity, another desirable goal. A further aspect discussed in this section of the thesis concerns mathematical methods, comparison, analogy and the inductive methods of experimental science (p. 19). Musil's creative work abounds with examples of comparisons and analogies between characters and situations, which will be discussed below in greater detail. His respect, even reverence, for the powers of mathematics endured throughout his life: 'Mathematics . . . (is) the new method of thought, pure intellect, the very well-spring of the times, the *fons et origo* of an unfathomable transformation.'[42] Ulrich, the man without qualities, having failed to achieve success in a military or a technological career, has finally become a mathematician before deciding to take a year's leave from his life. Even though the novel shows him passionately searching for another dimension to his existence, he envisages it as one that will complement, not replace, a mathematical outlook.

Thus, while he denies that Mach has succeeded in refuting orthodox epistemological theory, Musil welcomes his views as a clear exposition of modern scientific method (p. 31). Another section of the thesis considers Mach's treatment of the concepts of space, time and motion, which are presented not as absolutes, but as being possible only in relative contexts, i.e. in relation, for example, to another manifestation of a space. The argument here is that absolute space, time or motion cannot be found in experience and therefore do not exist (pp. 48 ff.). In view of these statements it is worth noting that Albert Einstein paid tribute to Mach, who had exerted a 'profound influence' upon his thinking in his youth.[43] Musil commends Mach's insistence on experience as a basis for theory; nevertheless he refutes the extension that *only* direct sense experience can be real (p. 53).

A further aspect of Musil's critique of Mach is concerned with the latter's arguments against the concept of causality. It is not possible to discover causes, only to establish connections between phenomena; thus modern science is concerned with representation of functional, instead of causal, relationships, and these are expressed in mathematical terms, primarily in differential equations (pp. 61 ff.). In this context Musil refers to important physicists of the period, such as Kirchhoff and Hertz, who claimed no wider validity for the equations representing the particular physical laws they had discovered beyond the validity inherent in the expression of those laws. Musil points out that such attitudes, as well as recent work on the nature of electricity, support Mach's contention that the purpose of scientific statements is not to explain, but only to describe.

The description of functional rather than causal relationships may equally well be applied to the human sphere, and in various works, particularly the two plays and the major novel, Musil makes use of the insights gained during his study of Mach. He recognises the complexity of action and interaction in human relationships and shows them in his fictional characters, especially perhaps in the area of morality, where circumstances, conditions, personalities and aims all play a part in influencing attitudes and decisions.[44] Nevertheless, Musil disagrees with Mach when the latter goes so far as to maintain that natural law or causality does not exist. Whereas Mach asserts that the connection of one fact with another resides solely in the functional equations that can be established between them, Musil says that such a connection must correspond to a real connection in nature (pp. 75–6). What the character of this connection, this natural law, may in fact be, is another question: Musil insists on the fallacy of assuming that analysis of sensations can reveal all facets of reality. He points out that the very exactitude of our thinking leads us to phenomena whose true structure we can never entirely apprehend with the means at our disposal (p. 123). Musil's scepticism is not confined, like Mach's, to 'traditional' concepts alone; it extends also to Mach's sweeping claim that adoption of the empirical methods of physics is capable of solving the problem of knowledge itself. Throughout the text Musil repeatedly points out that philosophical thinking on these topics is still changing and developing, and that no-one is yet entitled to claim that his opinions represent the last word on the subject.

Thus, in Musil's thesis, Mach, one of the most influential scientists of the age, was himself examined with true scientific scepticism. At the same time, it should not be forgotten that Stumpf, Musil's professor, held philosophical views opposed to those of Mach, being firmly based on a distinction between mind and matter, and emphasising psychical acts or functions. Naturally he was not very pleased to find his student supporting some of Mach's views, and it was only after repeated arguments that Stumpf could be persuaded to accept Musil's thesis.[45]

One of the greatest stumbling-blocks to an acceptance of Mach's theories is his abolition of the self or the mind. Mach calls it nothing but a useful concept, a tool invented for thinking purposes (p. 113); but if there is no mind, who or what does the thinking? Musil refuses to accept Mach's proposition that the basic elements of which matter is composed always remain constant, and only the method of observation determines whether in a particular case they are considered from the point of view of physics or that of psychology. According to Musil, Mach has not succeeded in proving the case for monism; therefore dualism must continue to be accepted (pp. 118 ff.).

Yet in spite of these reservations, there can be no doubt that Musil was stimulated and inspired by Mach's ideas. Echoes of his methods and his analytical approach are found not only in Musil's early works but throughout his mature writing, to such an extent that one may regard his study of Mach as the final stage in the metamorphosis of a scientist with literary ability into a writer with a scientific outlook.[46] More than a year before submitting his thesis, Musil had attracted public notice with his first novel, and to this we shall now turn.

Notes

1. M. Hamburger, *From Prophecy to Exorcism*, 1965, p. 48.
2. F. Nietzsche, *Werke*, ed. K. Schlechta, 1965, II, *Zur Genealogie der Moral*, pp. 761–900, p. 895(26); *The Genealogy of Morals*, trans. H. B. Samuel, 1974, vol. 13 of *Complete Works*, ed. Oscar Levy, p. 203.
3. Nietzsche I, *Menschliches, Allzumenschliches*, pp. 435–1008, p. 457(14); *Human, All-Too-Human* Part I, trans. H. Zimmern, 1974, *Complete Works*, vol. 6, p. 27.
4. TB I, pp. 27–35. Nietzsche II, *Der Fall Wagner*, pp. 901–38; *The Case of Wagner*, trans. A. M. Ludovici, 1974, *Complete Works*, vol. 8; ibid., *Götzendämmerung*, pp. 939–1034; *Twilight of the Idols* and *The Anti-Christ*, trans. R. J. Hollingdale, 1968.
5. R. W. Emerson, *Complete Works*, ed. E. W. Emerson, 1903, VI, *Conduct of Life*; *Lebensführung*, trans. H. Conrad, 1903.
6. Letter to Stefanie Tyrka, *Briefe*, 1981, pp. 5–7; also in TB I, pp. 21–2.

7. TB I, p. 32, from Nietzsche II, p. 955, *Twilight*, pp. 33–4.
8. TB I, p. 33; Nietzsche II, p. 968; *Twilight*, pp. 45–6.
9. TB I, p. 33; Nietzsche II, p. 969; *Twilight*, p. 46.
10. TB I, p. 34; Nietzsche II, p. 988; *Twilight*, p. 65.
11. Nietzsche II, p. 908; *The Case of Wagner*, p. 5.
12. Emerson VI, pp. 1–49; pp. 4–5.
13. F. Carpenter, *Emerson Handbook*, 1953, pp. 246–9.
14. Emerson VI, p. 23.
15. Carpenter, p. 248.
16. W. Wundt, *Beiträge zur Theorie der Sinneswahrnehmung*, 1862, p. XVI.
17. E. G. Boring, *A History of Experimental Psychology*, 1929, pp. 354–6.
18. Ibid., p. 605.
19. Ibid., pp. 377, 423–4.
20. Ibid., p. 351.
21. Ibid., pp. 357–8.
22. Ibid., pp. 359–60.
23. TB I, pp. 119–21; E. Husserl, *Logische Untersuchungen*, 1900, vol. 1, Chapters 4 and 7. Cf. further excerpts in TB II, pp. 69 ff.
24. TB I, p. 121; Husserl 1, Chapter 9.
25. TB I, pp. 123–4; Husserl 2, part 1, Chapter 5.
26. TB I, pp. 124–5; Husserl 2/I. Chapter 5.
27. TB I, pp. 127 ff.
28. GW I, e.g. pp. 517 ff.; MwQ, vol. 2, pp. 260 ff.
29. TB I, pp. 121 ff.; cf. H. Helmholtz, *Philosophische Aufsätze*, 1887. It was not possible to identify the exact source.
30. TB I, p. 126; cf. G. T. Fechner, *Elemente der Psychophysik*, 1860.
31. K. Dinklage, 'Musils Herkunft und Lebensgeschichte', in *Robert Musil. Leben, Werk, Wirkung*, ed. K. Dinklage, 1960, pp. 187–264, pp. 215–16. Further references will be to LWW. Cf. GW II, p. 944 (adapted).
32. Mach and Ehrenfels quoted by Boring, pp. 434–5.
33. TB I, pp. 131–2; S. Witasek, 'Über willkürliche Vorstellungsverbindung', in *Ztschr. f. Psych. u. Physiol. der Sinnesorgane*, 12, 1896, pp. 185–225.
34. J. Drever, *A Dictionary of Psychology*, 1969, p. 108.
35. GW I, pp. 871–2; MwQ, vol. 3, pp. 249–50.
36. Musil, 'Triëdere', GW II, pp. 518 ff.
37. Musil, 'Literat und Literatur. Randbemerkungen dazu', GW II, pp. 1203–25, pp. 1218 ff.
38. E. Mach, *Die Analyse der Empfindungen und das Verhältniss des Physischen zum Psychischen*, 1900, 2nd edn., pp. 5–21; *The Analysis of Sensations and the Relation of the Physical to the Psychical*, trans. C. M. Williams, revised S. Waterlow, 1959.
39. H. Bahr, 'Impressionismus', in *Zur Überwindung des Naturalismus*, ed. G. Wunberg, 1968, pp. 192–8, p. 198.
40. H. v. Hofmannsthal, *Gesammelte Werke*, ed. H. Steiner, 1945–59, *Prosa II*, 'Ein Brief', pp. 7–22; *Selected Prose*, trans. M. Hottinger *et al.*, 1952, pp. 129–41.
41. Musil, *Dissertation: Beitrag zur Beurteilung der Lehren Machs*, 1908, pp. 5–9, reprinted 1980; A Contribution to the Assessment of Mach's Theories.
42. GW I, p. 39; MwQ, vol. 1, p. 73.
43. P. A. Schilpp, ed., *Albert Einstein Philosopher-Scientist*, 1959, vol. I, p. 21. Quoted in A. Janik and S. Toulmin, *Wittgenstein's Vienna*, 1973, p. 133.
44. Cf. H. Arvon, 'Musil und der Positivismus', in *Robert Musil, Studien zu seinem Werk*, ed. K. Dinklage *et al.*, 1970, pp 200–13, p. 211. Further references to *Studien* 1970.
45. Dinklage, LWW, p. 217.
46. Arvon, p. 204.

2   THE DUAL VISION: *YOUNG TÖRLESS*

When Musil published his first short novel *Young Törless* in 1906,[1] the Berlin newspaper *Der Tag* in December of that year paid the relatively obscure student the compliment of a long and enthusiastic review. It was by Alfred Kerr, one of Germany's leading critics. After the novel had been rejected by several publishers Musil had appealed to Kerr, who advised him on various points of style and put in a good word for him at the Wiener Verlag. Yet the famous critic would scarcely have given the young author such positive support had he not seen real promise in the novel: 'The strength of his work lies in the unemotional . . . expression of hidden aspects of this life — which yet form part of it', he wrote. 'They have a right to be shown / The mood is not "painted", but arises from that which is presented', and so on, for eight columns.[2] Kerr gives an outline of the novel, pointing up its controversial subject-matter, concerned with sadism and homosexuality, justifying the manner in which the author treats such topics, and challenging the censor to do his worst. Not surprisingly, the work was afterwards understood by many to be written solely as a defence of homosexuality, something which Musil vigorously denied. Kerr had also praised its psychological acuity, and the perceptiveness with which the author presented a wide spectrum of states of mind in the central figure. Let us now consider the novel from these points of view.

At first reading, the work appears to be a rather sensational account of an episode concerning four adolescent boys. The protagonist, a boy of sixteen, is shown in a boarding school with a military bias, with two older boys who have strong, dominant personalities. Törless himself is shy, introverted, clever and has artistic leanings. A weak, effeminate boy commits a petty crime, and as a result is tortured and sexually abused by the two bullies. Törless becomes more and more involved, curiously unable to undertake independent action until near the end, when he warns the victim to expect yet more horrific tortures. The victim confesses to his theft and is expelled; Törless leaves of his own accord; and the school, with the two bullies, continues as before.

This outline summarises the outer action of one of the first novels of adolescence in Western literature, a story subtly observed and graphically told. It contains a good deal of autobiographical material and has rightly been interpreted as a strong criticism of the kind of educational establishment it portrays. In passing, we may note that the military boarding school Musil himself attended numbered amongst its pupils another famous literary figure, the poet Rilke, who has left a stark account of it in a short story entitled 'The Gym Lesson'.[3]

Musil's novel enjoyed an unexpected success, due at least in part to its frankness, considered scandalous in 1906, in describing the relationships between the four boys. The taboo in the society of that time on discussion of sexual matters was beginning to weaken, but very slowly. Arthur Schnitzler had been one of the first writers to defy it in his short stories and plays, for example *Anatol* (1893) and *Reigen* (filmed as *La Ronde*), published in 1900, but banned from stage performance for many years. Wedekind's *Spring's Awakening* (1891) was similarly banned by the censor until 1906, when it was staged in Berlin by Max Reinhardt. In the meantime, a number of medical publications, such as those by Krafft-Ebing and Hirschfeld, had openly discussed homosexuality and related topics. It was in this context that Freud during the 1890s formulated his theory of the sexual origin of neuroses. *The Interpretation of Dreams* (1900) is 'a historic landmark not only because it transmitted his work to a wider public than the medical profession but because here he lays the basis for his general theory of the power of sexuality and its pervasive presence in dreams, myths, art, in guilt feelings, sublimations, the super-ego and other reaction formations'.[4] In this work Freud put forward his theory of the Oedipus complex: 'It is the fate of all of us, perhaps, to direct our first sexual impulse towards our mother and our first hatred . . . towards our father.'[5]

Three years after *The Interpretation of Dreams* had met with a shocked reception, Weininger published *Sex and Character*. Weininger discusses the nature of the self and argues that sex determines character: a woman lives in the 'unconscious' state and is incapable of rational thought. He also suggests that homosexuality is at first only latent. Since all human beings contain masculine and feminine characteristics in varying proportions, *every* human being is a potential homosexual, according to the size of the share of the opposite sexual characteristics in his or her make-up.[6]

Since Musil's novel appeared in 1906, it has been argued that he must have known both *The Interpretation of Dreams* and *Sex and Character*. The notebooks of the time do not support this view, whereas other writers who interested him are freely quoted; nonetheless he might very well have seen reviews of these works. Musil's later references to Freud show considerable reservations, interpreted by some critics as evidence of a defensive attitude. Certain aspects of the early novel do have an affinity with the writings of Freud, but the same may be said of several other works of the period. In Austria before the First World War there was widespread uncertainty about all aspects of life; in a study of Schnitzler, Martin Swales comments: '. . . it is almost irrelevant whether writers of the time were directly influenced by Freud or not; his thinking is recognisably part of the spirit of the time.'[7]

Although the outer events related in the novel are indeed sensational, the reader's attention is soon caught by the inner action, tracing the development of the central figure, the boy Törless. Careful study of the text reveals that this inner development is closely linked to the boy's difficulties with perception and expression. Although the timespan of the novel is only a few weeks, the author uses a flashback technique to indicate that Törless had, from early childhood, possessed extraordinary sensitivity. His reactions to the people around him, to personalities, moods and physical characteristics, show an extreme sensibility; similarly he is aware of changes in his surroundings, of light and dark, trees and animals, benign or threatening moods in nature, to a quite remarkable degree. His basic problem lies in the fact that he can never succeed in expressing these experiences in words. This inability troubles him constantly, and eventually grows into an obsession; the discrepancy between the phenomena he observes all around him and the words available to express what he has perceived grows ever wider. Added to this is the fact that his parents, teachers and even his school friends appear not to notice any of the strange things he sees; the trees in a wood that seem to threaten him, or a wall in the school garden that appears to bend over and look at him silently. Törless concludes that he must be going mad, while his friends and others surrounding him are completely sane.

Suddenly the normality of the school scene is shattered by the petty theft, and the fact that the two bullies decide to exploit the culprit's vulnerability for their own purposes. Törless, forced to recognise that emotions and abnormality exist outside as well as in himself, is drawn into this outer action, but reluctantly. He is still preoccupied with his own problems of perception and expression; naturally a shy personality, the obsession with his quest for clarity seems to render him incapable of independent action. While the outcome thus remains uncertain, the author shows the boy seeking aid from various sources to help him understand the irrational and the unconscious. For a time he is drawn to Beineberg, one of the two bullies, a mystagogue who disguises his evil intentions behind a façade of quasi-philosophical tirades. When Törless receives no help from him, he turns to the mathematics master, who unfortunately is unable to offer an immediate solution to what he rightly describes as a philosophical problem, except by suggesting the works of Kant. Not surprisingly, the boy's attempt to unravel the *Critique of Pure Reason* founders on the footnotes. Eventually, Törless becomes involved with the thief, Basini, a weak, unreflective personality; for a time this boy holds an emotional fascination for him, but behind this lies the tempting idea that if he himself were to give up all questions and live from moment to moment like Basini, his own difficulties would disappear.

Meanwhile the outer action, with its suspicion, brutality and torture gathers momentum: a point is reached where even Törless, passive as he is, must see that if he continues to do nothing, Basini may be beaten to death. He warns Basini, who confesses his theft to the headmaster. There follows a stern inquiry; Basini is expelled, whereas Reiting and Beineberg succeed in evading all blame. Törless however, in the stress of being interrogated before the entire staff, is finally able to explain lucidly and cogently all that has troubled him for so long. All the words he needs are now at his command, and although he cannot yet answer all his own questions, he can at least express them and in doing so gains a new maturity.

Some interpretations of *Young Törless* emphasise the sociological aspects, seeing the novel as a critique of the prevailing system of education and, by extension, of the society maintaining that system. They point to oppression, cruelty and lack of regard for the individual in the outer action, particularly as shown by the two bullies, whom the author himself saw later as young precursors of the Nazi criminals.[8] Other interpretations concentrate on psychoanalytical aspects of the work and draw parallels with

Freud's early writings and those of Weininger.[9] While acknowledging the insights to be gained from these points of view, one may, however, try to approach the novel with a completely open mind, giving due recognition to its various elements. The horrifying outer happenings provide a framework for the intensity of the inner action, and the form, especially the imagery, is vital to the meaning of the whole.[10] Yet before considering the ideas and form of the novel, we should note certain elements in Musil's own life that may be connected with the writing of this work. Whereas no proof can be found that he was directly influenced by Freud[11] it has been argued that his own background might have predisposed him towards homosexuality. He had himself attended a school of the type he portrays, and the boy Törless is to some extent modelled on himself at that stage, while prototypes for the three other boys involved have also been identified.[12] The author denied however that the events took place in the manner related, and repeatedly stressed that his central interest lay in problems of perception and expression, and in the relationship between intellect and emotion, rather than in the outer action.

Nevertheless, it has been pointed out that Freud's later description of the possible origin of inversion in a mother fixation could very well apply to Musil himself.[13] His relationship with his own mother was not an easy one. She was a nervy, temperamental woman married to a quiet, reserved husband. A year after the birth of their son she met Heinrich Reiter, a teacher who became a friend of the family and in later years shared their apartment. The son's attitude to this 'intruder' is reflected in Musil's novella *Tonka*, to be discussed later. In this the young hero is constantly irritated by his mother's association with a similar figure. In autobiographical notes written towards the end of his life Musil refers to frequent quarrels with his own mother when he was about ten years old; eventually it was agreed to send him to boarding school.[14] His later attitude to his mother is mirrored in scattered notebook entries, such as those in Notebook 3. However, while the events of an author's life may be reflected in his work, it is the use he makes of his material which is of primary interest to his readers. Notebooks and essays illuminate the leading ideas and preoccupations at any one period, while influences that may be identified are helpful in following a particular train of thought. Events in his personal life obviously have a bearing on his work, but it is his creative writing itself, its ideas and the manner in which they are expressed, which must remain the focus of attention.

Returning to *Young Törless*, we may, however, consider the role of the boy's mother in the action. The author selects a few episodes to emphasise certain stages in the boy's development, gaining dramatic effect both from the manner of narration and from the placing of the episodes in relation to one another. At the very beginning of the work, the mother, an elegant lady, is shown taking an emotional farewell from her son at a railway station. Later that day, Törless and Beineberg visit Božena, the village prostitute. The author makes it clear that this is not their first visit, but that on each occasion, Törless had been filled with guilt and shame at the thought of what his parents might say if they could see him in the prostitute's dirty room. In his mind he regards his parents as models of propriety, and his mother, especially, appears to him as a pure angel above all earthly passions.

During the course of this visit Božena relates with evident enjoyment a story remembered from her time in the capital, showing Beineberg's mother in a compromising light. Törless, listening, is aghast. The prostitute's insinuating remarks concerning the other boy's mother make him suddenly aware that his own mother, regarded until now as an idealised, ethereal being, is a creature of flesh and blood, a woman like Božena. This insight fills him with shame, but he cannot dismiss it from his mind. He remembers occasions when his parents were walking in the garden together, their laughter, caresses — surely they too must experience the turmoils of love, in spite of their outward calm? He suspects unknown joys and feels excluded from their relationship with one another. They seem to be betraying him, just as he, in his visits to Božena, even in admitting a connection between the prostitute and his mother, has betrayed them. Bewildered and lost, the boy becomes easy prey for Božena.[15]

The unclear suspicion that his parents and all members of their highly respectable society must experience passions just as he does is confirmed by Basini's theft. Here is the proof that transition is possible between those who dwell in solid buildings and others uttering mad cries in tortuous passages; proof too that the two worlds lie very close to one another, with a borderline that may be crossed at any time. The letter in which his parents advise tolerance towards Basini further confirms these suspicions. The absolute standards he had hoped for, from them most of all, are lacking.[16]

Törless's horrified realisation that his mother is a woman like

Bożena coincides with his being involved ever more deeply in the intrigues of Reiting and Beineberg. In particular, the growing certainty that Basini, one of his schoolfellows, is a common thief, undermines his already fragile view of the world. The author devotes a considerable amount of space at the beginning of the work to a description of the boy's state of mind in his first years at the school, before the beginning of the present action. His sensibility and inventiveness are accompanied by an almost schizophrenic feeling of emptiness and lack of contact with others; only when he is writing or mentally occupied in some other way does he really come to life. Whereas a normally gregarious child is usually too involved in sport or group activities to worry overmuch about other people's lives, except in so far as they may impinge on his own, Törless in his inner helplessness seems to derive support from the belief that other people's behaviour is correct and therefore to be relied upon. When he learns, within a short space of time, firstly that his mother and the despised prostitute have much in common, secondly that a boy who shares his life at school is a criminal, his security is totally destroyed.

The opening sections of the novel also convey in a graphic manner the lonely existence of a young boy in a boarding school environment. Admittedly Törless is an unusually sensitive and introspective boy, but the author shows that the artificial isolation, a long way from home, intensifies his feeling of separateness. The school is reserved for the sons of the highest families in the land, is run on military lines and is situated in the depths of the country in order, as the narrator drily observes, to protect the pupils from the evil influences of the city.[17] Since neither his parents nor his teachers appear to understand or sympathise with Törless's wish to read literature and express himself creatively in writing, he is driven more and more into himself. The teachers are mostly soldiers, with a highly practical and utilitarian outlook, but even the chaplain and the mathematics teacher seem unable to appreciate that this particular boy perhaps needs to be treated in a somewhat more subtle manner than most of the others. The chaplain is kind but unimaginative; the mathematician genuinely tries to answer the boy's questions, but is himself so academic in his way of thinking that he cannot communicate with Törless at the latter's intellectual level.[18] As for his parents' attitude to things of the spirit, the narrator observes in a trenchant aside that this was largely responsible for his feeling of disorientation in the first place. At home the works of Goethe, Schiller and Kant were kept in a glass-fronted cabinet, never opened except on rare occasions. It was like the shrine of a deity, only reluctantly approached, and only worshipped because it was believed that thanks to its presence certain things could safely be neglected. Törless had been brought up to think that Kant had solved the problems of philosophy once and for all, while to attempt writing poetry after Goethe and Schiller was a waste of time. This warped attitude to philosophy and literature had had a serious effect on the boy's development by depriving him of the proper objects of his ambition. Left without a worth-while goal in life, he was easily dominated by Reiting and Beineberg. From time to time, however, his original interests reasserted themselves, leaving him each time with the feeling of having done something useless and ridiculous, and it was the constant conflict between his private inclinations and the rationalist and utilitarian ethos of the adult world which resulted in his insecurity and lack of confidence.[19]

Musil himself commented on the novel both at its time of publication and many years later. To those who assumed that his main concern was with the psychology of the adolescent, he replied that the choice of a youthful protagonist was nothing but a device to enable him to show the central problem more clearly than in an adult. Elsewhere he refers to the Maeterlinck motto which precedes the work as expressing the idea he wished to illustrate.[20] A letter written in March 1905, soon after the completion of *Young Törless*, illuminates his own view of the novel. The final section reads:[21]

A fact; The realm of the emotions and that of the intellect are incommensurable. Prime example: music. (How mistaken is the attempt to explain music by means of words and ideas!) This holds for all art . . . In other words: I know that at present I am the only person in this room to understand the painting, yet I do not know how or with what I do so. I can only convey my impressions with quite inexact words. And yet the certainty of understanding is quite indescribably strong . . . it is as if there were someone inside me to whom this painting speaks, whom it draws immediately into its circle etc., and that my real self which belongs to me (and we only think we belong to ourselves to the extent that we can intellectually understand ourselves) only grasps the shadow of this other being. *The self is literally split in two, it acquires a double floor and through the dim glass of the first and hitherto only one, we see mysterious movements without being able to interpret them.*

This seems to me a tragic experience. I took it as the real basis of my novel and called it *The Confusions of Young Törless*.

The letter confirms that the author saw problems of perception and expression as the central theme of the work. The experience of music and of looking at a painting cannot be expressed in words, at least not in adequate words. Yet the experience is overpowering; it speaks to another person within us, while our rational self only succeeds in grasping the shadow of this other, inexplicable self. The sensations described in the letter are in fact incorporated in the text of the novel: the boy remembers that on one occasion, standing with his father in front of a landscape painting, he had called out: 'Oh, it is beautiful', and had become embarrassed when his father was pleased. For he might just as easily have said, 'It is terribly sad'. 'It was a failure of words which tortured him then, a half-awareness that the words were only makeshift substitutes for what he had felt.'[22] Later in the narrative the boy recalls the powerful emotions associated with music: they were passions that had escaped out of the human beings, as out of cages that were too cramped, too commonplace for them. The music draws out the 'other' self from the cage of 'normal' existence.[23]

The two examples given in Musil's letter illustrate the many occasions throughout the novel where 'the self is literally split in two', and Törless sees not only himself but people, things and ideas in twofold form. Finally, after confusions and struggles he arrives at the point where, though he cannot explain, he can at least express what has troubled him and know that both rational and irrational ways of seeing the world have their own validity.

The dualism of intellect and feeling and the inadequacy of words to express what has been perceived, are the causes of Törless's deepest confusion. They affect him so profoundly that he suffers a split in his personality, a kind of schizophrenia. So long as he cannot solve this basic problem he does not know who he is; the inability to reconcile these two sides of his life seems to be tearing his soul apart, and, according to the narrator, remained the greatest threat to it for many years.[24] This fundamental handicap to the boy's development also renders him incapable of independent action. Quite early in the narrative we are told that his fertile mind could invent endless possibilities, but to select one of them as definitive and take action accordingly was beyond his powers.[25] This passivity continues throughout the novel to a point well beyond what most people would consider reasonable: Törless should either defend Basini against his torturers or warn him against them much sooner than he actually does. One commentator has interpreted this failure to act as moral ambiguity, almost an endorsement by the author of the sadism of Reiting and Beineberg,[26] but the matter is not so straightforward. Musil is concerned primarily with the development of the protagonist, and his curious inability to act, noted by the author as a problem in himself, recurs in other figures in his work, including Ulrich, the man without qualities.[27] Action is automatic in animals and unreflective characters like Basini, but for a person like Törless, with a finely-tuned mind aware of all possibilities, taking action is usually dependent on a conviction of necessity, arising from a sense of identity and one's own role in the world. Where these are lacking, as in Törless, Ulrich and others of Musil's figures, indecision and inaction are bound to result. The author does not endorse such passivity; on the contrary he presents it as a genuine problem, and it is indeed a noted characteristic of highly intellectual personalities, Hamlet being perhaps the most famous example.

The confusions of Törless may therefore be described as mainly epistemological, but also social. The problems of adolescence add to his difficulties, but it is not helpful to take them as central. The fact that the novel was published at the time when Freud's work was first becoming known does not necessarily prove any specific connection with him, because at the time he was only one among many other scientists and creative writers concerned with the unconscious and the ability of language to express it.

*   *   *

So one may distinguish three themes in this novel connected with the development of the protagonist: the theme of perception and expression, the theme of growth and personal development, and the theme of intellect versus emotion, this being closely linked with the other two. Each of these is associated with a group of characteristic images. The novel is preceded by a motto, as mentioned before, a quotation from Maeterlinck:[28]

In some strange way we devalue things as soon as we give utterance to them. We believe we have dived to the uttermost depths of the abyss, and yet when we return to the surface the drop of water on our pallid finger-tips no longer resembles the sea from which it came. We think we have discovered a hoard of wonderful treasure-trove, yet when we emerge again into the light of day we see that all we have brought back with us is false stones and chips of glass. But for all this, the treasure goes on glimmering in the darkness, unchanged.

This establishes the basic theme of perception and expression. Images of the sea recur in the text, particularly in the crucial section where the boy attempts to write down and analyse the various occasions when he has been most aware of the failure of words. His perception of the unconscious is graphically compared with the waves of a dark ocean breaking on a lighted shore, only becoming visible when they splash against the rocks.[29] Most frequently, the difficulty of perceiving the unconscious is expressed in images of a door, a gate or a threshold. At key points in the narrative the boy feels there is an insurmountable barrier between outer and inner events and his understanding: 'Between events and himself, indeed between his own feelings and some innermost self that craved understanding of them, there always remained a dividing-line, which receded before his desire, like a horizon, the closer he tried to come to it.'[30] Where the narrative involves real doors, gates, bridges or thresholds, these are presented symbolically; indeed, the name 'Törless' has been understood by some critics to mean 'he who cannot find the door'. In the red attic where the boys hold their secret meetings, Törless learns of Basini's theft. His reaction to the news is recounted in detail: outer silence over inner tension, a feeling of being threatened by events and by the malevolent surroundings, a realisation of links with the world of Božena: 'It was as though something had fallen, like a stone, into the vague solitude of his dreamy imaginings . . . There was nothing to be done about it. It was a reality. Yesterday Basini had been the same as himself. Now a trap-door had opened and Basini had plunged into it . . . / But then everything else was possible too.'[31] The underground passages of which *M. le vivisecteur* had spoken have turned into a yawning chasm, swallowing up Basini and threatening to engulf Törless with him.

Some of these images may be attributed to the influence of

Maeterlinck's essays; but whereas the Belgian writer uses them in almost random fashion, Musil incorporates them into a well-constructed novel. Similarly, here and there the detailed psychological descriptions of sensations and feelings may be linked with Musil's studies in visual psychology and his knowledge of Mach. Such passages serve to heighten concentration on the basic theme, whereas little space is given to conventional descriptions of the outer scene. A striking example occurs when Törless attempts one evening to write down his ideas while Basini sits reading in the same room. Törless, analysing the occasions when he has been aware of the unconscious, writes that people as well as things have recently appeared to him under a double aspect. Noting that this change is in some way associated with Basini, he looks at the latter, and suddenly a flood of remembered feelings surges into his mind, distorting his picture of the other boy so that he is aware only of a whirling sense of vertigo. He never really 'sees' Basini at all, for if it always seems as if a picture has just flashed across his mental screen, he never succeeds in catching this movement at the very moment it occurs.[32] The author then compares this mental process with the restlessness of watching a film, which also produces a false illusion of reality. The invention of cinematography in the previous decade no doubt stimulated psychological research in the visual field; Musil clearly found the cinematographic process fascinating, for he refers to it several times, especially in one of his major essays written in 1925.[33] The passage quoted is one of several in the novel where his knowledge of the tachistoscope and the chromatometer are evident; at the same time, however, such passages bear witness to his fundamental scepticism in the face of Mach's claim that analysis of sensations can reveal all facets of reality. On each occasion Törless is left with his doubts unresolved: the process of perception refuses to be perceived, the unconscious evades analysis.

Another optical instrument which provides Musil with an image for expression of the unconscious is the magnifying glass. Early in the novel the boys, walking through a village, flirt with the peasant women. Törless, younger than the others, does not join in, but his vivid imagination is all the more active. Inevitably, feelings of guilt accompany his erotic fantasies, but it seems to him that by putting them into actual words one would make them much worse than they are in the imagination. It would be like magnifying a picture to such a degree that one not only saw everything more distinctly, but also things which were *not there at all*.[34] In other words, magnification distorts, and elsewhere in the text Musil returns to this idea. Hofmannsthal, who had heard Mach lecture on the analysis of sensations, also employs the image of the magnifying glass to draw attention to possible anomalies in perception and expression. In the essay, the 'Chandos Letter', he uses this image to express his total despair at the failure of abstract words, of concepts. For Hofmannsthal's Lord Chandos things fall apart, and just as on one occasion, seeing his own skin through a magnifying glass, he had perceived it like a ploughed field full of holes and furrows, so now he perceives human beings and their actions as nothing but unrelated elements.[35]

Thus for Hofmannsthal, loss of words and concepts, expressed in the image of magnification, leads to *disintegration*. Only in the last section of the essay is a possible solution indicated: direct knowledge of the world through emotion, without any mediation of words. For Musil on the other hand, magnification produces *distortion*: the insistence on using words in situations where their use is inappropriate leads, it is true, to greater definition, as in a magnified image; but *ipso facto* the resulting excessive precision results in falsification of the original emotional experience. Hofmannsthal's Lord Chandos, during the crisis described in the essay, concludes that words have failed him and their use must be abandoned. Törless also feels the power of the irrational and the unconscious, but learns that expression, even if incomplete, and some measure of involvement enable the individual to rise above nameless threatening forces and gain at least some control over his own existence. Musil is concerned, both in *Young Törless* and in his later work, to establish those areas of life in which words can play a useful part, and those in which they cannot. The theme of the word pervades the novel and is examined with the precision of a *vivisecteur*. Musil undertakes an exploration of the means of communication, whether by word, sound or even silence; and a demonstration of the power of words over human beings in their lives and in their relations with one another.

In order to express what has been perceived, the mind needs to understand it; perception can take many forms, but in this novel the primary organ of perception is the eye. Eye imagery, and imagery based on light versus darkness is used throughout the text, for graphic presentation of the barrier between the conscious and unconscious. The eyes of people in the narrative are described as part of their personality, and in the important section where

Törless first begins to analyse his encounters with the unconscious and the irrational, the starting point of his reflections is his endeavour, while lying on the grass in the park, to lift himself by the power of his eyes up into the infinite blue of the sky: 'Infinity!' Suddenly he is startled to discover that this word, long familiar from mathematics lessons, possesses a wild, incomprehensible, threatening power, and that such power lurks behind most of the familiar concepts of his life. The difficulty of matching words and perception can operate in both directions. Some experiences are real when lived and known *directly*; however, when one tries to define them through words, the result is distortion. This was seen in the image of magnification; it is also the meaning of the quotation from Maeterlinck which Musil chose as his motto for the novel. However, the converse also holds: some events/persons/things appear strange and frightening from a distance, when we think of them with a 'wild surmise'. When we reach them and they demand action on our part, the strangeness dissolves like a dream, and the very necessity of having to act gives us the words and ideas required to master the situation.[36] These two linked statements, placed halfway through the narrative, sum up the tension between perception and expression, and Törless's inner development is dominated by his slow and painful progress towards accepting both statements as true.

The action of the novel ends with the assembled teachers interrogating Törless on his involvement in the brutalities which have come to light. At this stage he is no longer confused: in clear, confident, almost poetic words he explains why he became drawn into these events. The teachers, baffled by his reasoning, attempt to channel his account into a conventional social or religious framework, but the boy insists on his own interpretation of his state of mind. Finally, he affirms what he has learnt — the dual aspect of life is to be found not within external nature, nor within Basini, but in himself: 'There's something dark in me, deep under all my thoughts, something I can't measure out with thoughts, a sort of life that can't be expressed in words and which is my life, all the same . . .' In future he will look at things sometimes with the eyes of reason, sometimes with other eyes; both, he now feels, have their own validity.[37] His conclusion may be compared with Wittgenstein's statement written only a few years later: 'There are, indeed, things that cannot be put into words. They *make themselves manifest*. They are what is mystical.'[38] Wittgenstein, who like Musil had trained as an engineer before studying philosophy, was also concerned to define the function of language: 'Language disguises thought.' (4.002). The task of philosophy is to 'set limits to what can be thought; and, in doing so, to what cannot be thought', to 'signify what cannot be said, by presenting clearly what can be said' (4.114-5). He concludes that: 'What we cannot speak about we must pass over in silence' (7) but, as Janik and Toulmin have shown, this silence does not signify defeat or dismissiveness, but a readiness to acknowledge that the 'mystical' is not to be approached by means of the intellect, but through stillness, emotion and art.

As we saw in Chapter I, the young Musil, in his attempt to evaluate literary and moral decadence, drew on ideas from Nietzsche and Emerson. The theme of perception and expression was one on which Emerson had much to say, particularly in his essay 'The Poet' which Musil certainly knew: 'The man is only half himself, the other half is his expression', he quoted in 1905.[39] Even as early as 1902, discussing (in Notebook 4) the importance of giving form to one's ideas, Musil had referred indirectly to Emerson's remark: 'Words are also actions, and actions are a kind of words'.[40] The reference demonstrates Musil's view of the writer's task, and since it dates from the year when he probably began work on *Young Törless*, it may be connected with the novel in which the theme of communication plays such an essential role. We may then perhaps interpret the link with Emerson's conception of words as actions to mean that for the boy Törless, even though his ability to make decisions and to act is poorly developed, his painful striving for expression is to be counted as action, of equal value to actions of a more obvious kind. In Emerson's view, 'The poet is the sayer, the namer, and represents beauty . . . The poet does not wait for the hero or the sage, but, as they act and think primarily, so he writes primarily what will and must be spoken.'[41] Musil saw the boy Törless as one for whom the ability to express himself is crucial, perhaps as a future poet, and it is clear that in working out his own ideas he found Emerson's essay helpful.

The second main theme of the novel is connected with Törless's development towards maturity. The tension between perception and expression, emotion and intellect leads the boy through various confusions from which he finally emerges after achieving some sort of balance. Study of the text shows that his intellectual search for an explanation of his problems follows a steady progression, admittedly with some setbacks. His own attempts at clarification, usually after discussions with another character, proceed from occasions when he begins to see a link between his past experiences of the irrational up to the important section where he writes down what he has worked out. Several more sessions of thought are needed, however, before he arrives at the insights contained in his final speech. In his comments as narrator the author uses the specific word 'development', and as the story proceeds, he shows Törless becoming much more sure of himself in arguments with the other boys. From the social point of view the turning point is reached when he is at last able to take independent action to help the victim.[42] The long hesitation before he acts may indeed be regarded as selfish, but arises, as we have seen, from his personal lack of confidence and his obsession with problems of perception and expression. Once he has broken out of his passivity and become involved in action on behalf of another human being, he gains a measure of confidence which eventually helps him to achieve the mature expression of his ideas. Conversely, the author shows that this boy, so confused at the beginning of the novel, would never have acquired the courage to assert himself against Reiting and Beineberg without his initial painstaking efforts to analyse his problems. At the same time, it must be admitted that fear on his own account plays a part in his motivation when he finally rouses himself to warn Basini.

At key points in the narrative, the stages of personal development are expressed in imagery related to trees and growth, gardeners and plants. Towards the close of the novel the boy's soul is compared with the fruitful earth, under which the shoots are growing before they break out into the light of day. He longs to return home, although previously his feelings towards his parents had not been very warm; now, after the cataclysmic events in the school, he seeks the peaceful security of home, like a tree needing a sheltered place in which to grow.[43] Not every use of plant imagery in the novel is positive, however. The very first page of the text associates the characters in the narrative with the shrivelled trees at the railway station, unable to grow for the dust and soot covering their leaves. The mysterious forest surrounding the dilapidated tavern where the prostitute lives is evoked in a few lines worthy of tales by Grimm or E. T. A. Hoffman;[44] yet at the end of the novel, Törless, now older and wiser, sees it merely as a dusty thicket of insignificant trees.

The theme of growth and personal development, like that of perception and expression, owes something to Musil's knowledge of Emerson and Nietzsche. Emerson, who had studied classical literature and philosophy (including the neo-Platonists), knew the English and German Romantic writers, and the works of his contemporaries Carlyle and Goethe. The Romantics and Goethe were particularly concerned with the individual and his development. Emerson was also one of the first Western thinkers to read translations of the sacred Hindu books. He accepted the Hindu doctrine of the absolute unity of the world — of man and nature — under the various illusions or external appearances of things, and in his first book stated that 'The whole of nature is a metaphor of the human mind'.[45] In 'The Poet' he expounds this idea:[46]

> Nature offers all her creatures to him as a picture-language . . . We stand before the secret of the world, there where Being passes into Appearance and Unity into Variety./The Universe is the externisation of the soul/. . . The poet turns the world to glass, and shows us all things in their right series and procession. For through that better perception he stands one step nearer to things, and sees the flowing or metamorphosis . . . *that within the form of every creature is a force impelling it to ascend to a higher form*; and following with his eyes the life, uses the forms which express that life, and so his speech flows with the flowing of nature.

From the age of nineteen Musil knew Emerson's *Essays* well;[47] he quoted from this essay in Notebooks 4 and 11, as already mentioned. Thus it is tempting to find Emerson's portrait of the poet reflected in the figure of Törless, who by virtue of his 'better perception' sees those things which others fail to see, and strives for the power to 'express that life' and 'show us all things'. The novel charts his progress towards this ideal. In his search for enlightenment the boy has several conversations with Beineberg who, although he seems to be asking the same questions, comes up with quite different answers, which lead into the supernatural and justify the torture of Basini as a means of gaining knowledge. Törless, for his part, insists that what he seeks to understand, linked on the one hand with the use of imaginary numbers, and on the other with emotions associated with Basini, is not supernatural at all, but something natural inside himself.[48] The unity of man and nature, like the unity of the 'good' and 'bad' aspects of human life, was accepted by Musil's generation as a consequence of the theory of evolution, and was reinforced for Musil himself by the writings of Nietzsche and Emerson.

The inspired aphorisms of Nietzsche do not rank as systematic philosophy, yet they too exerted an immense influence. Much of their impact is due to his challenging and vivid style, an essential element of which is his use of plant and animal imagery. In Chapter I we saw the young Musil reading Nietzsche, for the second time, in 1902, and quoting especially from *The Case of Wagner* and *Twilight of the Idols*. Another of Nietzsche's works, *The Dawn of Day*, contains images connected with growth which are, perhaps unintentionally, echoed by Musil. For example, Nietzsche compares the state of pregnancy with personal development: as a future mother thinks only of the good of her unborn child, so human beings should act only in the faith that all their actions will benefit that which is coming to fruition within them.[49] Shortly after this, Nietzsche speaks of human growth through the image of a gardener, free to choose various methods of training his plants, with the ability to train even condemned elements to a useful purpose; he points out that men fatally limit their development by ignorance of their potential for growth. Musil uses such images to express the inner growth of Törless.[50]

The third main theme of the novel concerns the balance between intellect and emotion. For young writers of Musil's age, this constituted a basic dilemma. The outlook of their fathers' generation was based on positivism, and a belief in the power of science to solve all problems. The generation coming to maturity around 1900 could not share this confidence: whole areas of life, they thought, were not governable by reason, and human beings ignored emotions at their peril. Schopenhauer, Nietzsche and Dostoevsky had all contributed to this outlook, and psychiatrists were beginning to study the animal instincts evident in man. While the theory of evolution was widely accepted, and the novels of Zola and other naturalist writers emphasised the animal side of human nature, symbolist literature evoked indefinite moods and sensations, and 'decadence' became a fashionable term. As we saw in Chapter I, Musil's debate with himself on the subject of decadence in Notebook 4 sprang from his own acute awareness of the dichotomy between intellect and emotion.

It is instructive to consider the confusions of young Törless against this background. The boy becomes aware of irrational elements in nature and other people as well as in himself; yet he tries for a long time to find an explanation by intellectual means. After the failure of Beineberg as a possible confidant, he turns to the mathematics master for enlightenment. In particular, Törless is troubled by the function of imaginary numbers in a calculation, which he compares to a bridge whose central span is missing. The mathematician, unable to explain, encourages the boy simply to accept imaginary numbers as 'tools for thinking', in Mach's phrase, which can fulfil a useful function without themselves being understood. When he finally refers to Kant, Törless, heedless of the master's warning, tries to grasp the great man's abstract ideas by sheer willpower, but is utterly defeated by their complexity.[51]

His black despair after this failure of the intellect is illustrated in the dream sequence, and thereafter the emphasis, not surprisingly, shifts from intellect to emotion. Törless is morbidly fascinated by the thief Basini. His first reaction on learning of the theft had been an indignant refusal to have anything further to do with the boy, to denounce him and have him expelled. However, he is unable to persuade the others to agree, and Basini stays. Gradually it becomes clear to Törless that his indignant reaction was a defence not only against Basini, but also against himself: the thief represents the living embodiment of all the shameful thoughts and emotions which at various times have passed through his own mind. He resolves to study Basini, to make him the object of a psychological investigation. As the days pass, his interest becomes more personal and he finds himself caught up in an emotional relationship. He tries to persuade himself that his own problem would be solved by abandoning intellectual questions and living like Basini, from impulse to impulse, but soon realises that he cannot. After a time, the personal involvement wanes and is replaced by its opposite. At last the tortures Basini suffers at the hands of the other boys force Törless to take positive action to save him, and thus precipitate the novel's climax.

The imagery associated with feelings and the unconscious in this work is rich and varied. Sometimes the contrast between intellect and emotion is conveyed by the striking juxtaposition of light and dark, associated also with the act of perception. One of the finest examples occurs immediately before Törless's final triumphant speech, where the author explains how it is possible that the boy had apparently forgotten the insights gained earlier, during the writing scene: a great insight is reached only partly in the circle of light within the brain, the other half occurring in the dark soil of one's innermost being; above all, it is a condition of the soul, on whose outermost point the thought grows like a flower.[52] The boy had known the facts as facts, but the emotional awareness of their truth had eluded him until the final moment of crisis, when they came to life once more.

This beautiful image is clearly connected with Musil's reading of Novalis. He was greatly attracted to the Romantic poet who, like himself, was both a scientist and a creative writer. The early notebooks refer frequently to Novalis, and several quotations show that Musil was particularly interested in what he and other Romantic authors had to say concerning the relationship between the conscious and unconscious. Thus Novalis' fragment, quoted by Musil: 'If I am to understand something, it must develop organically within me', may be linked with the passage just quoted from the novel.[53]

Elsewhere the ebb and flow of emotion is associated with images of water or boiling liquid, often found in German literature. It is striking, however, to count the occasions in Musil's first novel where feelings are expressed in images associated with animals. Passion is described in terms of prowling wild beasts; on the other hand, when Törless becomes aware of his own sensuality the images are of spiders or butterflies.[54] Emotional situations connected with danger are often expressed in images of hunting, for instance where Basini enters the loft to be whipped; on other occasions the animal reference arises solely but graphically from the verb used, e.g. 'the fear that wriggled in his eyes', or again when the author speaks of feverish dreams that prowl around the soul, ready to attack.[55]

Bird images, on the other hand, have a different function. They are remarkable, firstly, only by their absence: in all the outdoor scenes except one a silent, hostile world is depicted. Birds are only mentioned on two occasions: one, where Törless remembers his vivid experience of music in Italy, and realises in a flash of insight that he is not insane, and that the composer of the music must have experienced the world in the same passionate way as himself: 'the passion of those arias was for him like the wing-beats of great dark birds, and it was as though he could feel the lines that their flight traced in his soul.'[56] This is the only place in the text where the author uses the word 'intuition'. On the second occasion, in the one exception to the other outdoor scenes, Törless sees a black crow silhouetted against the white landscape while he gives a lucid account of his confusions to the teachers.[57] These are the two climaxes of expression, the first where the boy himself realises and writes down the nature of his special gift, the second where, after overcoming bewilderment and terror, he is able to explain himself to others.

Musil employs the bird images in this novel as symbols of the 'living soul', to use Wordsworth's term:[58]

> . . . Until . . . we are laid asleep
> In body, and become a living soul:
> While with an eye made quiet by the power
> Of harmony, and the deep power of joy,
> We see into the life of things.

At such times Törless has second sight, as he himself says in his final speech. Yet the bird image may also be linked with Musil's knowledge of Nietzsche, in the sense that in his writings birds denote freedom.[59] Thus at the two climax points of the novel, birds become symbols of that condition of the soul which is able to perceive and express emotional, and perhaps even mystical, truth — free and unfettered.

In addition to these uses of animal imagery, the novel contains a large number of other instances, most of which serve to characterise the main figures. Beineberg is seen once as a bat, sometimes as a spider, at other times as a snake. The spider images are concentrated into a particular section of the novel, and draw attention to the cunning aspect of Beineberg's character. The snake image occurs, at times only implicitly, throughout the book. Beineberg's appearance leads Törless to imagine restless, winding movements; his words, proceeding in endless twists and turns, remind the other of ruined temples, idols and snakes versed in magic; his eyes glitter like two green stones. On other occasions he seems to be spitting poison or hypnotising his victim like a snake. Basini is seen as a small, vulnerable animal, often as a worm, also, like the snake, an ophidian image. After the whipping scene, the two bullies, to humiliate him further, make him say: 'I am a beast', and the sensual, animal aspect of his personality is mentioned repeatedly.[60] Various other references underline the view of Basini as a dirty, defenceless worm, unworthy, in Beineberg's eyes, of being treated as a human being. Törless sees himself as an insect: he compares his period at the school with the existence of a larva waiting to hatch, of no significance except with regard to the future.[61] On one occasion, where he feels annihilated by the silent, hostile world in the park, he sees himself as nothing but a tiny, living dot under the immensity of the dead sky.

Summing up the function of imagery in this novel, one may describe it in the following terms:

1. The theme of perception and expression or communication is most often stated in the metaphor of the door or gate;
2. the theme of growth is represented mainly by the metaphor of the tree, the image of the boy's development;
3. the role of emotion is often emphasised by animal imagery, and the function of ophidian imagery is to denote the two extremes of intellect and emotion between which Törless must find his way.

These three basic forms of metaphor occur, with variations, throughout the novel, to such an extent that one may justifiably speak of a metaphoric structure. Certain metaphors are so intrinsic to Musil's conception that they colour all the expressive material in those aspects of the work where each one applies: nouns, adjectives, verbs are directly or indirectly connected with the basic image. This gives the novel an extraordinary and poetic richness of texture. The imagery is never used for its own sake but constitutes an essential part of the meaning of the novel.[62]

Thus the work shows an epistemological, an existential, and also an ethical aspect. Törless's choice between intellect and emotion is not presented as an abstract one, for the two extremes are incorporated in the figures of Beineberg and Basini. At the beginning he sees himself as having no character at all, and looks for support to the two supposedly strong personalities. Reiting, the first, is uncomplicated: he is frankly a tyrant and a sadist; the author refers to him by an animal image only once.[63] Beineberg's character is much more complex, aptly expressed by the snake image: he distorts words and ideas, and attempts to dominate others by intellectual and spiritual means before assaulting them physically. He is by no means coldly rational: indeed, as the narrative proceeds his fanaticism becomes more and more apparent, yet he cleverly succeeds in projecting the appearance of a profound, rational thinker. His irrationality is masked by his ability to use words, and for this very reason Musil sees him as an insidious danger. Both he and Reiting are cruel sadists, but Beineberg twists the truth, as the Nazis did later. Looking back at his first novel, writing in the 1930s, Musil refers to these two characters as 'today's dictators *in nucleo*'.[64]

Basini, on the other hand, presented as a worm, weak, spineless and worthless, follows every impulse, never stops to reflect and is continually at the mercy of stronger personalities. He is unable to verbalise experience or to account for his actions. Yet Basini possesses a real beauty and charm which hold an increasing attraction for Törless as he fails to progress in his search for under-standing.

During the course of the novel, Törless is drawn first to Beineberg who appears to know all the answers; then, disillusioned with the intellect, he turns to Basini. Eventually he is able to act independently and work out within himself a balanced attitude to life. Following the author's use of animal metaphors for Beineberg and Basini, we may say that the snake-like Beineberg is opposed to the worm-like Basini. Beineberg himself is a symbol of over-reliance on words, which does not produce good results any more than over-reliance on the senses, symbolised by Basini. Törless is torn between these two extremes, and only achieves a balanced outlook when he has freed himself from their influence. The image of the snake, customarily a symbol of the fall of man, is an inspired choice; the two aspects in which Musil shows it, the cunning serpent and the despicable worm, symbolise its two extremes.

Thus the author links the theme of intellect versus emotion with the basic theme of communication; neither too great a dependence on words nor complete abandonment of them provides a solution: what is needed is balance. It seems permissible, in fact, to see both Beineberg and Basini as variations on the theme of Törless: they are *possibilities*, showing what he might become.[65]

The device of projecting separate aspects of one complex personality on to several fictional characters had been used by Strindberg, for example in *To Damascus* (1898). W. H. Sokel states of this play: 'The beggar is an aspect of the main character', and, of the first expressionist dramas: 'All characters are conceived in terms of an aesthetic attribute. Each character plays the role of a musical leitmotiv, expressing an aspect or a possibility of the hero'.[66] Musil later remarks that his generation regarded Strindberg, rather than Goethe, as belonging to themselves, and he may well have seen plays by the Swedish dramatist while studying in Vienna in 1897, or in Berlin, where they were staged from 1902 onwards.[67] The idea of mentally dividing one personality into its constituent parts clearly appealed to him; already in one of the *M. le vivisecteur* sketches he recounts a dream in which he experienced people in this manner. In his doctoral thesis Musil also quoted approvingly from Mach's exposition of the function of analogy in scientific method.[68] In his later creative writing analogy and variation are effectively used as a means of revealing different aspects of the main characters. In this first novel, the two opposing possibilities of Törless are incorporated in Beineberg and Basini, the snake and the worm: the boy veers from one to the other before he is able to work out his own salvation.

Another possible source for Musil's use of ophidian symmetry may be found elsewhere. It has already been mentioned that in seeking to reach a balance for himself, Musil refers to Emerson; the latter's essay on 'Compensation' expounds the idea that nature as a whole, and, especially, human life tends towards a state of balance. The image of two snakes or intertwining serpents is known in Kundalini yoga as a symbol of growth between two opposites; the same symbol appears in the caduceus, the staff of the Greek god Hermes. Musil, actively interested in the visual arts, might well have seen paintings or sculptures showing Hermes with the caduceus. The question remains, however, why he should use this symbol in its Eastern significance of growth between two opposites. It is possible that the link was here provided by Emerson.

The name Hermes was applied by the Greeks not only to the messenger of the gods and the conductor of souls, but also to Hermes Trismegistus, their name for the Egyptian god Thoth the Thrice-Greatest, who invented all the arts and sciences, above all, writing. As inventor of hieroglyphs, he was named 'Lord of Holy Words'. His books of magic 'commanded all the forces of nature'. In the Middle Ages, he was known as master of the Hermetic art of alchemy.[69] Hermes Trismegistus is mentioned several times by Emerson, particularly in the essay on 'Intellect': 'The Trismegisti, the expounders of the principles of thought from age to age . . . Hermes, Heraclitus, Empedocles, Plato, Plotinus, Olympiodorus,

Proclus, Synesius and the rest, have somewhat so vast in their logic, so primary in their thinking, that it seems antecedent to all the ordinary distinctions of rhetoric and literature, and to be at once poetry and music and dancing and astronomy and mathematics'.[70]

The notion of a way of thinking that embraces all the branches of knowledge and art, usually kept separate in our late Western culture, is one that would appeal to Musil. He may thus have followed up the name Hermes Trismegistus and discovered the association with the holy books of the East, which are linked in the novel with Beineberg's father. The 'Lord of Holy Words' thus becomes closely associated with a novel concerned with problems of perception and expression. At the same time, in the symbol of Hermes, the intertwining serpents provide the image to express Törless's growth towards a balanced life.

The metaphoric structure in Musil's first novel may therefore be said to operate in three dimensions. Doors or gates, bridges or frontiers lead Torless from the conscious to unconscious, or vice versa, from perception to expression. The tree is the basic metaphor of his development. Lastly, ophidian symmetry presents Beineberg and Basini as possibilities of Törless; from his relationships with them he will emerge with a new awareness of his own identity. The scientist in Musil notes minute details of thought and sensation, while the poet incorporates them in images appealing directly to our senses, in an artistic whole. The limitations of language, fundamental for the protagonist, are regarded as a challenge by the author: 'My aim is not to make the reader comprehend, but feel'.[71] The problem of conveying the inexpressible in simple, vivid language, in imagery vibrant with associations, in evocative descriptions of significant moments, is brilliantly solved.

Notes

1. R. Musil, *Die Verwirrungen des Zöglings Törless*, GW II, pp. 7–140; *Young Törless*, trans. E. Wilkins and E. Kaiser, 1971. Further references will be to YT. A film of the novel has been made by Volker Schlöndorff.

2. A. Kerr, in 'Der Tag', 21 December 1906. Quoted in K. Corino, 'Robert Musil und Alfred Kerr', *Studien*, 1970, pp. 236–83, pp. 240–1.

3. R. M. Rilke, 'Turnstunde', 'The Gym Lesson', *Sämtliche Werke*, ed. E. Zinn *et al.*, IV, 1961, pp. 601–9.

4. R. Pascal, *From Naturalism to Expressionism*, 1973, p. 202.

5. S. Freud, *Die Traumdeutung*, 1909, pp. 182–7; *Complete Works*, standard edn, 1953–74, IV, *The Interpretation of Dreams*, trans. J. Strachey *et al.*, pp.

261–4.
6. O. Weininger, *Geschlecht und Charakter*, 18th edn, 1919, pp. 51 ff.
7. M. Swales, *Arthur Schnitzler. A Critical Study*, 1971, p. 13.
8. Pascal, 1973, pp. 223–5; U. Baur, 'Zeit- und Gesellschaftskritik in Robert Musils Roman "Die Verwirrungen des Zöglings Törless" ', *Musil-Studien*, 4, 1973, pp. 19–45.
9. H. Goldgar, 'The Square Root of Minus One: Freud and Robert Musil's *Törless*', *Comparative Literature*, XVII, 1965, pp. 117–32; K. Corino, 'Ödipus oder Orest? Robert Musil und die Psychoanalyse', *Musil-Studien*, 4, 1973, pp. 123–235.
10. E. Stopp, 'Musil's "Törless": Content and Form', *MLR*, 63, 1, January 1968, pp. 94–118; A. Reniers, 'Törless: Freudsche Verwirrungen?', *Studien*, 1970, pp. 26–39; G. Müller, *Dichtung und Wissenschaft. Studien zu Robert Musils Romanen "Die Verwirrungen des Zöglings Törless" und "Der Mann ohne Eigenschaften"*, 1971.
11. A. Reniers, 'Törless . . .', 1970, pp. 29 ff.
12. K. Corino, 'Törless ignotus', *Text und Kritik*, 21–22, December 1968, pp. 18–25.
13. Corino, 1973, p. 133; Freud, *Drei Abhandlungen zur Sexualtheorie*, 1961, pp. 21 f. standard edn, VII, *Three Essays on Sexuality*, p. 145.
14. TB I, p. 935.
15. GW II, pp. 28–36; YT, pp. 39–48.
16. GW II, p. 52; YT, p. 69.
17. GW II, p. 8; YT, p. 12.
18. GW II, pp. 74–8; YT, pp. 100–4.
19. GW II, pp. 78–9; YT, pp. 105–6.
20. Letter to Matthias di Gaspero, 1907, *Briefe* 1981, I, p. 47.
21. Letter to Stefanie Tyrka, 1905, *Briefe* 1981, I, pp. 13–14. My emphasis.
22. GW II, p. 65; YT, p. 86.
23. GW II, p. 92; YT, p. 123.
24. GW II, pp. 25–6; YT, pp. 34–5.
25. GW II, p. 41; YT, p. 55.
26. D. Turner, 'The Evasions of the Aesthete Törless', *Forum for Modern Language Studies*, X, 1, January 1974, pp. 19–44.
27. TB I, pp. 138, 955.
28. Maeterlinck, 'La Morale Mystique' in *Le Trésor des Humbles*, 1896, pp. 65–6. Translated in *Young Törless*, see above.
29. GW II, p. 90; YT, p. 121.
30. GW II, p. 25; YT, pp. 34–5.
31. GW II, p. 46; YT, p. 61.
32. GW II, pp. 90–1; YT, pp. 119–22.
33. GW II, pp. 1137–54. See Chapter 5 of this study.
34. GW II, p. 18; YT, p. 24.
35. Hofmannsthal, *Prosa* II, p. 14. *Selected Prose*, p. 134.
36. GW II, pp. 62–5; YT, pp. 82–6.
37. GW II, pp. 137–8; YT, pp. 184–5.
38. L. Wittgenstein, *Tractatus*, 1974, 6.522, p. 73. Emphasis in the original. Cf. Janik and Toulmin, 1973.
39. TB I, p. 170; Emerson III, *Essays, Second Series*, 'The Poet', pp. 1–42, p. 5.
40. TB I, p. 17; Emerson, p. 8.
41. Emerson, p. 7. Cf. H. Hickman, 'Der junge Musil und R. W. Emerson', *Musil-Forum* 6, 1980, 1, pp. 3–13.
42. GW II, pp. 128–9; YT, pp. 171–3.
43. GW II, p. 128; YT, p. 171. Cf. Stopp 1968, p. 109.

44. GW II, p. 27; YT, p. 36.
45. Emerson I, *Nature*, 'Language', pp. 25–35, p. 32.
46. Emerson III, pp. 13–21. My emphasis.
47. A. Reniers, 'Drei Briefe Robert Musils an Josef Nadler und ihr Hintergrund', *Studien* 1970, pp. 284–93, p. 287. Cf. *Briefe* 1981.
48. GW II, p. 83; YT, p. 112.
49. Nietzsche, *Werke* I, *Morgenröte*, pp. 1009–1279, pp. 1271–2, no. 552; *The Dawn of Day*, trans. J. M. Kennedy, 1974, *Complete Works* vol. 9, pp. 383–5.
50. Ibid., p. 1,275, no. 560; ibid., pp. 388–9. Cf. GW II, pp. 128, 131, 140; YT, pp. 171, 177, 188.
51. GW II, pp. 74–8; YT, pp. 102–8.
52. GW II, p. 137; YT, p. 183.
53. Novalis, *Gesammelte Werke*, ed. H. and W. Kohlschmidt, 1967, *Blütenstaub* no. 18, p. 337; TB I, p. 957.
54. GW II, pp. 18, 70, 86; YT, pp. 24, 94, 116.
55. GW II, pp. 69, 45, 140; YT, pp. 91, 60, 188.
56. GW II, p. 91; YT, pp. 122–3.
57. GW II, p. 136; YT, p. 182.
58. W. Wordsworth, *Poetical Works*, ed. T. Hutchinson, 1936, 'Lines Composed above Tintern Abbey', pp. 163–5, lines 42 ff.
59. Nietzsche, *Werke* I, *Menschliches, Allzumenschliches*, p. 441; *Human, All Too Human*, p. 7; *Morgenröte*, p. 1279, no. 575; *The Dawn of Day*, p. 394.
60. GW II, pp. 72, 109–10; YT, pp. 96, 146.
61. GW II, p. 41; YT, p. 55.
62. Cf. Stopp 1968, p. 108.
63. GW II, p. 60; YT, p. 79.
64. TB I, p. 914.
65. Cf. A. Reniers-Servranckx, *Robert Musil*, 1972, pp. 77–84.
66. W. H. Sokel, *The Writer in Extremis*, 1959, pp. 35–6.
67. TB I, p. 493.
68. Musil, *Dissertation*, pp. 18–19. See also Chapter 1.
69. J. Viau, 'Egyptian Mythology', *Larousse Encyclopedia of Mythology*, 1962, pp. 8–48, p. 26.
70. Emerson II, *Essays* I, 'Intellect', pp. 323–47, p. 346.
71. Letter to Paul Wiegler, 1906. TB II, pp. 1217–18; *Briefe* 1981, I, p. 24.

3 FINDING A VOICE: *UNIONS*, EARLY ESSAYS AND SKETCHES

Nine months after Musil had been awarded his doctorate at the University of Berlin, he was invited to become assistant to Alexius von Meinong, founder of the first Austrian laboratory in experimental psychology at the University of Graz. After the unexpected success of *Young Törless* two years previously, the young author had begun to think seriously of becoming a writer; the offer from Meinong now forced him to choose between the scientific and literary sides of his personality, at least with regard to a career. Had he wished to continue with academic research in psychology, this post would have provided a splendid beginning; nevertheless, after hesitating for three weeks, he declined the offer. His letter to Meinong, though couched in formal terms, shows that he regarded the choice as a fateful one, and more than thirty years later he still wondered if he had made the right decision.[1] Although not himself active in experimental psychology, he followed its development and referred later to works by Wolfgang Köhler, Erich Maria von Hornbostel, Ernst Kretschmer, Kurt Lewin and others.[2] The fact that he read these and related works throughout his life shows the earnestness of his resolve to explore all facets of the human psyche; just as Törless, at the end of the novel, explains that in future he will sometimes look at things with the eyes of reason, sometimes with other eyes, so Musil in his later work attempts to analyse both the rational and emotional aspects of human life, striving to create a synthesis between them.[3]

In the meantime Musil stayed in Berlin. Some insight into his life there since 1903 is gained from the story 'Tonka', notes for which have been found from 1905, although it was not published until 1924.[4] The story is largely autobiographical, Tonka being identified with Herma Dietz, whom he had probably first met in Brünn, and who came to Berlin with him.[5] In the text, Tonka is shown as a girl from a humble background who follows the young scientist to a large city. The association is frowned upon by his mother, who regards the girl as socially unsuitable to marry her son, but the real causes for its tragic outcome lie deeper. Musil shows the impossibility of true communication between a young man who pretends to be deaf to any questions not admitting a clear-cut solution, and the simple, uneducated girl with, apparently, nothing but a kind heart. The isolation of the big city, the lack of money and finally Tonka's pregnancy which, according to the calendar, began on a date when her lover was away, drive them ever further apart. When it becomes clear that she is also suffering from venereal disease, he convinces himself, in spite of her denials, that she must have been unfaithful to him, and she dies in hospital. Tortured by doubts right up to the end, he cannot bring himself to say the one saving word to express his trust in her. Once she is dead, however, the blindness seems to fall from his eyes, and he feels her being as a small warm shadow upon his life. Tonka's fate is 'the symbolic embodiment of the fact that in some respects one simply cannot rely on the intellect.'[6]

Information given in the notebooks makes it difficult to judge to what extent the ending of the story is based on fact, but other documents indicate that Herma died in circumstances similar to those described in 'Tonka', and she is mentioned for the last time in 1907.[7] About this time Musil met the woman who was to be his wife, of whom he writes in 1910: '. . . she is not something I have won or achieved, but something I have become and that has become myself.'[8] Martha Marcovaldi, née Heimann, born in 1874, was the daughter of a prosperous Jewish family in Berlin, and had studied painting with Lovis Corinth. After a first marriage cut tragically short by the early death of her young husband in Florence, she remained in Italy to paint. In 1898, she married an Italian businessman, Enrico Marcovaldi, by whom she had a son and daughter; a few years later, however, she left her husband and returned with the children to Berlin. Musil first mentions her name in 1907,[9] and the relationship between them soon became close; however, it was a long time before she could obtain a divorce, so that her marriage to Musil did not take place until Easter 1911. Martha's warm personality, her artist's eye and clear judgement gave Musil the support which enabled him to reach maturity as a writer. Although a gifted artist, she had little personal ambition, devoting herself to him and his work. He talked over his projects with her, discussed contemporary literature and read to her work in progress; sometimes she would read and summarise books for him.[10] Yet the relationship was by no means only an intellectual one, as scattered notebook references show.[11] In all the practical aspects of everyday life he relied more and more on his wife, particularly in his last years, and it was she who took upon herself the responsibility of publishing the last part of *The Man without Qualities* after Musil's death in exile in 1942.

From 1908 onwards, having made a positive decision to become a writer, Musil concentrated on forging a personal style. Almost from the beginning of the notebooks, the analytical pieces of *M. le vivisecteur* had alternated with sketches in a more decadent manner typical of *fin de siècle* writing. Later, and throughout the Berlin years, he wrote critiques of Hamsun, D'Annunzio and other writers of the period, showing his keen awareness of the importance of style, structure and form. In order to achieve an artistic whole, he notes, some central focal point must be found, or even a series of focal points; this is essential, for artistic expression necessarily implies 'tactics of the inner line'. It is not possible to create a work of art by including everything; the writer must select and construct, he must choose his own method of approaching the work as a whole and the persons depicted in it from all those available. The naturalist writers, in his opinion, had failed to define their aims clearly enough; Musil's notebook entries discuss their work and his own from many angles, enabling us to follow the development of his thought.[12]

The effort of the next two-and-a-half years was channelled almost entirely into two novellas which appeared in 1911. Musil had published an earlier version of one story, 'The Enchanted House', in 1908, in the periodical *Hyperion*. When the editor, Franz Blei, asked for a second piece, Musil readily agreed, hoping to complete it within a week or two; in fact it grew into a desperate venture absorbing every ounce of energy, yet he refused to abandon it. Together with this novella, 'The Perfecting of a Love', he published a revised version of the original story, now called 'The Temptation of Quiet Veronica'; the whole volume was entitled *Unions*. Apart from a few critics who saluted Musil's ability to reveal the inner life of the human soul, the response to the book was entirely negative — a bitter disappointment for the author.

What was it about this work which made Musil so determined to finish it, knowing, as he must have done, that it was never likely to achieve popular success? In a series of autobiographical notes dating from about 1936, he analyses his intentions during this period, and takes the opportunity to discuss the relationship of psychology to literature. The use of psychological elements in a literary work is not to be regarded as equivalent to the practice of psychology as an academic discipline, and the lack of distinction between them has, in Musil's view, resulted in a great deal of confusion. He defines the distinction thus: 'Literature does not convey learning and knowledge./But: literature makes use of learning and knowledge. And, of course, concerning the inner world as much as the outer one'.[13] Literature claims to depict segments of life as they are. It is therefore dependent on the current state of knowledge, on facts created by research. Musil proceeds to consider the example of psychoanalysis, which was beginning to be known in non-medical circles by the time he was writing the novellas. Since psychoanalysis attracted such widespread public notice, were writers therefore obliged to make use of its formulae and opinions? According to Musil, this did not happen. Literature, he writes, is 'a different world' and cannot be tied to an ideological system.

During the writing of the novellas, he recalls, he was working out his solution to the problem of the relationship between realism and truth in literature. Realism, by which here he appears to mean naturalism, had aimed to present a truthful picture of the surface of life, of things as they really are; his purpose was to go beyond this, to penetrate beneath the surface, to organise in depth.[14] Literature gives meaning to life and interprets it, not only by means of the intellect but even more through the emotions. After this, Musil returns to the relationship of literature to psychology. 'The Perfecting of a Love' describes how a woman, Claudine, moves within three days from deep love of her husband to committing adultery with a complete stranger. Academic psychology, he suggests, would select one or two possible ways of explaining such a case and classify it according to type. The writer's approach is a different one. Musil chose to describe the action and particularly the mental state of the characters in terms of the 'smallest steps, the most gradual, unnoticeable transition'. He claims a moral value for this procedure, in demonstrating the constant possibility of moving from one position to its opposite. Most important for him however was what he calls the 'principle of motivated steps', that is, all that happens should be related to the innermost nature of the characters, and no part of the action should proceed mechanically.[15]

As with Musil's first novel, so in the two novellas the literary work rests upon a foundation of biographical fact, in this case the life of Martha Musil. Corino shows that Martha, like 'Veronica', grew up in the home of an aunt together with four male cousins, one of whom became her first husband. Later, when she already knew Musil, an incident similar to that described in 'The Perfecting of a Love' took place in Berlin. Martha had gone to visit a former fiancé with the intention of breaking off her relationship with him. In a note on this episode Musil states she regarded it as a turning-point, a paradoxical confirmation of her enduring love for himself.[16]

The action of 'The Perfecting of a Love'[17] begins with a scene showing husband and wife together one evening at home. The room in which they sit is described in terms of stillness, beauty and light. It is shut off from the dark streets outside, and everything in it contributes to a sense of timeless perfection, expressing the harmony of their life together. One begins to wonder if anything can make this love more perfect than it is already — is the title ironic? The two people in the room are talking, however, about a character in a book they have been reading who is a rapist; they are trying to understand his state of mind, and this leads them on to talk about themselves and their relationship with one another. The next day Claudine leaves for a visit to the distant boarding-school where her daughter is a pupil; the birth of this child, now aged thirteen, took place during Claudine's first marriage, but was the result of a casual affair. Claudine's unregulated life at that time had changed suddenly when she met her present husband; a deep, intense love now unites them.

During the railway journey Claudine begins to think about her husband and their mutual love; although their life together appears so perfect, it seems to her that in that very fact lies a danger of a rigidity which she has observed with horror in the lives of other people. She feels, and not for the first time, that in their exclusive concentration on each other they have lost contact with the outside world. As the journey continues and she looks out of the window at the fields and bushes, this feeling of lost contact, of emptiness, becomes so strong that it causes her physical pain. She experiences an agonising sense of isolation, of lack of meaning in her existence. It is not so much the fear of unknown dangers felt by Törless, as the anguished dread of Hofmannsthal's Lord Chandos who cannot relate to the world outside himself. She senses out there an unconscious life, a life which normally, in her civilised existence with her husband, lies outside her awareness. She has a sudden premonition that this journey may lead to some crisis for herself. Her life seems to be out of balance: the very perfection of her marriage is pulling her along by its own momentum, whereas she experiences from time to time an overwhelming need to stop and think things out alone. Up until then her real life has been an isolated one: her child far away at school, her husband apparently absorbed for much of the time by the demands of his work. As Claudine thinks back to their home, she suddenly feels that she has been imprisoned in it. Now, she gradually becomes aware of being free, as in her former existence, but it is clear that she recoils from the idea of returning permanently to that dissolute mode of life.

Eventually Claudine ceases to fight in her mind against the sensation of strangeness. But she wonders who she really is, feeling uneasily that she might have become someone quite different if circumstances had been otherwise, the wife for instance of one of the teachers at her daughter's school, whom she regards only with distaste. What is her real identity? Here, as so often, Musil points to the various possibilities of human existence; for Claudine this becomes a question which drives her to the edge of her reason. One may have to break faith with one's surface identity in order to remain true to oneself at the deepest level.[18] More and more, she convinces herself that unless she is able to share in the incomprehensible world of feeling beneath the level of words, her life will become petrified and worthless. She senses that only by living at the deepest level of emotion can she truly be herself, and in order to preserve her love for her distant husband, she may have to act out her own sensuality by being unfaithful to him.

The greater part of the story consists of Claudine debating these questions with herself. The 'other' man, a senior government official of some kind, worldly and self-assured, first appears on the train, and like Claudine is detained in the isolated village for several days and nights by heavy snow. She visits the school and speaks to the teachers, but forgets to see her daughter for whose sake she undertook the journey, since her own problems drive everything else out of her mind. During the second night, while the compulsion of her own sensuality grows ever stronger, she experiences a vivid feeling of being united with her husband, a sense of his nearness and understanding of her actions. This gives her release from her feverish thoughts and she knows with inner certainty that their love is so deep that nothing can destroy it. The next day she ceases to think and allows events to take their course. She gives herself to the stranger, who glows with satisfaction at his conquest; however, by then Claudine finds his presence almost irrelevant, while at the deepest level she now feels united with the whole world, and truly herself.

Most of the text records Claudine's own thoughts, described by the author in minute detail using the stream of consciousness technique. A remarkable feature of the style are the images in which her emotions are expressed. Her feeling of isolation on the journey and in the village is underlined by the snowy landscape and the sleigh ride from the railway station; during the train journey, the stranger speaks of 'an enchanted island' as he looks out at the view, emphasising the sense of strangeness. Claudine's feeling of emptiness is echoed by the cold light over the fields. As in *Young Törless*, the emotional aspect of the characters is often expressed by animal imagery, and an analysis of these associated with Claudine herself shows how she gradually changes from an ostensibly rational person to a woman dominated by her unconscious.[19] Many of the expressions in this work relating to the unconscious recall Musil's novel, and a parallel clearly exists between Claudine and Basini, also seen as an animal, for both are shown as primarily sensual beings. Unlike Basini, Claudine tries to justify her actions to herself, but her attitude is largely passive. The temptation to abandon oneself to sensual experience, to the irrational, is fundamental to many of Musil's characters, not only in the early works but, as we shall see later, in his drama *The Visionaries* and also in *The Man without Qualities*.

'The Temptation of Quiet Veronica',[20] the second novella of 1911, is in some ways the most abstruse of Musil's published texts; yet it repays careful reading. The narrative gives a description, from the inside as it were, of the feelings and mental state of the central figure, a woman on the verge of middle age living in a large old house with an elderly aunt. Two men, perhaps cousins of Veronica, also appear: Demeter, sensual and aggressive, and Johannes, imaginative and apparently indecisive. The outer action is reduced to an absolute minimum; on the other hand the thoughts and feelings of Johannes and, especially, Veronica are narrated in great detail. Musil commented that the text might be regarded simply as an account of an almost pathological case bordering on psychasthenia. Yet actual case studies, he felt, should be left to psychiatrists and psychologists; in his view it is not the creative writer's task to recount clinical facts, but to describe and illuminate an emotional context.[21]

The way in which Musil describes the development of Veronica's mental and emotional state is detailed and complex, but again made vivid for the reader by the abundance of imagery. Veronica has lived in the dark old house with her aunt, completely isolated from the outside world, for so many years that she seems to have lost all individuality. Her empty life proceeds mechanically from day to day, from year to year, without her being aware of the meaning of time. Her emotional responses to such events as do occur in her monotonous existence seem to be entirely negative. The only person to whom she talks about anything beyond household affairs is Johannes, and in the first part of the narrative the author relates fragments of their conversations without any clear indication of a temporal sequence. Johannes had once intended to become a priest, but it appears that he now lacks any definite faith, being engaged in a constant search for a truth beyond everyday reality: '. . . things beyond the horizon of consciousness . . . premonitions of some wholeness that it was still too soon to apprehend'.[22]

Veronica, too, is seeking to understand certain aspects of her own life, but has the greatest difficulty in putting them into words. In part, she seems to be aware of a mysterious spiritual dimension, like that which Johannes tries to adumbrate. On the other hand, it emerges during the narrative that, like Törless, but at a much later age, she is increasingly aware of her own sensuality, whose development has been inhibited by the conditions of her existence. On three occasions this is made explicit by reference to animals. Eventually, Veronica explains to Johannes that Demeter had once brutally taunted her with the prospect of being imprisoned in the house for ever, growing into the same ageless, sexless creature that her aunt appears to be; profiting from her shocked reaction, he had then attempted to seduce her. For a moment she had almost yielded, seeing herself and Demeter doomed to remain in the old house for ever as in a world apart; but then, remembering Johannes, she had rejected him. Her appeal to Johannes for his help leads him to suggest that they leave together, but at the last moment she refuses, whereupon he departs alone, declaring that he intends to commit suicide.

From the point where Veronica decides to remain in the old house, the author subtly builds up our understanding of her state of mind. Animals in her surroundings and animal images gain an increasing hold over her. Demeter, dark and sensual, reminds her of an animal, but Johannes, more intellectual, cannot understand her unformulated allusions. The memory of an episode with a large dog, with whom she used to play during adolescence, begins to dominate her mind, providing a focus for her sensuality; suddenly the real Johannes is in her way. She wants instead to give herself up to the wind caressing her like an animal, or else to overwhelm Johannes with her own emotions. She begins to feel that she herself may be capable of experiencing the outer world directly through her senses, without the need for 'love'.

Once Johannes has left, Veronica experiences a period of extraordinary happiness which seems to be strangely linked with his impending death. It is as though his decision to kill himself on her account has liberated her from repression and given her the strength she previously lacked to live her life in her own person. She wakes through the night, intending to keep watch for his death; but instead the night becomes one when 'all that had ever taken form under the twilit blanket of the long malaise that her existence was, all that had been dammed off from reality . . . at long last . . . had the force to break through into her consciousness'.[23] The space between her and the objects in the room around her, which for so long had been empty and lifeless, now assumes tension and meaning. The objects themselves acquire a life of their own, the moments live and shape themselves around Veronica, and she feels more intensely than ever before that she herself is a part of this outer life. An exaltation takes hold of her mind, and in this state of trance she feels that Johannes too must now exist in such an altered reality. She suddenly remembers dreams in which she had known similar experiences. As dawn approaches, she begins to realise that Johannes is probably still alive. She feels a great tenderness, for it seems that she owes this climax of experience to him; her awareness of his love for her produces a sense of mysterious spiritual union with him, although he is far away.

The next day brings a letter from him. He is indeed still alive: the ordinary life of the outside world has held him fast and prevented his suicide. The idea that he should die had come from something said by Veronica; he had seized on it as a noble gesture, but without inner conviction. Reading the letter, Veronica is stunned, and feels rejected. She appears to fall back into her previous autistic frame of mind, yet at times succeeds in catching a glimpse of her own feelings during that one exalted night, when her relationship with her surroundings was direct and immediate. A shadow of that heightened reality still lies on her everyday life, giving her secret joy; no longer does she feel threatened by Demeter, but looks forward with some curiosity to the return of Johannes.

This brief summary of 'The Temptation of Quiet Veronica' can only give an outline of the text. As in 'The Perfecting of a Love', there is very little outward action, all the emphasis being concentrated on the development of the characters' states of mind, and, again, the key role of imagery is a remarkable aspect of the writing. The author hardly appears as narrator at all, since almost all the material is given as conversation, or as Veronica's own thoughts; but the deeper levels of meaning are indicated by the imagery in which her thoughts are expressed. Animals and animal images constantly recur to draw attention to sensuality; but sensual experience is also sometimes associated with emptiness and dissolution, with images of liquids and the sea. Johannes had intended to commit suicide at sea, before becoming once again rooted in the everyday world which Veronica has never known. During her night of self-discovery she experiences the whole space around her and the objects within it as having a heightened spatial reality, characterised by unusually intensive light, contrasting with the gloom of her normal life.[24] Musil often uses such spatial and light imagery to underline this sense of an immediate link with something beyond the frontiers of consciousness; at times the contrast between light and darkness operates in the reverse direction, but here the emphasis is on a combination of perception and knowledge, as in Törless's first climax of perception and expression in the writing scene.[25] As in the first novel, so in 'Veronica' there are constant references to the difficulty of expressing oneself. Comments by the author show that in the novellas he was intentionally describing people on the verge of insanity; the importance of expression and communication to the equilibrium of human life is very much in his mind, and on one occasion he refers to the characters in 'Veronica' as 'people whose final bid for salvation consists in speaking'.[26]

'The Temptation of Quiet Veronica' may be seen as a parable: both the main figures are searching for 'some wholeness that it [is] still too soon to apprehend', 'though it betrays its nearness only in a stirring like that of a music not yet audible . . ., in heavy folds vaguely outlined in the yet impenetrable curtain of things far off'.[27] The basic theme is similar to that of *Young Törless*, but whereas there the narrator from time to time sums up the underlying ideas, here they are incorporated in the reflections of the characters them- selves. Vital as expression and communication are, the life expressed in words is only half of life — there is another dimension if we open ourselves to it. Sensuality and sensibility lead us towards it, but it is not only sexual; emotion can be associated with many aspects of life, and direct immediate experience through feeling is as essential to human beings as reasoned thinking expressed in words. Hofmannsthal's Lord Chandos, after his depair at his inability to trust in abstract words or to relate to things outside himself, finally arrives at a point where the simplest objects in his surroundings can give him intense happiness, so long as he perceives them through emotion alone.[28] Throughout Musil's work runs the endeavour to explore this other condition, but, unlike Chandos, he wishes to do so without abandoning reason. The characters he creates are often unbalanced in one way or another, to the point of being almost casebook studies in the novellas of 1911, but his own purpose, as stated in 1926, was to show how a synthesis between the rational and emotional sides of life might be achieved.[29]

Claudine's and Veronica's split personalities and their alienation from the 'normal' world may be linked not only with Törless and Lord Chandos, but also with Mach's assertion that the self is nothing but a fiction and has no real existence (see Chapter 1). Musil was writing the novellas from 1908–11. During this period, Freud was becoming widely known, and as we have mentioned, although there is no record of Musil having studied his works at this time, he must at least have read accounts of Freud's main ideas. After comparing successive versions of 'Veronica', Corino concludes that Musil must have known Freud and Breuer's *Studies on Hysteria* (1895). In his view, changes were made in the final version of the story to remove any appearance of Freudian influence.[30] He certainly knew P. Janet's *Les Obsessions et la Psychasthénie* (1903) and probably Binet's *Les Altérations de la Personnalité* (1892). At various times during these years Musil made notes on apperception, judgement formation, the psychology of feeling and different kinds of personality disorders, to provide background information for the type of characters he wished to portray.[31] Some of the descriptions of Claudine's and Veronica's states of mind correspond closely to statements by Binet, Janet and other writers in the field of psychopathology, and, like them, he is concerned with the nature of the self in all its manifestations.[32] In the novellas he presents characters who have already crossed the frontier of 'normality', although it would not be correct to describe them as insane. He also follows the progress of their particular lives descriptively in terms of the 'smallest steps'; in later works and the essays he discusses the whole area of irrational experience which formed one of his main fields of interest, from mystics to pathological cases. Yet, as we saw earlier in this chapter, while Musil studies the specialist literature and makes detailed notes, often with critical comments, he sees himself not as a researcher patiently collecting facts, but as a creative writer. The intellectual inquiry helps to prepare the ground for his fiction and drama, where he chooses figures in a particular situation and follows their lives through to a conclusion. The exceedingly detailed manner in which this is done in the novellas leads, however, to a narrative almost totally devoid of momentum, no doubt one of the chief reasons for the book's poor reception in 1911. Musil, who had 'almost destroyed himself' during the writing,[33] never again published anything so extreme, but, in his last years, this was the only one of his works he occasionally liked to read.[34]

*   *   *

During the time Musil remained in Berlin after his graduation, he made contact with a number of writers and critics, and, in September 1910 tried to obtain a position as critic with the *Berliner Zeitung*. When this failed, he was forced to accede to his father's request that he should return to Austria. Almost thirty years old, Musil was still being supported by his parents who, once he had announced his intention of marrying, insisted that from then on he should earn his own living. Despite his son's reluctance to leave Berlin, Musil's father set about finding employment for him, and was able to obtain a post in the library of the Technological University of Vienna. Before starting work there in the spring of 1911, Musil spent three months in Italy with Martha Marcovaldi.

This Italian visit made an indelible impression on him; the warmth, light and clarity which had drawn Goethe, Nietzsche and so many German writers and artists towards the south affected him deeply, and are reflected in the early drafts of his major novel, particularly the section called 'The Voyage to Paradise'.[35] During a second visit in 1913, while on sick leave from his post in Vienna,

Musil began to write a number of short sketches later published in newspapers and periodicals. These were eventually collected with others into a volume entitled *Legacy in My Lifetime*, not published until 1936; a recent study has, however, established the dates of composition, thus enabling us to relate the separate pieces to their immediate background.[36] The first section of the book is entitled 'Pictures', and one of the early pieces in it consists of a series of portraits of staff and guests in a German boarding-house in Rome, Pension Nimmermehr. They are far removed from the expressionist subtleties of the novellas; these pieces are short, graphic and down to earth, and recounted in a gently humorous tone. A very different spirit appears in the first piece of the collection, also the first to be published. It was originally called 'Roman Summer (From a Diary)', and later 'The Fly-Paper'. It describes in two short pages the behaviour of flies alighting on a fly-paper, their desperate struggle to escape, their resignation, agony and eventual death. This sketch is presented with a brevity and concentration that render it all the more effective; the human parallels are drawn without emphasis, yet the total impression is horrifying. In the preface to the collection published in 1936, Musil draws attention to this piece, with another one, remarking that it would be easy to see them as a veiled description of later conditions. Such pieces, he writes, are rather a kind of prophecy, and may be composed by anyone who observes human life in its small, unguarded manifestations, anyone prepared to watch and record seemingly meaningless details until the moment arrives that reveals their significance.[37] With hindsight, we see that it is no accident for Musil to have written a piece like this in the year before the outbreak of the Great War. Just as *Young Törless* has been called 'perhaps the most clairvoyant book . . . written before the First World War',[38] so 'The Fly-Paper' is a parable of human beings inextricably caught up in a fate they might, perhaps, have avoided. In the previous year, Kafka, also living in the Austro-Hungarian empire, had written 'Metamorphosis', a much longer tale which shocks the reader in a different way, but also one invoking animal imagery to shed light on human behaviour.

The Man without Qualities is set in this same year, 1913, and its wide-ranging panorama of the period will be discussed in later chapters; one element already mentioned of this vast novel, however, is the author's interest in mental disorders. During his Italian visit of 1913, Musil was taken round the Manicomio, the Mental

Hospital of Rome, where he knew one of the doctors; he recorded his impressions in great detail.[39] This material is associated in his major novel with the figure Clarisse, based on Alice, the wife of Musil's childhood friend Gustav Donath. Alice began to show increasing signs of mental imbalance from September 1910 onwards, and her abnormal behaviour, sayings and various adventures are carefully described in Musil's notebooks.[40] He refers particularly to her greatly heightened awareness of the symbolism in life, seeing 'connections between all things, which sane people merely fail to see'. He is fascinated by the development of her illness and remarks that his previous notes on apperception exactly fit her case.

Although Musil resented being tied by his library duties, his work there must have pleased his superiors, for by the end of 1911 he had been promoted. During the year 1913 he was granted two periods of sick leave, which gave him time to write. Since leaving Berlin in the autumn of 1910 he had kept in touch with the literary world of the German capital, through figures such as Alfred Kerr and the publisher Samuel Fischer; from 1911 onwards he began to publish essays, sketches and criticism in the expressionist periodicals *Die Aktion* and *Die weissen Blätter*, and became a regular contributor to *Der Lose Vogel* and *Die Neue Rundschau*. A review in the last-mentioned periodical in August 1914, for instance, discusses a volume of *Stories* by Robert Walser (1914), as well as the first two published works of Franz Kafka, *Contemplation* and *The Stoker* (both 1913). The latter wins much praise from Musil, who finds in it 'intentional naïveté', 'moral delicacy', and the mark of a skilled artist.[41] These reviews and others of the time show Musil writing for publication with a confidence and authority previously lacking in his work. He was now sufficiently well known in literary circles to be invited to write for other papers as well as these periodicals, a fact which must have given him much-needed encouragement after the disappointing reception of the novellas.

Another cause of the greater sureness and maturity apparent in the writing of this period is to be found in his marriage to Martha Marcovaldi at Easter 1911. It had proved extremely difficult for her to obtain a divorce, and their relief at overcoming all the obstacles to their marriage must have been considerable. For almost the first time since childhood Musil knew a settled home life, and with Martha he experienced erotic love, beauty and a sense of security which have been compared to the light, beauty and life brought by the lady from Portugal into the dark castle of Herr von Ketten, in the story called after her.[42] Marie-Louise Roth finds an unmistakable link between the change in Musil's personal life brought about by Martha, the introduction to the light and clarity of Italy, which he also owed to her, and the changes in his writing at this period. She points out that plans for 'The Lady from Portugal' date from 1913, although it was not published until 1924, and that the episode where Herr von Ketten climbs a sheer rock face to prove that he has regained his will for action may be linked with the writer's new-found maturity. Musil, from then on, turned increasingly from the shadowy sphere of the novellas towards the real world around him. The detailed observation of facts, whether in the Mental Hospital or the streets of Rome, the humorous portraits of individuals or the symbolic recording of an incident in animal life, are all based on the visible world outside the writer, who reflects upon and transmutes his material, but no longer seeks it largely within himself. At the same time, his assessments of other writers become more comprehensive and yet more precise than previously, as shown by the notebooks. From 1911, the first essays begin to appear, some of which may be said to continue the theoretical work of his university years, not, however, concentrated on one specific area of study, but engaging in public discussion of issues of the day.

It is perhaps salutary to recall at this stage in Musil's life that in addition to the two volumes of fiction of 1906 and 1911, he had published his thesis on Ernst Mach, and even before that, two technical articles on 'Motor Engines for Small Businesses' and 'Heating for Domestic Purposes'.[43] These earlier publications may serve to remind us that the extreme psychological tendency of the novellas, which he himself once described as a kind of 'literary exercise', represents only one side of Musil's mind. Trained in engineering, mathematics, philosophy and experimental psychology, he sought to think clearly and logically in areas where it was appropriate, while never ceasing to point out that in emotional and artistic fields logical categories could not be applied, and a different system of values must obtain. The essay with which he entered the wider forum of public debate, 'Obscenity and Disease in Art',[44] appeared in the periodical *Pan* in March 1911, and was intended as a contribution to the dispute then going on between the head of the Berlin police, Herr von Jagow, and Alfred Kerr, on the question of censorship. Two earlier numbers of *Pan* (January and February 1911) had been suppressed for printing the travel journals of Gustave Flaubert, considered by the police as unfit for publication. In the essay, Musil attacks the censor's decision in this and two similar cases, and then proceeds to spell out his own views on the differences between obscenity in life and in art. If a writer, or a visual artist, chooses subject-matter which may be described as obscene or diseased, such a description no longer applies to the work of art produced by him. He presents the chosen topic or object in its relations to other phenomena in order to make the reader or spectator understand it both intellectually and emotionally; this is not so very different from the methods of science, where understanding is also based on establishing analogies and connections. Art, like science, seeks knowledge; it presents that which is obscene and diseased in its relationships with that which is decent and healthy, and so increases understanding of the latter. The original impression received by the artist dissolves in his mind, and the component parts of that impression, released from their normal associations, suddenly acquire unexpected links with often quite different objects. 'In this way relationships are created and associations disrupted, while consciousness bores a way through. The result is a mental picture, usually far from precise, of the process to be described, yet surrounded by faint echoes of psychic relationships, a slow stirring of far-reaching emotional, intentional and intellectual associations.'[45] This process in the artist's mind must then be echoed in the mind of the recipient, who, by receiving this artistic whole, will benefit from the purifying effect of art, which lifts the original subject-matter into a higher, more general sphere.

The difference between science and art, according to Musil, lies in the fact that whereas science is interested in concepts, general rules and causal relations, art operates through the senses, and chooses individual examples. Not concrete reality, but emotional associations and increased knowledge of what is humanly possible form the artist's goal: 'To love something as an artist means, then, to be moved not by its value or lack of value in itself, but by an aspect of it which suddenly appears. Art, if it has any value, reveals things hitherto only seen by a few.' If this definition is true, Musil continues, the ability of art to reveal new aspects applies as much to obscene or diseased areas of life as to others. It is a serious error, in his view, to regard the boundary between mental health and disease, or between morality and immorality, as a simple line.

There are no psychic poisons as such, but only the poisonous effects of a functional imbalance of one or other of the psychic components; every action, emotion, volition or intention can be healthy or diseased, every healthy psyche possesses elements similar to those in sick ones, and the final outcome depends only upon the individual whole and its highly complex web of many different relationships. Therefore, since it is no longer possible to draw a firm borderline between morality and immorality in life, the justification for doing so in art has disappeared.

In this essay Musil expresses a view of the relationship between art and morality already apparent in his reaction to critics of *Young Törless*. His statement that art can have a purifying effect goes back to Aristotle, whose *Poetics* he had read and annotated possibly as early as 1898.[46] In a late notebook entry he writes: 'Since my youth I have regarded aesthetics as equivalent to ethics,' a statement also made by Wittgenstein in the *Tractatus*.[47] Musil's emphasis on a functional view of morality provides an early indication of one of the main threads in *The Man without Qualities*, where Ulrich, the hero, is confronted with the psychopath Moosbrugger and obliged to recognise the links between himself and the criminal condemned by society.[48] In 1911, the year this essay appeared, the work of Freud, Weininger and others was pervading intellectual circles in Germany and Austria, but society at large was not yet prepared to accept such potentially 'dangerous' views.

Musil's description of the processes in the artist's mind, where his impression of the original subject-matter dissolves into its component parts, which then acquire totally new associations, recalls early developments in twentieth-century painting. His interest in the visual arts is documented in a number of references in the essays, and he reviewed exhibitions in Vienna in 1922 and 1924.[49] As a student, Musil used to visit art galleries in Berlin with his friend Johannes von Allesch, and in 1921 reviewed the latter's book, *Looking at Art*, on publication.[50] In one of the reviews of art exhibitions in 1924 he mentions Kandinsky's *On the Spiritual in Art* (1912), one of the 'decisive documents of the modern movement . . . in which . . . for the first time an abstract "art of internal necessity" was proclaimed and justified as a contemporary phenomenon'.[51] Among the thousands of unpublished papers left after Musil's death, four pages of notes on this book have been identified. Marie-Louise Roth shows that Musil finds himself in

agreement with many of Kandinsky's ideas, especially his conception of art as a part of the 'life' of the spirit, the function of art
being not mimesis, but the intensification of reality. Roth also
refers to other unpublished notes in which Musil collected material
for a planned article on Vincent Van Gogh, who is mentioned a
number of times throughout the *Notebooks* and *Collected Works*.[52]
In his paintings Musil sensed an awareness of the connection
between ethical and aesthetic aspects of life akin to his own. It
would be possible, he writes in a book review of 1913, to love
reason and yet value mysticism, 'which since the beginning of time
has enlarged our knowledge of what it means to be human by
experiences at the frontiers of understanding; in our age we owe
such experiences to the eyes of Van Gogh, when he looked at a
coffee pot or a garden path.'[53]

It is thus evident that Musil's first published essay, 'Obscenity
and Disease in Art', was based on deep convictions with regard to
the nature and function of art, both literary and visual (he wrote
much less about music). His ideas were developed partly through
conversations with friends, partly by reading, and were in some
ways close to those expressed by Kandinsky, although the latter's
book did not appear until the following year. At the same time,
Musil's descriptions in this essay of the processes of the artist's
mind recall his studies in visual perception, together with Allesch,
Wertheimer and other founders of *Gestalt* psychology, and his
detailed study of Mach's theories on the analysis of sensations. His
continuing interest in the visual arts was greatly stimulated by the
fact that his wife was a trained artist. Although she drew little in
later years, she was undoubtedly gifted, to judge by the few
portraits to have survived, and Musil was proud of her talents and
her unerring eye for character.[54]

The essays Musil wrote during the four years from 1911 cover a
number of different fields. Several are concerned with politics,
particularly Austrian politics of these years. Prophetic insights and
scepticism go hand in hand: 'As yet all is quiet, and we sit as in a
glass cage, not daring to move lest the whole edifice shatter into
fragments' (1913).[55] Other essays discuss the connections between
society, religion and modernism; the nature of morality or the relationship of good and evil; or topical questions such as women's
emancipation. In 'Concerning the Books of Robert Musil' (1913)
he invents a discussion between himself, speaking anonymously in
the first person, and two critics, one a young adherent of the 'new

school' of literature, the other an established writer.[56] The meeting takes place in a surrealist mountain landscape identified as the brain of Robert Musil. The attacks on his work from either side provide him with an opportunity to state his own view of the two books published in 1906 and 1911. To the objection that *Young Törless* pays far too much attention to studying the psychology of a boy of sixteen, he retorts that a young protagonist was chosen deliberately, to enable him to show aspects of the psyche that in an adult would be hidden by too many other factors. His central objective at the time was not the portrayal of this particular individual, but rather to demonstrate through him what it is that in such a person is still incomplete and growing to maturity. Psychology in art, he writes, is nothing but a tool, it is the carriage in which you sit; if, in this author's work, you merely note the psychology he employs, you are looking for the landscape inside the carriage. As conflicting opinions are flung to and fro, Musil steadily expounds his conception of the nature and function of literature. Contrary to what some believe, ideas are essential in a literary work, and the writer must search out new ways of combining ideas with means of expression. Emotion by itself is not sufficient; individual experience alone renders it unique, and the writer, in depicting great emotions, creates a fusion of feeling and intellect. Thus he uses the original experience as the focal point for several others, together with all related intellectual and emotional associations. Writers who fail to take account of the deep-seated web of ideas and emotions governing the lives of their fictional characters can only assume how the latter will behave in a given situation; real literature must penetrate the essential core of human beings, their ideas and emotions, and the relationships between these, for they often reveal unexpected significance and provide the only basis for creating characters that are true to life.[57]

The reader approaching these essays with a knowledge of *The Man without Qualities*, whose first volume was not published until 1930, is struck time and again by comments, phrases, and indications of possible lines of thought which find mature expression in the major novel, but already engaged the author's serious attention twenty years earlier. Of no essay is this more true than the one entitled 'The Mathematical Man' (1913).[58] For Musil, mathematics is the highest and purest form of reason, and Ulrich, having become disillusioned with a military and then a technological career, is shown at the beginning of the novel as a mathematician.

In the essay Musil first enumerates some aspects of modern mathematics, and salutes its capacity to predict in principle all possible eventualities: a triumph of mental organisation, of epistemological economy. The uses of mathematics in modern civilisation are well known. Yet for mathematicians themselves, mathematics has a deeper meaning; those who devote their lives to it are not motivated by its potential applications, but by a passionate desire for truth. In a brilliant passage, Musil shows how the whole of modern life is pervaded by mathematics: 'With the exception of the small number of hand-made pieces of furniture, clothes, shoes, and of children, we obtain everything by means of mathematical calculations.' The pioneers of mathematics had worked out certain basic ideas leading to results; these were seized upon by the physicists and finally by the technologists who built the machines:[59]

> And suddenly, after everything had been arranged in the best possible fashion, the mathematicians . . . discovered that in the foundations of the whole edifice there was something seriously wrong; no doubt about it, they checked the very lowest level and found that the whole building was suspended in the air. But the machines were working! We must therefore assume that our existence is nothing but a fantasy; we live it, but only on the basis of an error. No one living today can experience such a feeling of unreality as the mathematician.

This passage, written eight years after Einstein had announced his Special Theory of Relativity, reflects the shock administered by him and other leading thinkers to the certainties of the nineteenth century outlook. The paradox at the heart of mathematics is used by Musil to draw attention to the irrational, inexplicable aspects of life pointed out earlier by Nietzsche, Bergson and Freud, as well as by many creative writers. Such a paradox, as we have seen, lies at the very centre of Musil's thought, from the early *M. le vivisecteur*, who expects the street to cave in under him at any moment, through Törless, who finds in imaginary numbers a powerful symbol of the irrational, and on to the later works. Musil rebels against the one-sided positivism of the older generation, yet is quick to point out the folly of allowing the pendulum to swing too far in the opposite direction, of abandoning the intellect altogether. In the essay under discussion, he comments that in recent years reason has acquired a bad name, especially among novelists. Novels consisting solely of emotion, such as some contemporary German ones, are likely, however, to induce in the reader nothing but an uncomfortable feeling of satiety. It is not the authors of works like these, but mathematicians who are his ideal, for their clear thinking can and should be applied not only in technology, but equally to the realms of the spirit.

The essays and criticism published during these years attracted the notice of Samuel Fischer, who offered Musil a post as editor with *Die Neue Rundschau*; in December 1913, therefore, he moved back to Berlin, delighted with a new position which left him plenty of time for writing. His satisfaction was to be short-lived. By August 1914 Europe was at war, and Musil, who until 1913 had been an officer of the Austrian reserves, immediately returned to Austria to enlist in the army.

Notes

1. *Briefe* 1981, I, pp. 61–64. Cf. TB I, p. 918.
2. W. Köhler, *Die physischen Gestalten in Ruhe und im stationären Zustand*, 1920, cf. GW II, p. 1085; E.M. v. Hornbostel, cf. GW II, p. 1224; E. Kretschmer, *Medizinische Psychologie*, 1922, cf. GW II, p. 1141; K. Lewin, several references and excerpts, cf. TB I, p. 801, II, pp. 583–4, 1213–15, and Nachlass-Mappe 6/1. See also TB II for a bibliography of Musil's reading, and Chapter 7, n.32.
3. Cf. Musil, 'Analyse und Synthese', 1913, GW II, pp. 1008–9.
4. Musil, 'Tonka', GW II, pp. 270–306; cf. TB I, p. 171; English translation in *Tonka and other stories*, trans. E. Kaiser and E. Wilkins, 1965, pp. 169–222.
5. Dinklage, LWW, pp. 211, 220.
6. TB I, p. 100. See also Chapter 4.
7. Ibid., p. 211. Cf. K. Corino, *Robert Musils "Vereinigungen"*. *Studien zu einer historisch-kritischen Ausgabe*, Musil-Studien, 5, 1974, pp. 30. 44.
8. TB I, p. 226.
9. Ibid., p. 210.
10. Dinklage, LWW, pp. 218–21.
11. E.g., TB I, p. 306.
12. Ibid., pp. 148–9, 217–18.
13. GW II, pp. 967–73, p. 967.
14. Ibid., p. 970.
15. Ibid., p. 972.
16. Corino 1974, pp. 32 ff., 46–7.
17. Musil, 'Die Vollendung der Liebe', GW II, pp. 156–94; 'The Perfecting of a Love', trans. E. Kaiser and E. Wilkins, in *Tonka* . . . 1965, pp. 13–67.
18. Ibid., p. 179; ibid., p. 45.
19. U. Karthaus, *Der Andere Zustand. Zeitstrukturen im Werke Robert Musils*, 1965, pp. 93–103.
20. Musil, 'Die Versuchung der stillen Veronika', GW II, pp. 194–223; 'The Temptation of Quiet Veronica', trans. E. Kaiser and E. Wilkins, in *Tonka* . . ., 1965, pp. 68–112.
21. Nachlass-Mappe 4/3, p. 118 f., 'A88', quoted in Corino 1973, p. 180.

22. GW II, p. 196; 'Temptation . . .', p. 71.

23. Ibid., p. 214; ibid., p. 98.

24. Ibid., p. 214; ibid., p. 99. Cf. R. Zeller, ' "Die Versuchung der stillen Veronika". Eine Untersuchung ihres Bedeutungsaufbaus', in: *Sprachästhetische Sinnvermittlung*, ed. D. Farda and U. Karthaus, 1982.

25. GW II, p. 92.

26. TB I, pp. 220–1.

27. GW II, p. 194; 'Temptation . . .', p. 68.

28. Hofmannsthal, *Prosa* II, pp. 17 ff.; *Selected Prose*, pp. 136 ff.

29. GW II, p. 942.

30. Corino 1974, pp. 239 ff.

31. J. Magnou, 'Grenzfall und Identitätsproblem (oder Die Rolle der Psychopathologie) in der literarischen Praxis und Theorie Musils anhand der Novellen "Vereinigungen" ', in *Sprachästhetische Sinnvermittlung*. Cf. Marie-Louise Roth, *Robert Musil. Ethik und Ästhetik*, 1972, pp. 353, 357.

32. Magnou, pp. 5–6.

33. GW II, p. 957.

34. Ibid., p. 969.

35. GW I, pp. 1536, 1651 ff.

36. Musil, *Nachlass zu Lebzeiten*; 'Legacy in My Lifetime', GW II, pp. 471–562. Cf. Marie-Louise Roth, Robert Musil, *Les Oeuvres Pré-Posthumes*, I *Biographie et Écriture*, II *Genèse et Commentaire*, 1980.

37. GW II, p. 474.

38. W. Berghahn, *Robert Musil in Selbstzeugnissen und Bilddokumenten*, 1969, p. 33.

39. TB I, pp. 278–81.

40. Ibid., pp. 227–30.

41. GW II, pp. 1,467–9. Musil was one of the first critics to praise Kafka's work.

42. Musil, 'Die Portugiesin', GW II, pp. 252–70; 'The Lady from Portugal', trans. E. Kaiser and E. Wilkins, in *Tonka* . . . 1965, pp. 142–68. Cf. Marie-Louise Roth 1980, I, p. 40. See also Chapter 4.

43. Musil, 'Die Kraftmaschinen des Kleingewerbes'; 'Motor Engines for Small Businesses', 1903; 'Die Beheizung der Wohnräume'; 'Heating for Domestic Purposes', 1904–5. Details in Roth 1972, p. 510.

44. Musil, 'Das Unanständige und Kranke in der Kunst'; 'Obscenity and Disease in Art', GW II, pp. 977–83.

45. Ibid., p. 980.

46. TB I, pp. 54–8.

47. Ibid., p. 777; Wittgenstein, *Tractatus* 6.421, p. 71.

48. GW I, p. 121.

49. GW II, pp. 1585–7; 1640–4; 1656–9.

50. Ibid., pp. 1517–21.

51. H. Read, *A Concise History of Modern Painting*, 1969, p. 33.

52. Cf. Roth 1972, pp. 316–18, 321–4, 494–8. See also *Musil-Nachlass*, Mappen 7/11, pp. 190–3; 4/3, pp. 252–68, and references in TB I.

53. GW II, pp. 1447.

54. Cf. ibid., p. 974.

55. Musil, 'Politisches Bekenntnis eines jungen Mannes'; 'Political Credo of a Young Man', GW II, pp. 1009–15, p. 1014.

56. Musil, 'Über Robert Musils Bücher'; 'Concerning the Books of Robert Musil', GW II, pp. 995–1001.

57. Ibid., pp. 1000–1.

58. Musil, 'Der mathematische Mensch'; 'The Mathematical Man', GW II, pp. 1004–8.

59. Ibid., p. 1006.

4 A CHANGED WORLD: THE FIRST WORLD WAR AND *THREE WOMEN*

Musil's first reaction to the outbreak of war in 1914 was one of loyal patriotism. In August, he enlisted as a lieutenant with an infantry regiment that was soon ordered to defend the South Tyrolean border between Austria and Italy. He spent the first three years of the war in the then Austrian region of the Dolomites and on the frontier north of Trieste, the whole area being threatened by the claims of the Italian Irredentist movement. Italy had at first announced her neutrality, but declared war on Austria-Hungary in 1915, after the Treaty of London had promised her territorial gains in the Tyrol and along the Adriatic coast.[1] Musil, soon promoted to battalion adjutant, was responsible for organising different sectors of the front in turn, and took part in a number of battles both in the Dolomites and on the much-disputed Isonzo River frontier around Gorizia. The notebooks of this period record little of daily life under these conditions, but a citation for the Bronze Military Medal awarded to Musil in 1916 speaks of his devotion to duty, courage under fire and selfless rescue work during an avalanche.[2]

After a period of serious illness in the spring of 1916, Musil was released from front-line service and eventually transferred to Group Headquarters in Bolzano. Here he was given an assignment for which he was particularly well fitted, namely the editorship of the regional army newspaper. Karl Dinklage shows that in comparison with earlier numbers of this publication, consisting merely of a series of reports by army personnel, the new version under Musil's direction became a professionally run newspaper with leading articles and outspoken comments on topical issues. It stood firmly for a united Austria, playing down references to the regions and removing the name 'Tyrol' from the original title. Moreover, it did not flinch from criticising the current state of politics or the opportunism and profiteering encouraged by the war. A few of the pieces contributed by Musil himself were reprinted in 1960.[3]

Musil directed this newspaper for about ten months, during which time he enjoyed a relatively normal life in Bolzano, made even happier by the fact that after long months of separation Martha was able to join him there. Unfortunately, changes in the

77

High Command had the effect of forcing the paper to close, and Musil was transferred to the Isonzo army in the east. By March 1918, however, he had returned to Vienna to become editor of another official publication, established to sustain the morale of the army by reporting the military and diplomatic successes of the monarchy in the face of the disruptive agitations of nationalist groups all over the empire. This weekly paper appeared until October 1918.

On October 28–9, 1918, Czech troops mutinied and began to return home from the front. In Bohemia and Moravia the nationalists took control; Croatia and Dalmatia announced a union with Serbia; Poland proclaimed its independence. Inside Austria, a coalition government was formed. On November 3 Austria signed the Armistice; on November 11 the Emperor Karl abdicated; on November 12 a German Austrian Republic was proclaimed. It was the revolution: the empire had finally and inevitably collapsed.

Russia had withdrawn from the war after the success of the Bolshevik revolution in October 1917. In Germany, during November 1918, workers' and soldiers' councils assumed control locally in Berlin and elsewhere, and the German Emperor was forced to abdicate too. In April 1919 a soviet republic was set up in Munich, and Communist-inspired demonstrations took place in Vienna. In the cities of Austria people were starving, and the Entente powers, Britain and France, threatened to cut off supplies if a soviet republic were declared there. In September 1919 the Austrian parliament accepted the Treaty of Versailles.[4]

This was the background to Musil's return to civilian life at the end of the war. For about a year, unable to find anything more appropriate to his training, he took a clerical post in the Foreign Office archives, compiling an index of press-cuttings. A friend reported a meeting with him during this period in a kind of soup kitchen run by ladies of the aristocracy for the benefit of needy intellectuals. He described the meticulous politeness with which Musil, known for his high standards in matters of food and dress, forced himself to taste the various dishes being served which had the appearance of soup, vegetables or meat, but were all substitutes. Afterwards they would adjourn to a café to talk for hours over endless cups of coffee, a life-long habit with Musil, whose home accommodation consisted mostly of small, cramped apartments, and at this time amounted to no more than a room or two.[5]

In 1920 the Austrian War Ministry invited him to join the staff of its officer training department. Having tried without success to regain the editorial post in Berlin that he had been obliged to resign in 1914, Musil accepted this position, in Vienna. He was appointed as one of four civilian consultants who were to advise army tutors on non-military aspects of the training of the officers in their charge. The work was reasonably interesting and well paid and, most important, left much free time for writing. Unfortunately the worsening economic situation of Austria led to the post being done away with by the spring of 1923, when Musil was made redundant. Once again he found himself wondering if at an earlier stage of his life he should have taken academic or other regular employment with a pension. Various comments in the notebooks bear witness to his painful realisation that he had acted naïvely when in 1908 he had decided to earn his living by writing alone, a prospect that now looked very different, in the inflationary post-war world. And yet . . . 'Writing is not an activity but a condition. Therefore, if you have a job and happen to have a free half day, you cannot simply resume work.'[6] His mission as a creative writer, as he saw it, outweighed all other considerations, and despite the increasing uncertainty of his financial position, some of his greatest work was produced during the following years.

The beginning of the war was felt by Musil and many others as a kind of religious experience. The endless years of stagnation and ossification in the old Austro-Hungarian empire, the indecision in almost every area of life, the 'uncertainty of man concerning the worth or perhaps also the true nature of himself and those nearest to him'[7] were swept away overnight by the necessity of defending one's country against aggression. The demands of life had suddenly become clear and unequivocal; loyalty, courage and other military virtues came to the fore. In September 1914, at the height of the emotional upsurge that marked the beginning of the war, Musil admits in an essay that writers and intellectuals had believed in an ideal of European man which had little to do with the existing forms of life; he goes on to link their forward-looking and courageous attitudes with the military courage now evident on all sides. He describes the feeling in Austria and Germany during the first hours of the war that the whole of Europe was engaged in a conspiracy to exterminate them; there was an overwhelming awareness of their common language, a national bond which united the two peoples, despite previous differences. No doubt, he writes, the nations on the opposite side were experiencing the same emotions, those who were our friends perhaps being swept along by the current in spite of recognising the wrongness of their cause. We are all caught up in the elemental necessity of protecting the tribe, he writes; it is a feeling no-one can explain, and beyond the gravity of the hour an overpowering certainty and joy.[8]

Today, looking back to 1914 after two major wars with their attendant atrocities committed in the name of nationalism, Musil's readers may question the tone of such sentiments; at least he admits that those on the other side are likely to be imbued with the same patriotic feelings. Yet in a notebook of the time, he describes a rather less lofty aspect of the outbreak of war, the panic and frenzy he witnessed in Berlin: the uprooted intellectuals, the shrill tones of the newspapers, mass hysteria in the streets, the breakdown of normal rules of behaviour, soldiers stealing from one another. The lists of the fallen: . . . dead . . . dead . . . dead, a grim litany.[9] In a later notebook he reflects on the implications of the war: '. . . millions of people have lost their nearest and dearest or their means of existence. That *must* rend the nation apart, one of those suppressed experiences which avenge themselves as hysteria' — a prophetic comment whose truth was soon to become apparent. The war was irrational, it swept up everyone in a fervour of patriotism; but, he writes, for himself the exaltation did not last long, except when face to face with death, out in the open.[10] On another page he returns to his own attempts to achieve factual understanding of the world, 'the real background against which I may construct my unreality'. The essays play an essential part in Musil's continuing efforts to work out a theoretical framework as a basis for his creative writing. But by 1919 he was forced to recognise that time was not on his side: 'The five years of slavery during the war have . . . torn the best part out of my life.' He renounces the plan to work out a systematic, scientifically-founded appraisal of the state of the world, resolving only to set out his views and the reasons for them as occasion arises.[11]

In the course of this attempt to clarify to himself and others the state of the contemporary world, Musil published in March 1919 a long essay on the proposal to unite Austria and Germany into one political entity. When Hitler actually carried out the *Anschluss* in 1938, it was seen by many as the working out of National Socialist megalomania, but the idea in fact had a very long history. During the Middle Ages the Holy Roman Empire of the German Nation had consisted of Austria and a number of other German states, and historically, the Austro-Hungarian Empire was its heir. Following the rise of Prussia in the eighteenth and nineteenth centuries, an intense rivalry had grown up between Prussia and Austria, coming to a head in the war of 1866 when Austria was decisively defeated at the battle of Sadowa. As a result she was obliged to renounce her claims to leadership of the German states, most of which were henceforth united under Prussia.[12]

After the First World War, the Treaty of Versailles forbade Austria's union with Germany except under the auspices of the League of Nations; nevertheless the idea still enjoyed considerable support. Musil's essay, written before the terms of the treaty were finally agreed, makes out a strong case. Undeterred by the sensitive state of national feeling in Austria after defeat and the collapse of the empire, he examines the position in 1919, and argues that the idea of the separate national state is generally treated with a veneration it does not deserve. After giving examples of great thinkers maltreated by the state, he points out that in one respect states behave far worse than the average man: that is, in their relations with other states. The basic laws of human behaviour, enshrined in the Ten Commandments, enjoin human beings not to kill, not to lie, not to desire their neighbours' goods and so on, but are replaced in inter-state relationships by the single law of national advantage. While states seeking this are of course recognised as criminal by the inhabitants of other states, they manage, by extraordinary means, to appear to their own citizens as the embodiment of honour and morality. These obvious comments, he writes, should not need to be repeated, were it not for the fact that all the talk at the present time of 'guilty' states shows how little the real nature of the state is as yet understood.

Looking to the future, Musil continues, the sensible way to organise larger communities would be on the basis of a common language, especially in a case like that of Germany and Austria, two states that are immediate neighbours and share a long cultural history. He then considers objections to such a plan. These emanate on the one hand from the Communists, who see all nation states as obsolescent, and on the other from those wearied by the quarrels between nationalist groups in the Austrian empire. Musil recalls that difficulties with the nationalist factions were usually blamed for lack of progress in the empire, but conversely, he suggests, perhaps these only assumed such importance because in the years following Austria's defeat by Prussia the life of the empire had virtually stood still. The economic links with Hungary since 1867, and the inability of any one group to assume real leadership, had slowed down economic development to a dangerous extent, depriving the state of any national vigour. But who in any case was the state? It was merely an anonymous administrative organism without body, mind or spirit of its own: a ghost.

These then were the conditions in which, it was said, the unique Austrian culture was able to flourish. Musil denies that any such common culture existed after 1867; if the inhabitants of Austria-Hungary since that date were not prepared to speak with the same enthusiasm of their *modern* culture, then they were merely indulging in nostalgia. Austria before the war was an anachronism: 'The Austrian face smiled because it no longer possessed any facial muscles'. Elegance and finesse were no substitutes for all that was lacking. Comparing Austria and Germany, with regard to financial support for universities, number and size of important libraries, art collections, theatres, books published, and so on, Musil argues that the culture of a state must surely lie in such things, if anywhere. On the last page he emphasises that his strictures are directed at the state, not at the individual Austrian, who is indeed cultured and hard-working. Life in Austria, he concedes, almost regretfully, is more intense, less rushed, more open to outside influences than in Germany. But, he repeats, if it is the task of the state to provide the conditions in which individuals may produce and promote spiritual values, then the Austrian state would need to be changed, from top to bottom. Union with Germany would be a much simpler way of achieving this goal, and would benefit Germany by the infusion of specifically Austrian virtues.[13]

Some of these critical observations reappear later, clad in affectionate irony, in the major novel, under the heading Kakania; in 1919 however Musil puts them forward as a serious contribution to a topical debate. The political essays written before the war were equally outspoken. Musil never joined a political party, although in 1918 he signed the programme of the Activists, a group, led by Kurt Hiller, which was committed to political involvement by artists and intellectuals.[14] Yet although Musil was not actively involved in politics, the notebooks show that he was very much aware of the contemporary political scene. This is one of the aspects of his essays and notebooks which make them of value today; he is the thoughtful, analytical observer of developments which were to have a decisive effect on the course of twentieth-century history, and his comments, placing each event in context, help us to understand the various factors involved.

*　　*　　*

Musil's war service is reflected in notebook entries and sketches published in various journals and later reprinted in *Legacy in My Lifetime*. The most striking work to come out of the war years is found in the two novellas 'Grigia' and 'The Lady from Portugal', which appeared with 'Tonka' in 1924 under the title *Three Women*, although each tale is mainly told from the point of view of the man involved. 'Grigia'[15] and 'The Lady from Portugal' are both at first reading remarkable for their graphic descriptions of the Tyrol. In a few words Musil evokes the astonishing landscape of this region, whose deep valleys are framed by walls of mountains, with secret villages hidden away at the end of contorted and sometimes dangerous tracks. Above the forests tower cliffs of rock that form the boundaries of this strange world. The hero of 'Grigia', a geologist whose name is given simply as Homo, agrees one day on the spur of the moment to take part in a speculative venture to reopen some old Venetian gold-mines in the Férsina valley. This decision is made at a critical juncture of his life, a time when it seems to hesitate, as if to change direction. We are told that his wife, whom he loves dearly, has gone with their young son, who is ill, to a health resort. Homo had refused to accompany them, pleading the need to continue work at home; yet two days later he plunges without reflection into unpremeditated adventure.

The mountain village chosen as the base for the expedition is described as a mysterious and fantastic territory. The houses, perched on a steep hillside, are supported on poles like prehistoric lake dwellings. The people, whose ancestors came to the valley in medieval times, form a German-speaking enclave in an Italian region, their language full of enigmatic expressions. Homo and his companions are welcomed like gods because they bring work, money and goods into the poverty-stricken community; the villagers do not, as anyone else might, stop to ask what kind of men they are, but respond to them with love and gratitude. Homo finds himself more and more absorbed by the magical nature of the world in which he now lives, and where his previous self seems somehow irrelevant. Yet, although he no longer answers his wife's letters, he has not forgotten her. Lying in an alpine meadow brilliant with flowers, encircled by green larch trees as in a fairy-tale, he experiences a feeling of intense closeness with his distant wife. For some reason he has a premonition that he will die in this place, and at the same time a sudden and irrational certainty that their love will endure beyond the grave. In a moment of ecstasy he feels united with her and at the same time with the trees and flowers around him, the gold and precious stones in the ground under his feet. From that day onwards he is no longer afraid of death.

While work on the old mines slowly proceeds, the whole district is organised to make it possible. All the villagers are involved in one way or another, and horses and many guard dogs are brought in so that the valley is full of animals, underlining the primitive, even brutal aspect of life there: '. . . nature is anything but natural, she is earthy, angular, poisonous and inhuman wherever man does not impose his will upon her.'[16] The five men in charge of the work meet every evening for dinner, their gatherings increasingly pervaded by unutterable boredom and emptiness, which a creaking gramophone does little to dispel. Homo is sickened by the atmosphere of decay and senselessness that reminds him of the worst aspects of the European civilisation he has left behind. By contrast, the age-old traditions of village life associated with herding cattle and hay-making have a freshness and authenticity which fascinate him, and these are personified by the local women. Within a short time he drifts into an affair with a young woman he calls Grigia (after the name of her cow), without seeing in this any betrayal of his love for his wife. He feels himself completely detached from his former existence; it has lost all vitality, like a butterfly in autumn. Throughout the summer, he lives as in a dream, but one day Grigia refuses to meet him in a barn, as she has before. He persuades her to enter a disused mine-shaft where they make love for the last time; suddenly he sees in the doorway her husband, who had been working in the mines and whose existence he had completely forgotten, and a moment later the entrance is blocked by an enormous stone. After many hours Grigia finds another way out of the prison, but Homo is too exhausted — or too irresolute — to attempt escape, and dies.

This story, considerably shorter than either of the novellas of 1911, is also much easier to read, partly on account of the superb descriptions of the setting, partly because the author makes greater use of traditional methods of narration. Nevertheless, the central figure is presented in depth, and the process by which he meets his end unfolds against a background rich in imagery. The setting itself, in the remote mountain valley, provides that removal from the familiar scene which all Musil's heroes seem to need, to a greater or lesser extent, if they are to achieve knowledge of themselves. For Törless it is the red attic or the loneliness of the park; for Claudine the snow-bound village; for Veronica the transformation of her own room into a space full of light. Homo drifts into the adventure which is to lead him to the mountains, as he drifts into the affair with Grigia; but between these two events lies the moment of apocalyptic vision when it becomes clear to him that his life no longer possesses real meaning, and that he will remain united with his wife in a love beyond earthly existence.

Looking back from this point to the outset, we note that the story contains many signs of disintegration and death. It starts in the month the mountain snows are beginning to thaw, giving the air a softness unknown during winter. An old farmer salutes the strangers with his scythe, like Death himself. The wildness of the animals surfaces from time to time, or else they are cruelly treated by the labourers; a fly's lingering death prefigures Homo's own. The idea of dissolution appears on the first page and is suggested many times thereafter. So we find ourselves asking: what was Homo's life before his journey to the mountains, and why does he accept its dissolution without resistance? The answer is found, at least in part, on the opening page. Except for 'books and plans', all his previous life had, it seems, been centred on companionship with his wife, but once the child began to develop needs of his own which the mother was obliged to put first, Homo's love for her diminished. It does not seem to have occurred to him that he might have a duty to help care for his own sick child. Yet this was not because he had urgent work to do; he had no specific plans for the summer when he so readily accepted the invitation to join the mining venture. Homo's former life gives the impression of having no definable identity, of non-involvement with both work and family; he idealises his wife so long as she is there for him alone, but is unwilling to accept his share of family responsibilities. He seems primarily a thinker who, when required to act, lacks willpower and allows things to happen to him, a man so intent on the fine details of the situation in which he finds himself that he overlooks its real nature. The passive intellectual is a figure Musil draws again and again, being well aware of his own leanings in that direction. At the same time he clearly regards Homo as exemplifying an attitude of mind treated ironically elsewhere in his work, that of the city dweller who looks at 'Nature' through romantic spectacles, who even assumes in his arrogance that the countryside and its inhabitants are there for his benefit alone, but who is too effete to survive contact with nature in the raw. Homo abandons himself to a dream of life in the magic village with Grigia, the child of nature, without once thinking of her husband; but when the latter appears, it is as the agent of death, and the stone rolled in front of Homo's tomb has a brutal and final reality.

A further dimension is shown in the few pages devoted to the gatherings of the expedition leaders: wine, the gramophone churning out popular songs and arias from *Tosca*, smoke, dirty jokes, boredom, quarrels over trifles, challenges to duels which come to nothing, killing time. 'They no longer talked to each other, they merely talked' — a sign language, as between animals.[17] And floating over it all, in the music, 'the lust which enters into all that goes on in the cities', into manslaughter, jealousy, business, car racing; no, not lust, but a longing for adventure, not even that, but a knife, a sword from heaven, an angel of destruction, madness, war? The fatal emptiness of so-called civilised man before 1914 is linked with Homo's own emptiness, and the author shows how a conflagration may break out for no other reason than that people are weary to death of their own senseless existence.

'The Lady from Portugal'[18] is also set in the Dolomites, but in medieval times. The focal point of the action is a castle high on a steep mountainside, isolated from the outer world both by the sheer cliff on which it stands and by the roaring of the torrent below. Herr von Ketten, its lord, is the leader of the knights of the region in their long-standing quarrel with the Bishop of Trent, a war that has continued for generations. His wife is a lady from Portugal whom he wooed and brought home twelve years ago; she is a beautiful, mysterious woman whom the soldiers call a sorceress, and reads books filled with esoteric symbols. While she rules over the castle and brings up their two sons, Herr von Ketten lives in the saddle, and after eleven years of scheming and fighting scores a decisive victory which ends the war.

On his way home he is stung by a poisonous mosquito, and immediately falls into a dangerous fever. After being bled and wrapped in poultices for two days, he is carried home; the fever takes its course, but Herr von Ketten survives, if as a shadow of his former self. It seems to him that he has already departed this life; he lies there passively until the day when he realises that unless he summons up all his willpower, he will surely die. Suddenly the fever leaves him, and from that day onwards he begins a slow and painful recovery. As the weeks drag by, a number of happenings, insignificant in themselves, forcibly remind him of his vanished strength. The presence of a young wolf, reared by his wife during his years of absence, rouses him to anger, but his arm is too weak to bend his bow; instead he commands a servant to destroy it. He notices that his fur cap no longer fits as tightly as it used to, yet it is almost new; his head must have grown smaller. The chaplain, the scribe and a wandering scholar, all eating at his table, openly make jokes at his expense; he strikes the worst offender in the face, but does not throw him out. The lowest point in von Ketten's humiliation is reached when a young nobleman, a childhood friend of the Portuguese lady, arrives at the castle. Frau von Ketten delights in the company of the young man, as he reminds her of home. A handsome, amusing courtier, he makes her laugh amid the uncouth surroundings, and shows no inclination to leave. Her husband is consumed with jealousy, exacerbated by his inability to understand the language in which they converse, yet the rules of hospitality forbid that he should ask the stranger to depart. A wise woman prophesies that he will only regain his health by achieving something, but refuses to say what this might be.

As the tension between the three people mounts day by day, an unexpected visitor enters the castle. It is a little cat, young and playful; unlike other cats, it does not hunt in cellars and attics, but prefers to stay with the human inhabitants who are perhaps glad to play with it and forget their own problems. It soon becomes clear that it is sick, yet no-one can bear to give the order to kill it. While the cat suffers almost like a human being, the three adults watch, and none of them can escape the thought that it is his own fate which has passed into the animal. Finally, the lady asks a servant to end its suffering; afterwards she and her husband meet by chance, and neither can find a word to say. The little cat was a sign, but how are they to interpret it?

On the same day Herr von Ketten decides that if his wife does not send the stranger away by nightfall, he must kill him. Evening comes, but he cannot bring himself to arm and fight, as his whole former mode of life now appears senseless. Yet, on the other hand, he is not prepared to suffer indefinitely. Suddenly he resolves to accept a quite different challenge, and almost in a trance, begins to climb up the bare rock-face below the castle. In the moonlight the cracks and footholds in the cliff are just visible. He knows that this ascent is a crazy undertaking, yet the very danger makes strength flow back into his limbs. The only way to enter the castle at the top is through a window: it is the stranger's room, and it is empty. Silently he moves to his wife's room: she is alone, sleeping peacefully; a servant informs him that the stranger left at moonrise. When he is reunited with his wife, she says: 'If God could become man, he could become a cat, too', and to his ears it does not sound like blasphemy.

This novella is perhaps the most perfect of Musil's shorter works; the dramatic setting plays a vital part, but forms only one element in its success. The centre of the stage is held by two evenly-matched figures, for although the author does not devote as much space to the lady from Portugal as to her husband, he says enough to portray her as an individual with an essential role. Herr von Ketten is shown as the man of action, for whom the year spent with his beautiful young wife after their marriage marks a brief pause in a lifetime of fighting. The main narrative begins at the point when, by winning the war, he has lost the justification of his professional skills: 'Othello's occupation's gone'. Like Homo, he is shown at a turning-point in his life, a moment when his former being is suddenly deprived of all meaning. In the case of von Ketten, this climacteric is further marked by the sting of the insignificant mosquito, as a result of which he almost dies; thus he loses not only his occupation, but the physical strength and toughness that constituted the basis of his soldier's identity. At the moment of victory, the successful general is carried home helpless, a parcel of bandages.

What is to become of him? Is he to give in, to yield to his body's longing for an end to the struggle? That is not von Ketten's way; he is a fighter, and he fights for his life. During the long convalescence he must endure not only the shame of his own weakness, but also the humiliations of daily life in the castle. His resentment of the young wolf's vigour is satisfied by a word of command, but other problems are not so easily solved. The agony of jealousy is intensified by the knowledge that in former times he would not have hesitated to attack his rival; now, even though his body is more or less restored, his inner self is unable to reach a decision.

The sudden, irrational resolve to climb up the bare rock-face is the act of will-power the wise woman had prophesied as needful, and with it he finds not only himself, but his wife again.

As was mentioned earlier, Musil often presents figures in complementary pairs: Beineberg and Basini as possibilities of Törless, Johannes and Demeter on either side of Veronica. A similar link may be seen between Homo and Herr von Ketten, both of whom face a crisis in which they must find a new mode of being. These two figures illustrate the dichotomy between reflection and action, one of Musil's constant themes in *Young Törless* as well as the later works. Faced with the challenge of an unfamiliar situation, the two men react very differently. Homo, the intellectual, has lost the hold on his life from the beginning; neither work nor family are strong enough to bind him, and he allows himself to be drawn into a dubious adventure. The affair with Grigia finally appears as the natural means to his inevitable end, yet with greater strength of will he might have escaped from the mine where he dies. Herr von Ketten on the other hand, although reduced to a shadow by the fever, is threatened not only by the taunts of lesser men but by the presence of a rival for his wife's affections, but asserts himself by sheer physical daring, thus gaining a new life. In passing it may be noted that Musil set great store by physical fitness and took part regularly in various kinds of sport, a characteristic also reflected in Ulrich, the man without qualities.

Another aspect of 'The Lady from Portugal' is the significant part played by animals. The fever that transforms Herr von Ketten is caused by a mosquito, a sign of the unpredictable. His wife rears a wolf cub found in the forest, its sinewy body reminding her of her absent lord; but when her lord himself, wasted by disease, is confronted by the animal, his first action on the way to recovery is to order its death. The little cat walks into seemingly insoluble tension between the three people who watch it suffer; while it lingers and dies, each of them associates the animal's fate with his own, and draws conclusions from it. In this story, the animals act as signs, reflections of the human situation at a particular juncture, illuminating aspects of that situation for the characters involved. In *Young Törless* and the two novellas of 1911, on the other hand, animal imagery is used rather for characterisation; the human beings see either themselves or others in terms of animals, and certain animal attributes are emphasised in each case. As we saw earlier, Musil's life-long interest in animal psychology was developed by his early reading of works in the field of evolutionary theory (see Chapter 1), but equally by his reverence for Nietzsche, Emerson and Novalis, who frequently employ animal parallels in their work, particularly to show links between the conscious and unconscious (see Chapter 2). Frau von Ketten's final words, suggesting that the little cat was indeed a sign from God are quoted almost verbatim from Novalis.[19] The notebooks of the Romantic poet and scientist contain other statements that may be linked with important aspects of this story, for example Herr von Ketten's sudden and illuminating discovery of what he must do to master what has seemed an impossible situation. In 'Tonka', the last story in this volume, Novalis's *Fragments* are mentioned by name.

'Tonka', the last novella in *Three Women*, was briefly referred to in Chapter 3.[20] The story describes the relationship between an unnamed young scientist and Tonka, a girl from a humble background. The young man is a passionate adherent of the rational yet imaginative spirit of the age, the adventurous spirit of inventors and engineers; he pretends to be deaf to any questions not admitting a clear-cut solution, thinks logically and sees himself as one of Nietzsche's 'free spirits' soaring bravely through unknown skies. His father is a kindly man, but unwell; his mother represents all the bourgeois conventions which infuriate her son. His revolt against home is reinforced by the constant presence of a friend of the family, a civil servant and writer of popular novels who is an admirer of the young man's mother. Her affirmation of the norms of upper-class society, his habit of discoursing upon historical and philosophical questions in large but meaningless terms, have shaped her son's opposition. Even his offer to look after Tonka owes something to defiance, since he is convinced that the girl, who had nursed his grandmother, has been badly treated by his family.

The young man moves to a large city and takes Tonka with him; while he devotes himself to his research, she works in a shop. After some years of living together, she becomes pregnant and shortly afterwards shows symptoms of venereal disease; the beginnings of the pregnancy and the disease, however, appear to fall on a date when he was absent. From this point onwards the narrative is concerned with the agonising doubts of the young man in face of Tonka's steadfast denials that she has been unfaithful to him, and with her reaction to his lack of trust. In spite of the doctors' warnings that she needs care and consideration if she is to survive, he tortures her as well as himself by his obsessive preoccupation with the facts of the case; their material situation grows steadily worse, and eventually she dies in hospital.

From the beginning, the author emphasises Tonka's nature. She is seen as an unassuming, kind-hearted girl who loves the young man for himself alone, although she comes from a milieu where prostitutes are not unknown. He, the intellectual, loves her for her freshness and simplicity and her genuine goodness, in contrast with the conventional attitudes of his mother and her circle. The young man and the girl may be seen as representatives of intellect and feeling; she seems to come from an irrational, emotional, fairy-tale world, as do Grigia and the lady from Portugal. The encounter between them turns in the end on the question of what constitutes truth or reality, also one of the central themes of *Young Törless*; in 'Tonka' the problem is intensified to the point of agony by the fact that the young man is a scientist whose thinking is governed by probability theory. Medical opinion and common sense combine to produce a high probability that Tonka has been unfaithful; is he then to fly in the face of the obvious conclusion? Yet Tonka denies the charge and soon refuses to answer any further questions; against all the arguments pointing to her guilt, he must set her essential nature, her goodness and devotion to him. What is truth? What is he to believe? Even in his scientific world a measure of faith is required to believe in the existence of objects and processes, otherwise all that remains, according to Mach's theories, is a heap of unrelated elements. Thus by his insistence on facts and probability the young scientist manoeuvres himself into a position where he is not prepared to offer Tonka even the trust underlying his relationships with things, and by that lack of trust she is destroyed.

Other factors complicate the situation. If he admits to being the father of the child, this implies that he himself has venereal disease, which is not supported by medical evidence. Despite their growing estrangement, he still feels responsible for Tonka, since it was he who brought her to the city, and although his mother applies increasing pressure to end the liaison, he resists it without committing himself wholeheartedly to the girl. One of the main themes of the story, again as in *Young Törless*, is that of language and communication. Tonka and the young scientist are separated by differences of sex, class, intellect and language: she is Czech, he is

German. Musil grew up in Brno (Brünn) in Moravia, where, as in the Prague of Kafka and Rilke, the educated classes spoke German while the people spoke Czech, and this no doubt sharpened his awareness of the vital importance of communication. Both 'Grigia' and 'The Lady from Portugal' are set in a language-frontier area, and just as Homo is fascinated by Grigia's strange vocabulary, so also Herr von Ketten suffers from being unable to understand what his wife and the young Portuguese courtier are saying to each other. When the young scientist, proud of his effortless way with words, asks Tonka to explain her feelings, she cannot answer; but when she sings her own folk-songs, it is he who is left speechless. Although he senses that her inability to express her thoughts and feelings is a serious handicap, he is not prepared to make allowances on that account. In Notebook 11 Musil quotes Emerson's remark: 'The man is only half himself, the other half is his expression' with a later reference to this novella.[21] Later in the story, the young man's dreams are haunted by Tonka; even in waking hours he suspects that his rational way of looking at life is inadequate, that perhaps he is the guilty one. But still his intellect will not allow him to admit it. Even when she is near death he cannot speak one saving word to show he believes in her. Yet after she has died, the blindness falls from his eyes, and he recognises, too late, that some areas of life cannot be ruled by the intellect, that goodness and love possess a truth of their own.

The publication of the notebooks, which Musil could not have foreseen, has provided some evidence of links between 'Tonka' and his own life in the period up to 1907. The notebooks reveal the author reflecting upon, and shaping his own experience, in order to bring out certain aspects; at the time of the entries concerning 'Tonka', the story was still intended to form part of the major novel, but by 1924 he had decided to include it in *Three Women*. All Musil's fiction and drama can be shown to relate in one way or another to his own experiences or to those of people he had known, but it is not for this reason they are worth reading today. As Musil reflects in Notebook 10, the basic elements constitute no more than the 'building bricks' of the writer's creative task: 'he copies parts of the real world and combines them into a whole' that only exists in a particular work.[22] In constructing this new reality, the writer analyses and illuminates the ordinary world. He transmutes his own experience and fuses it with other elements according to very deep-seated ideas, which find expressive form in structures and imagery that may not even be present in his conscious mind when he begins to write. Analysing the tension between ideas and expression in his work in 1910, during the writing of *Unions*, Musil finds that in contrast with scientific thinking, always controlled by exact goals and methods, creative writing can easily become shapeless if it is not structured by imagery. It might be thought that the writer invents suitable images in a haphazard fashion, but this is not so, for '. . . the original images are created out of the conception one has of the whole', and these then dominate the work as it proceeds.[23]

In *Three Women* much of the imagery, or the symbolic description of outer reality, shows the strange, irrational world in which the three men become involved, not necessarily because of the three women, but through them. The author seems to be pointing to the vulnerability of those who think themselves secure. The use of animal images, with their emphasis on instinct, underlines this aspect. Other images, again as in earlier works, are based on the contrast of light and darkness, on spatial separation, or on separation brought about by the sound of a roaring torrent. When Herr von Ketten and his wife can find nothing to say to one another, they are enclosed in a 'dome of silence'. This spatial manner of seeing the movements of the principal figures extends also to their movements within the dimension of time. In all three novellas time plays an essential part. In each one the author points out that the action relates to a time of life when one is particularly vulnerable, and then reinforces this awareness through the text. For Homo, the moment of decision occurs in the blocked-up mine, for von Ketten when he at last faces up to the need to act. The young scientist is caught up in a web of uncertainties, but while he hesitates, Tonka's pregnancy takes its inexorable course, demonstrating one kind of reality about which there can be no doubt whatsoever.

In 1918 Musil published an essay entitled 'Skizze der Erkenntnis des Dichters', an outline of the nature and function of the creative writer's mind.[24] The German word *Dichter*, by which Musil described himself, denotes not only a lyric poet, but a writer of literature in all its forms; the essay sets out his conception of the creative writer's mind and of the way he sees the world. He begins by describing the writer as the one who is most aware of the utter loneliness of the self in the world, and among other human beings, the one who is most sensitive to the imponderable and intangible elements of life. To make the distinction between the 'non-rational' writer and his opposite absolutely clear, Musil then draws a portrait of the 'rational' man, who operates, particularly in science, with facts and figures, with laws and concepts, and with material that can be analysed, defined and arranged in categories. In the rational sphere, facts may be considered in isolation; yet in any particular area, repetitions often occur. Numbers, colours, weights, speeds and so on are capable of being described exactly, and without ambiguity. This view of the world is governed by concepts of firmness, solidity and stability, and although exceptions to the rules do occur, rational men are not disposed to take them very seriously, and hope to eliminate them in time.

Since this rational outlook has been so successful in uniting the minds of men, it is not to be wondered at if they seek to apply the same procedures in the field of morality. Here, as in the area of facts, attempts are made to firm up essentially shifting ground by a foundation of rigid concepts supporting a network of laws and rules. Our system of ethics, he writes, is still a static one based on the concept of solidity. Character, right and wrong, norms and other regulators are invoked as the basis for the moral decisions of daily life. But here things are much less straightforward, for the spirit of man is anything but firm and stable. This is the non-rational domain, the realm of exceptions rather than rules, and in order to understand it a complete reversal of mental attitude is required. Here facts do not conform, and laws are like a sieve in which the holes are no less important than the mesh; events do not repeat themselves but are immeasurably varied and individual. It is the sphere of values and value judgements, of ethical and aesthetic relationships and of ideas. Whereas concepts or scientific judgements can be valid without reference to persons or circumstances, an idea is always dependent on both, and a statement like 'no belief deserves the sacrifice of one's life' may be interpreted in various ways, in which circumstances, experience and personal choice all play a part. In this sphere ideas, facts and relationships are infinite and incalculable.

This is the realm where the creative writer is at home. While his counterpart, the rational man, is satisfied if he can set up as many equations as there are unknowns, here there is no limit to the number of unknowns, equations or possible solutions. The writer's task is: 'constantly to discover new solutions, connections, constellations, variables, to depict prototypes of courses of events, enticing models of possible human beings, to *invent* the inner man'.[25] What Musil advocates is not a 'psychological', scientific approach to the study of human nature, but one that will do justice to the infinity of possible variations in the workings of the human soul.

Writers are often thought of as exceptional beings, not necessarily in a good sense. This, according to Musil, is a fallacy; it would be more useful to describe them as those who are concerned with the exceptions, but are not themselves exceptional. A writer is not 'mad', not a 'visionary' nor a 'child'. The methods by which he or she gains knowledge of the world are not really different from those of the scientist, since facts and skill in combining them are needed in both fields; the difference lies in what they see, for the scientist is concerned with outer reality, the writer with the human spirit. Finally, in the fourth year of the war, Musil rejects an attitude of mind that expects writers to do nothing but glorify their own age and its ideas, or to abandon the critical faculty and give voice to unbridled emotion. His understanding of their function is a loftier one, resting on his profound conviction that the writer has a mission to fulfil. By drawing attention to aspects of life that cannot be measured, cannot be imprisoned in systems or categories, yet possess literally vital significance, the writer follows a vocation defined not by his own talents, but by 'the structure *of the world itself*'.[26]

The distinction in this essay between rational and non-rational ways of knowing the world, expressing clearly what had been implicit in much of his earlier writing, formed the basis of Musil's work from this time onwards. His view of the writer's task also remained constant and was stated once again in the interview with Oskar Maurus Fontana in 1926, when, asked for his aims in writing *The Man without Qualities*, he replied: 'To provide help in understanding and coming to terms with the world'.[27]

Notes

1. C. E. Williams, *The Broken Eagle. The Politics of Austrian Literature from Empire to Anschluss*, 1974, pp. 243–4.
2. Dinklage, LWW, pp. 226–7.
3. Ibid., pp. 227–9; 265–72.
4. Williams, pp. 248–50.

5. Berghahn, 1969, p. 76.

6. TB I, p. 470.

7. GW II, p. 956.

8. Musil, 'Europäertum, Krieg, Deutschtum'; 'On Being a European, War, On Being a German', GW II, pp. 1020−2.

9. TB I, pp. 298−9.

10. Ibid., pp. 543−4.

11. Ibid., p. 527.

12. D. Richards, *An Illustrated History of Modern Europe*, 1967, pp. 176−80.

13. Musil, 'Der Anschluss an Deutschland'; 'Union with Germany', GW II, pp. 1033−42.

14. J. C. Thöming, 'Der optimistische Pessimismus eines passiven Aktivisten', *Studien*, 1970, pp. 214−35, pp. 220 ff.

15. Musil, 'Grigia', GW II, pp. 234−52; 'Grigia', trans. E. Kaiser and E. Wilkins, in *Tonka* . . ., 1965, pp. 115−141.

16. Ibid., p. 245; ibid., p. 131.

17. Ibid., p. 243; ibid., p. 128.

18. Musil, 'Die Portugiesin', ibid., pp. 252−70; 'The Lady from Portugal', in: *Tonka* . . ., 1965, pp. 142−168.

19. Novalis, *Fragmente vermischten Inhalts*, no. 144, *Gesammelte Werke*, p. 397.

20. Musil, 'Tonka', GW II, pp. 270−306; 'Tonka', in *Tonka* . . ., 1965, pp. 169−222.

21. TB I, pp. 170, 171; Emerson III, p. 5.

22. TB I, p. 448.

23. Ibid., pp. 214−15.

24. Musil, 'Skizze der Erkenntnis des Dichters'; 'The Mind of the Writer', GW II, pp. 1025−30.

25. Ibid., p. 1029. Emphasis in the original.

26. Ibid. Emphasis in the original.

27. Ibid., p. 942.

5

THE MATURE WRITER: ESSAYS, *THE
VISIONARIES* AND *VINCENT AND THE
MISTRESS OF IMPORTANT MEN*

After the insecurity of the immediate post-war period, Musil's life became somewhat more settled in the years 1920–3. In addition to working as an educational consultant for the Austrian War Ministry, he acted as Viennese art and theatre critic for two German-language newspapers in Prague, first the *Prager Presse* and then *Bohemia*, from March 1921 until December 1922. The reviews he wrote, and others up to 1930, are reprinted in GW II and cover such events as Max Reinhardt's début in Vienna, a performance of Strindberg's *Dream Play*, an appearance by Yvette Guilbert, an exhibition of Russian art, and a performance of Shaw's *Saint Joan*, as well as many plays by German and Austrian dramatists. Almost one hundred notices, including some book reviews, provide a record of the varied cultural scene in Vienna during the years when the Republic of Austria was becoming established.

Financially, Musil was better off up to 1923 than at any time before or since. His relatively steady income enabled him to rent an apartment in Vienna large enough to contain one room for use as a study, where he worked at a huge old dining table covered with papers. This apartment, at Number 20 Rasumofskygasse, in a stately old building near the centre of the city, remained the home of Robert and Martha Musil until they moved to Berlin in 1931.[1]

In Chapter 4 the discussion of *Three Women* was linked with Musil's experiences during the war, out of which two of the stories arose. His first work to be published after the war was, however, the drama *The Visionaries*.[2] Notes for this play are found in the notebooks as early as 1908, and then in 1911, 1912 and 1918; the manuscript was completed by 1920 and published in 1921.[3] Although critical opinion was favourable, no producer was prepared to put it on; not until April 1929 was the play given a stage performance in Berlin, and this was a disaster. In spite of Musil's protests, the text was drastically shortened so that it failed to make sense, the actors rebelled, and in the auditorium booing and laughter drowned the applause. A friend who accompanied the author on this occasion recalls how afterwards they wandered through the dark streets of Berlin, too distressed for words, and sees this humiliating failure as helping to undermine Musil's health.[4]

It must be admitted that *The Visionaries* is a play which would need highly sympathetic acting to make it a success on stage. The four main characters are shown at a crisis in their relationships which is only resolved by a change of role and a change of partner. This would no doubt constitute a useful plot for comedy, or even for farce, but Musil treats their problems seriously, although comic elements are not entirely lacking. The action is set in a country house inhabited by Thomas, an academic, and his wife Maria, said to be calm and very beautiful; her sister, Regine, described as 'dark, indefinable . . . a magic bird', and Regine's lover Anselm have recently arrived. The four people have always known one another and spent their childhood together in the house. Since that time Regine has been married twice, first to Johannes, who died very young, but whom she has never forgotten, and then to Josef, a university professor whose arrival in pursuit of his wife precipitates the crisis. Outraged that Thomas has agreed to shelter Regine and her lover, Josef threatens to ruin his career unless he ceases to protect them.

During the course of the action, however, it becomes apparent that none of the four principal characters is quite what he or she seems at first sight. Regine emerges as a highly complex personality. She has visions of Johannes, her first husband, and her marriage to Josef has clearly not progressed far beyond a formal union. He attributed this coldness to a saintly disposition, and blames Anselm for her flight from home; but a small notebook in her handwriting reveals her in a very different light, showing that over many years she tried to give meaning to her empty, senseless life by affairs with a series of lovers, all of whom she called Johannes. Anselm points out that Johannes committed suicide because Regine would love him only as a sister, and interprets her behaviour since then as an attempt to keep faith with him after his death, or with an inner reality which only she can perceive. When, in the second act, Regine is heard crying hysterically off-stage, Anselm observes that she does not really believe in all that, any more than she believes that her crying will do any good. 'She simply does it . . . It is the last, accidental, inappropriate means of expressing herself she has left.'[5] Yet Regine herself, at the beginning of the play, sees her life in larger terms; she speaks of the unlimited powers with which every human being enters the world: 'But then life always forces him to choose between two possibilities, and he always feels: one of them is missing . . . the undiscovered third possibility.'[6] Thus one ends by never doing what one really wanted to do, and one's original talents eventually wither away. Up to then she has believed that it is possible to separate the inner self from the actions of the outer person by an effort of will, and hoped to begin a new life together with Anselm; but in the course of the play her view of herself and her own future is completely changed.

Anselm is the male counterpart to Regine: he drifts from one situation to the next, guided only by his feelings. Formerly a lecturer like Thomas, he soon relinquished his post and disappeared for many years. He has lived abroad, was a monk for a time, has known all kinds of adventures, some of them of a dubious nature; he has never settled anywhere for long, yet he has a wife somewhere at home. Anselm is dominated by emotion and his relationships with other people, but only if they meet him on equal terms; anyone who insists on treating him with cold reason fills him with fear. His deepest conviction is that human nature is grounded in love, in the widest sense, 'in a nameless state of nearness and relatedness' to things and people, the relationship between man and woman being only one overrated instance of this general condition.[7] This is the 'other condition' seen by Musil as the antithesis to the intellect, yet not, in the ideal case, supplanting reason. Musil's view is rather that the perfect human being should combine both aspects. Anselm confesses to Maria that he never intended to marry Regine; he sought only to help her live again, to awaken her feelings and lead her out of the haunted emptiness of her former life. When Regine insists that she wants to live with him, he refuses to listen; instead of her hysterical outbursts, he now longs for the serene, natural beauty of Maria who, in his eyes, represents the ideal. When Josef and Thomas face him with incriminating evidence of his past misdeeds, he makes no attempt to deny them; but when Maria turns away from him, he pretends to commit suicide. Although Josef is obliged to admit that Regine left home of her own free will, he still intends to humiliate Anselm; but by next morning the latter has disappeared.

While Anselm is irrational, imaginative and free, Thomas seems to be the complete opposite: a rational being, an academic with a trained mind, happily married and established in the old family home. We are told that Josef's visit was prompted by a letter from Thomas, anxious to regularise the position of his sister-in-law. Josef's revelations, aided by the detective he has employed, completely alter the relationships of the four characters with one another. It proves impossible to avoid discussing Regine's and Anselm's actions and motivation, embarrassing as it may be to everyone concerned, and in the course of this, Maria tends more and more to take Anselm's part. Thomas's reaction is twofold. On the one hand he is tempted to discount Anselm as a lightweight who, though gifted, has achieved nothing. On the other hand, being scrupulously honest, he must admit that Anselm possesses qualities he lacks and that Maria is right when she reproaches him with being too cerebral, with seeing everything in terms of the intellect. He cannot deny it; but recognising the fact does not shield him against the torment of common jealousy. In a painful scene Maria proclaims her need to feel, not think, to experience words, music and life directly and without explanation. She concludes that her life with and for Thomas has not given her real fulfilment, and leaves to join Anselm. Thomas, though sad at her going, acknowledges her right to choose, and, defying Josef's threats with regard to his own career, refuses to pursue Anselm any further. To his own surprise, he defends Anselm's open outlook against's Josef's narrow one, and proclaims the vital truth that all the scientific advances of humanity will ultimately achieve nothing, so long as the fatal division between soul and intellect persists.[8]

In contrast with these four characters, the remaining three figures all have their feet placed firmly on the ground. Fräulein Mertens, Regine's companion, is a worthy but unimaginative lady of uncertain age who acts as a dramatic foil to Regine's fantasies. Josef, the rational man *par excellence*, is convinced not only that he has justice on his side, but that his interpretation of Regine's behaviour is the only correct one. Momentarily shaken by evidence to the contrary, he soon recovers his equilibrium and is concerned up to the end with the facts of the case, contained in a large folder which provides some light relief in the last act. Most of this material has been assembled by Stader, the detective, whose invention is a master-stroke. Formerly a servant and café singer, he now owns a detective agency, Newton, Galilei and Stader, run according to the latest methods: graphology, probability theory, psychology and half-a-dozen other areas of science all have their part to play in his investigations. Nothing is left to chance, for according to Stader chance does not exist, facts do not exist, nothing exists but scientific laws and scientific relationships. Stader's reverence for statistics is accompanied by a distinct lack of concern with interpretation, and indicates the author's ironic view of scientific method gone mad. At the same time it should be noted that Stader is quite prepared to resort to blackmail in order to achieve his ends;[9] in other words, his command of knowledge is no guarantee that this knowledge will be used in a responsible manner. The comic figure of the detective, a travesty of rationalism, shows that the intellect alone is as capable of producing extremes as the irrationalism of the visionaries.

Despite his bitter disappointment at the play's lack of success, Musil believed that it expressed the essence of his thinking, and even after his death Martha Musil quoted his view that *Törless* and *The Visionaries* led directly to *The Man without Qualities*.[10] It has been said that while Musil's pre-war work shows the irruption of the irrational into reality, his post-war work is concerned with the extension of reality.[11] Even the stage directions of this play indicate that things are not quite what they seem: the scenery is to be constructed so that its unreal nature is never overlooked, the floor is to be painted in fantastic colours, and instead of a ceiling, the room on stage is to be open to the sky.[12] This deliberately artificial set reminds one of Brecht and his theory of alienation, but Musil's play had already been published by the time Brecht's first play was performed in 1922, and Brecht's first theoretical writings did not appear until 1930. Yet although Musil did not regard himself as an expressionist, he was a member of the expressionist generation, and as early as 1913 reviewed one of the first important expressionist dramas, *The Beggar* by Reinhard Johannes Sorge. He praised the play's combination of 'normal' scenes with intense and visionary elements.[13] Such fantastic elements are already found in Strindberg, particularly in his *Dream Play* (1902) reviewed by Musil in 1922, and in a notebook entry around 1920 Musil recalls that in his youth, he and his contemporaries responded eagerly to the Swedish dramatist.[14]

Musil's post-war work is indeed concerned with the extension of reality, but this statement may be interpreted in two different ways. Like other members of his generation in Austria and Germany, Musil had experienced the horror of war, the collapse of the political order and the hunger and penury of the first years of peace. After the downfall of the monarchy, the military defeat and the ensuing chaos, there was a widespread longing for a new beginning, a spiritual transfiguration of mankind. Some writers expressed their own apocalyptic vision of the future, while others pointed to revolution and a new social order, but for Musil any fundamental change in society had to begin at the personal level with the regeneration of the individual man and woman. The content of this play is revolutionary indeed, viewed from the standpoint of traditional morality, but the outward form of the 'experiment' is still a conventional one, and only the anti-naturalist décor indicates what is to come. On the other hand, one may see the whole of Musil's work as an attempt to explore ways by which men and women may become more truly themselves; if his pre-war works place the emphasis on the irruption of the irrational into 'normal' life, the later works seek to illuminate human life from various angles, in order to reveal new possibilities, 'to depict prototypes of courses of events . . . models of possible human beings, to *invent* the inner man'.[15] This quotation from his essay on the nature and function of the creative writer's mind admirably sums up what he was trying to do, and correspondences between the text of the essay and of *The Visionaries* show that the drama is conceived in the same spirit.

If one regards the four principal characters as models of possible human beings, their progression throughout the play becomes somewhat clearer. Each of them develops in some way during the course of the action, while the other three figures remain static. The development of the principal characters, however, makes it very difficult to define their identity: Thomas begins as an intellectual, but finishes by pleading for an end to the division between soul and intellect; Anselm, who has lived by emotion and fantasy, seeks greater reality in the person of Maria. Maria's decision to leave Thomas is justified in terms of her need for a more direct, non-intellectual mode of being, while in the final scene, Regine appears cured of her hysteria and perhaps at last able to assume responsibility for her own life. Each of them has moved some way towards an ideal combination of intellect and emotion, but since they all begin at a different point and have different needs, the solution for each of them must be different too. As elsewhere in his work, Musil illuminates his meaning by the use of variation and analogy, and here the minor characters also have an important part to play. Fräulein Mertens, contrasted with the two other women, seems to lack spontaneity and imagination; the author presents her as the embodiment of bourgeois convention, lacking a genuine personality of her own. Josef, in his self-importance and rigidity of outlook, is contrasted with Thomas, while another aspect of intellectual man is demonstrated by Stader, with his thirst for knowledge which he then uses for his own lucrative ends.

The four visionaries are searching, each in his or her own way, for a mode of life in which reason and feeling, rational and non-rational, are in balance. As we have seen, this has been Musil's central concern since the writing of *Young Törless*, and will ultimately constitute the mainspring of the action of *The Man without Qualities*. Soon after the beginning of the drama Regine speaks of the unlimited powers inherent in every human being; later Anselm describes other forces at work in nature, in animals, between people — the power of feeling, the truth of immediate understanding. These are things, he says, which Thomas may *know*, but does not trust, for they do not fit his intellectual view of the world.[16] Maria, according to Anselm, possesses these powers without being aware of them, for Thomas has suppressed them in her, unable to tolerate powers other than his own; but now Thomas is beginning to realise that his own life is incomplete. Anselm goes so far as to suggest that if Maria leaves, the shock will startle Thomas out of his self-imposed isolation, and the final act bears this out. For by then Thomas is proclaiming his need for an open way of life offering unknown possibilities. Regine, on the other hand, progresses from an empty life filled with meaningless sensuality, to a stage where she can, perhaps for the first time, participate in a responsible adult relationship. Thomas and Anselm may, in a sense, be regarded as two halves of a single whole, and here one thinks of Ulrich who, taking stock of his life, perceives it in the image of two trees, the tree of reason and the tree of feeling, flourishing but divided. To achieve a union between these two separate halves of his being eventually becomes the goal for which he lives (See Chapter 6.)

As so often in Musil's work, the dichotomy between intellect and feeling is associated in the drama with the problem of action. Anselm makes the point that Thomas's outward success has been achieved at the cost of a lack of human contact. The intellect sees everything in terms of words and ideas, and denies validity to whatever refuses to fit into its schematic view of the world. But real life requires actions, not words: '. . . one has to act in such a way that one cannot say, or think, or even understand it, but simply do something! No-one today knows how to act.'[17] It will be remembered that Törless, at a crucial point in the novel, is faced with the necessity to act, to become involved with another human being, and like him, other figures in Musil's work find difficulty in taking even the simplest action on their own initiative. At the time of writing *The Visionaries* Musil was making notes on the relationship between the rational and non-rational elements in human beings, amplifying sections of early notebooks and adding further material. In this context he returned to the essays of Emerson, particularly to the one entitled 'Circles', and made a series of excerpts which have recently been transcribed.[18] It is illuminating to compare some of these with the text of the drama: for example, where Anselm speaks of the truth of immediate understanding between two people, we find Musil, under the heading *Other Condition*, quoting the following: '. . . for these moments confer a sort of omnipresence and omnipotence . . . without time'.[19] At another point on the same sheet Musil places the heading: '*Living Action* — Cf. Visionaries' and then quotes two sections from the end of the Emerson essay. The first excerpt may be linked with Anselm's open outlook, aimless or filled with potential according to one's point of view, and later shared by Thomas: ' "A man," said Oliver Cromwell, "never rises so high as when he knows not whither he is going".' The length of the final excerpt shows the significance Musil attached to Emerson's thought, and is clearly reflected in Anselm's plea for action, quoted above:

> The one thing which we seek with insatiable desire is to forget ourselves, to be surprised out of our propriety, to lose our sempiternal memory, and to do something without knowing how or why; in short, to draw a new circle. Nothing great was ever achieved without enthusiasm. The way of life is wonderful: it is by abandonment.

Thus in *The Visionaries* Musil shows four contemporary figures attempting to achieve a balance between intellect, reason and awareness on the one hand, and instinct, emotion and intuition on the other. In working out these ideas he found Emerson very helpful; in some respects Emerson was the heir of the Romantic movement, but he had also read the neo-Platonists whose teachings were concerned with intuition and the relationship between the spiritual and material worlds. At an earlier stage Musil had encountered related ideas in the essays of Maeterlinck, from which he made excerpts under the heading *Intuition*; he included quotations from Plotinus describing intuitive knowledge and the means of attaining it.[20] In the years after writing *The Visionaries* Musil became more and more interested in studying intuition, mysticism and the whole area of the 'other condition', and some of this work will be considered later.

Musil wrote only one other play, the farce *Vincent and the Mistress of Important Men*; published in 1923, it was performed the same year in Berlin and the following year in Prague and Vienna.[21] It was on the whole well received, and revived after the Second World War in Germany and Austria, in Paris in 1969 and in Poznań, Poland in 1972. During the interval of the first post-war performance in Cologne in 1957, a gentleman in the audience was heard to ask who had translated this ultra-modern play so excellently into German. Pronouncing Musil's name in the French manner, he evidently assumed that the author was a member of the Parisian avant-garde theatrical movement, together with Ionesco, Adamov and Samuel Beckett.[22] After the first performance in 1923, some critics wrote of *Vincent* as being to a greater or lesser extent an imitation of earlier works, particularly of Wedekind's *Lulu* plays. In a notebook entry of 1924 Musil refuted this criticism, arguing that the line of development into which his play would fit was rather the one leading from the poet Christian Morgenstern via Dada to Joachim Ringelnatz, and 'the pranks of Brecht and Bronnen'.[23] Egon Naganowski has investigated some of these connections, and also shows correspondences between *Vincent* and more recent plays.

The heroine of Musil's farce is a beautiful woman named Alpha, who is surrounded by a host of admirers, including a scholar, a politician, a famous pianist, a reformer, and the young heir of a rich industrialist. In the normal way she receives these gentlemen one at a time; to each in turn she offers understanding and appreciation, while opening his eyes to the incompleteness of his own life. All of them adore her, and each one sees in her his soul, or in Jungian terms his *anima*. The stage set consists of a boudoir separated by a curtain from a bedroom at the rear, yet it is never made absolutely clear whether Alpha's meetings with these leaders of society include a physical as well as a spiritual dimension. At the beginning of the play Alpha returns at three o'clock in the morning from an evening out with Herr Bärli, a millionaire businessman who, impatient of being kept at arm's length like her other suitors, demands that she marry him. When she prevaricates, he ties her up and threatens to shoot her, but at this moment Vincent enters. Alpha retires behind the curtain while Vincent introduces himself, first to Bärli and then to the next visitor, Dr Halm, married to Alpha but separated from her. A little later her admirers arrive with presents for Alpha's name-day, invited by the lady herself to visit her at this unusual hour.

Vincent, it appears, has been away for sixteen years, after failing to keep a promise made to Alpha when they were both very young. Her marriage to Halm has not been a success, and so she has built up an independent existence. Vincent himself is a character who is difficult to define. At present he earns his living as an actuary, but during the course of the play evolves grandiose plans, based on his mathematical expertise, for breaking the bank at one casino after another, so that he and Alpha may live in unimaginable luxury. In the meantime he is not above taking money in return for various services, first from Halm and then from Bärli, and he is finally unmasked as a swindler. Fortunately for everyone concerned it is not thought necessary to summon the police, and at the end Vincent departs to take up new employment as a servant. Having failed to make a success of his own career, he concludes that the only rational course is to be of service to another person's life; but he might as well be paid for it! And so the dreamer finally comes down to earth, at least for the time being. Apart from the excitement brought into the action by Vincent's fertile imagination, the proceedings on stage are anything but dull. In the first act the gifts brought by Alpha's admirers include a number of exotic items of clothing, at the sight of which Halm exhibits unmistakable transvestite tendencies, while a girlfriend of the heroine reveals herself as bisexual. In the second act, after an ecstatic reunion between Alpha and Vincent which ends behind the curtain, Bärli carries out his earlier threat to shoot both Alpha and himself, although with blank cartridges. It emerges, however, that this melodramatic charade has been organised by Vincent to cure Bärli once and for all of his passion for the soul, Alpha, so that, freed from this troublesome infatuation, he may henceforth devote himself to the pursuit of money alone.

Alpha, who owes her success to the fact that she can be all things to all men, describes herself on two occasions as an anarchist. Solid worth apparently means nothing to her: 'She says to the scholar, you are no businessman, to the musician, you are no scholar, to the businessman, you are no musician, in short to each and all: you are no human being. And every one of them suddenly understands that his life is senseless'.[24] She has never taken her admirers seriously, never ceased to hope that one day she will find her place in life. Under the spell of Vincent's dreams for their future together, she calls him the magic bird who will carry her away, but when she realises that his projects are nothing but make-believe, she decides that any improvement in her life can only result from her own initiative. One might indeed see her as an early feminist, were it not for the unexpected ending: scornful of the assembled admirers and their plans for her future, she reaches for the telephone and accepts the proposal of marriage of a wealthy baron.

This ironic outcome is in keeping with the tone of the whole play, and with Vincent's decision to go into service. He, too, is at heart an anarchist: like Anselm in *The Visionaries* he is independent, imaginative and flexible, a personification of the creative mind. As with Anselm, the author implies that such a person may on occasion behave in an anti-social manner, and in the farce Vincent allows free rein, at least in imagination, to his criminal tendencies. When Alpha reproaches him with telling fantastic lies, he counters by pointing out that it is the facts which are fantastic: according to the latest research, it is as true to say that the sun turns round the earth as that the earth turns round the sun; fire destroys and fire nourishes, and so on. 'What contributes more to the uncertainty in the world: if I say two different things on two successive days, or if your six friends hold six different views of the world at one and the same time?'[25] These ideas recur in the first book of *The Man without Qualities*, where Musil develops the theme that it is as valid to say that something could be the case as that something is the case. Vincent's lack of respect for what is generally called reality is connected with the fact that he has no real profession, which allows him the freedom to analyse these matters from the position of an outsider. At the same time, he cannot take himself seriously, either, not even to the extent of profiting in any substantial way from his undoubted talents.

Vincent's scepticism and irony lie at the heart of this play, while the brilliant effect of the whole work results from the combination of the author's mastery of language with the tragi-comic happenings on stage. Vincent is contrasted with the pillars of society around Alpha, each of whom has been taken over by his professional identity to such a degree that he does not even possess a name of his own, the only exceptions being the young man, a student of technology, and Bärli, the businessman, both of whom are seen as having some contact with everyday reality. Scepticism, irony and fantastic stage performances were also characteristic of the Dada movement which began in Zürich in 1916, with the aim of showing up the absurdity of the world, and provoking the bourgeois public. Musil himself named this movement among the possible antecedents of his farce, and in 1923, when the play appeared, wrote a favourable review of performances by three small theatre groups from Russia, noting their links with Dada and praising their artistry, their magical combination of sense and nonsense, the unreal and the surreal.[26] *Vincent* may also be linked with a number of twentieth-century plays, including works by Goll, Ionesco, Dürrenmatt and Sartre, and may indeed be regarded as a precursor of the theatre of the absurd.[27]

Musil's farce is his first work to demonstrate at length his command of irony, later to be used to superb effect in *The Man without Qualities*. In *Vincent*, irony is deployed in the construction of the characters, in the farcical situations on stage, but above all in the language. Alpha unsettles Bärli right from the start by refusing to listen to his declarations of love, expressed in the forthright terms he employs for business; instead of saying: 'Either you marry me or I kill us both', he ought, she informs him mockingly, to clothe such sentiments in the language of the romantic novel. However, when he tries out a few suitable phrases, she coolly points out that he is hampered by his lack of vocabulary. To this he replies with increasing signs of desperation that his wealth no longer matters to him since she has begun to call him stupid. He sees now that he ought to reflect upon his life, but cannot do so: 'I've never learnt how to do that. Or I've forgotten how. That's why I live helplessly like an animal'.[28] He is the successful man of action, the man who acts without thinking, at the opposite pole from the detached intellectual who so often faces him in Musil's work; but Alpha makes him realise that his lack of words is a serious handicap. Alpha, on the other hand, can do anything with language, and therein lies one of the secrets of the fascination she exerts on representatives of the real world. Her magic words flash through the air, clad in brilliant colours, like birds of a tropical forest. 'One can join together things which don't belong to each other, just with words, in such a way that no-one is any the wiser.'[29]

Vincent too is a master of language; his agile mind weaves a web of fantasy by which even Alpha is taken in. When Bärli inquires about his profession, Vincent replies: 'Word-maker': not writer or poet, but a maker of words, a namer of names. Seemingly insignificant beside the successful businessman and the other self-righteous figures, he yet manipulates them all, and some of them even pay him for it. With his grasp of mathematics and his mastery of language, Vincent is bound to fall on his feet in any situation; but, perhaps from necessity, probably by choice, he will always remain alone. In contrast with Vincent, the figure of Halm provides a highly unflattering portrait of a certain kind of professional writer. He declares that the style and ideas for which Alpha is universally admired are secretly supplied by him, but complains that no-one will acknowledge his contribution to her success; at the same time, however, he blandly states that all his ideas are derived from others.[30] He regards Alpha as entirely his own creation, and, in a sort of parody of Shaw's *Pygmalion*, intends to sell her to Bärli in return for public recognition. Yet, when she finally decides to marry into the aristocracy, he is all obsequiousness. Musil seems to imply that Halm is prepared to prostitute himself and his talents, seeking acclaim and reward wherever and however they may be found; meanwhile there can be little doubt that the author's sympathies lie with Vincent, the fantastic and unsuccessful dreamer, but a genuine human being.

*   *   *

Musil now began to be more widely known, and in November 1923 was elected Vice-President of the Society of German Writers in Austria, whose President was Hugo von Hofmannsthal. The latter asked for a copy of *Vincent*, and in the letter sent with it Musil expresses appreciation for Hofmannsthal's support.[31] Most of Musil's letters reprinted in LWW are to his friend Johannes von Allesch, but the same volume, published in 1960, contains articles by a number of Musil's friends who have since died, giving their impressions of the man and the writer. All agree that he kept aloof from public life, especially that part of it in which some literary figures of the day sought the limelight, largely because a man of his scholarly temperament did not care to participate in the social round, partly because he regarded some authors who achieved acclaim, such as Anton Wildgans, with undisguised contempt. For a time he used to meet friends once a week in the Café Central in Vienna: this circle included Oskar Maurus Fontana, Franz Blei, Robert Müller and others. Fontana helped to win recognition for Musil by writing reviews and an interview in 1926; Blei was a writer and editor who had promoted Musil's work since before the war. Another friend was Efraim Frisch in Munich, editor of *Der Neue Merkur*, while Alfred Kerr, the famous Berlin critic who had supported the publication of *Törless* in such positive terms, wrote a favourable review of *Vincent*. In 1923, Musil was awarded the Kleist Prize for *The Visionaries*, and in 1924 the Literature Prize of the city of Vienna.

The year 1924 was a significant one in Musil's life. Both his mother and father died within months of one another, and although he had not seen much of them in the immediately preceding years, the loss affected him deeply.[32] The money he inherited became worthless in the catastrophic post-war inflation, and as he had by this time lost his post at the War Ministry, his financial position was precarious. On the other hand, he now had a contract for what was to be his major novel, with Rowohlt, who had published *Three Women* and *Vincent*, and was able to devote the greater part of his time to this work. Advance payments arrived at regular intervals, but in a letter to Allesch of 1925, Musil voiced his concern that Rowohlt had not acknowledged the receipt of the first hundred pages of the novel. Allesch's intercession with the publisher immediately led to an appreciative telegram and a further payment.[33]

At the end of the war Musil had resumed his practice of using his notebooks partly to work out ideas for his own writing, partly to note down titles and excerpts from all kinds of books. A random selection of the topics and writers mentioned during the first post-war years produces the following list: consciousness and perception, probability theory, Thomas Mann, Rudolf Kassner, early Christian sects, Gustave Flaubert, the life of insects, Friedrich Schiller on the theatre, Houston Stewart Chamberlain and Ludwig Klages. A series of short pieces for the *Prager Presse* in 1923 bears the general heading *Cultural Chronicle*, and includes such diverse subjects as the philosophy of vitalistic biology, the 'knocking' of internal combustion engines, the flight speed of aircraft, tuberculosis, theories of planetary motion, E. R. Jaensch and eidetic imaging, and various aspects of economics.[34] This remarkable range of subjects reflects Musil's wide and varied interests, and in the essays of these years, facts and ideas from many sources are deployed in the service of a mission to which he devoted himself single-mindedly for the rest of his life.

While the two plays were concerned with setting up 'models of possible human beings', one seriously, the other through the medium of satire, Musil's major essays written during the period sought to tackle related questions on a much larger scale. In each of the essays the emphasis lies in a different direction, yet it is clear that they all form part of a larger debate in the author's mind. For some time Musil had considered publishing a volume of his essays, either in their original form or reworked into a continuous whole; Notebooks 25 and 26 are entirely devoted to this project and allow us to observe how he develops some key ideas. The provisional title of Notebook 25 is 'Attempts to find a different human being'; on the next page he reminds himself that he must show *why* he thinks differently from other people, the reason being that he is a trained engineer and used to tackling problems in a practical manner. In all the activities of daily life people set about solving their problems first in one way, then in another, until at last they succeed; even a dog trying to get through a door with a stick in his mouth will follow the same procedure. Only in the realms of law and morals are rigidity and immutability held to be sacred.[35] In Notebook 25 he remarks that the title concerning 'a different human being' might well be applied to his entire *oeuvre*. At the beginning, however, he considers a subtitle, 'The German as a Symptom'; when Musil speaks of Germans he includes German-speaking Austrians, and the essays show that his analysis of the contemporary situation in Germany and Austria is intended to apply in many respects to Western civilisation as a whole. In Notebook 8 (1920) he speaks of 'this grotesque Austria' as being nothing but a particularly clear example of the modern world.[36]

In a period of transition and fundamental readjustment, when the inhabitants of both Germany and Austria had to accept defeat and opprobrium while learning a democratic way of life, Musil attempted in these essays to provide an analysis and assessment of the contemporary cultural situation. They represent a serious endeavour to see the position clearly and isolate various factors; to help remove outworn modes of thought and suggest new directions. In the present survey it is not possible to discuss his arguments in as much detail as they deserve; nevertheless, some of his ideas may be considered with special reference to four essays: 'Spirit and Experience', a discussion of Oswald Spengler's *The Decay of the West* (Volume 1, 1918); 'The Nation as Ideal and as Reality'; 'The Helplessness of Europe'; and 'The "Decay" of the Theatre' (Section 3: 'Crisis in Education'). The proposed book on the symptomatic nature of the contemporary situation in Germany, an enlarged and systematically reworked version of the essays, survives in note form but was never published in Musil's lifetime,[37] since he eventually decided to incorporate much of this material in *The Man without Qualities*, Book I, as a theoretical basis for the whole work. In 1931, after the publication of Book I, he stated that the second part would have to be rewritten, since it had been finished before the first part was written at all.[38] The complex history of the genesis of the major novel need not concern us here; in the years after the First World War Musil was working steadily on successive drafts for his *magnum opus*, for instance in Notebooks 8 and 21, but in the course of this work the title, emphasis and details of the underlying plan were changed several times.

The essay on Spengler, published in 1921, is not so much a review as an opportunity for Musil to attack what he sees as wrong and dangerous thinking. He refers to the first volume of Spengler's work, *Der Untergang des Abendlandes* (1918), which must, according to Hans Kohn, be translated as *The Decay of the West*, since the rendering 'decline' is too weak.[39] Kohn places Spengler's book in the context of Germanophile, anti-Western tendencies voiced during and after the war by men like Moeller van den Bruck, author of *Das Dritte Reich* (*The Third Reich*, 1923), Ernst Jünger and other nationalist writers. They believed 'that the lost war could turn into a German victory, if the Germans would realise that they represented the spirit of the times . . . Young nations . . . had new ideas, while the aged West was a continuation of the outdated eighteenth century'.[40] Spengler had gained a large number of readers with his *Preussentum und Sozialismus* (*Prussianism and Socialism*, 1919), a fervent appeal to German youth, to national pride and military virtues. *The Decay of the West* proclaimed that 'the victorious West was doomed . . . Spengler predicted the coming of new caesars who with their warrior élites would break the dictatorship of money together with its political weapon, democracy. Before the breakthrough of elemental forces, the intellectual world built up by the conscious mind would vanish'.[41] Truth and justice would be overcome by vitality and power. To some extent, such views reflect the influence of Nietzsche, but Kohn points out that Nietzsche was an individualist who would have resisted the emphasis on the German state. Spengler saw history as a succession of closed systems, regarding democracy and objectivity in science, for example, as characteristics of bourgeois society, out of place in the new martial age. To him, 'as to Hegel and Marx, history was subject to inexorable laws; his laws, however, did not belong to the realm of the idea or of society, but to biology . . . Marx believed in men, while Spengler was a nihilist'.[42]

The English-speaking reader may find some difficulty in understanding how such ideas could permeate German society sufficiently to allow a National Socialist government to be formed and to dominate the state. Yet earlier influences should not be overlooked. After the failure of German liberals in 1848 to establish a democratic constitution for the whole of Germany, it was Bismarck who from 1862 became the most powerful influence in Prussia, and then in the German empire. Bismarck, whose first priority was the unification of Germany under Prussian leadership, was aggressive, anti-democratic and hostile to the humanitarian and liberal spirit represented in the eighteenth century by Goethe and Schiller. It has been said that the traditions of the Bismarckian empire were the principal factor in the destruction of the Weimar Republic.[43] Another factor in shaping attitudes among the leaders of Germany was the work of Thomas Carlyle. Hugh Trevor-Roper has shown that his *Life of Frederick the Great* of Prussia was warmly received by Bismarck, and later by Hitler and Goebbels. 'In the intellectual pedigree of Nazism, Carlyle cannot be refused a place. Reacting against the rational eighteenth century, he believed in the insufficiency of human reason and extolled the direct intuitive knowledge of the visionary man . . . / When Hitler wrote, in 1924, that once in many centuries the political philosopher and the statesman might converge in one man who would then be able to end an old age of history and begin a new', such ideas, although not immediately inspired by Carlyle, corresponded to the latter's doctrine of the hero.[44] Hitler's words as well as Musil's essays must be seen against the background of the unsettled state of Germany during these years. After the Armistice of 1918, civil wars continued in Germany and Eastern Europe at least until 1923, and the confused and disturbed conditions seriously undermined the successful development of Germany's first republic, whose constitution had been drawn up in Weimar, the home of Goethe, in 1919. Conservative nationalists on the right and socialist revolutionaries on the left shared a fervent revolutionary mood, both expecting the millennium. 'The two movements were bitterly hostile, though from time to time they co-operated against the common enemy, the West'.[45]

Musil's discussion of Spengler's book needs to be seen in this context. His primary objective is to show that Spengler's thinking is muddled and inaccurate, and Spengler's conclusions, therefore, worthless. He begins the attack by selecting a number of statements from *The Decay of the West* where the author has made a point by reference to mathematics; Musil shows that every one of these statements is wrong, and drily observes that they may be taken as examples both of the universality and of the style of reasoning of the work. This lack of precision in scientific areas where accuracy is essential is, according to Musil, characteristic of a way of thinking which he then parodies in merciless fashion: since butterflies and the Chinese are both coloured yellow, one may say that the butterfly is the Central European winged dwarf Chinese . . . 'Here for the first time attention is drawn to the remarkable coincidence between the great age of Lepidoptera and that of Chinese culture', and so on.[46] The brilliant illogicality of this nonsense should not divert attention from Musil's very serious criticism of Spengler and others like him who fail to understand the empirical methods of thought dominant in the modern world, and even take a perverse pride in this failure. Spengler and his associates look down on empiricism as being narrow, unimaginative and lacking in depth (the German word *Verstand* often used derogatively by them may be translated as mind, understanding, reason, sense), while claiming to be the sole representatives of *Geist* (spirit, mind, life, vitality, the essence of a thing).[47] The central thrust of Musil's arguments is that *Geist* and *Verstand* cannot, and must not, be separated, and that the way in which Spengler does so can only result in speculation, mystification and falsehood.

Musil next considers Spengler's references to science and shows that here too a number of errors may be detected, not necessarily errors of fact but of interpretation, based on inadequate understanding. Spengler states that since research in physics, for instance, is dependent in the last resort on the particular individuals who carry it out, physical systems are subjective creations just like the creations of drama, music and painting. Musil replies scornfully that even a monkey knows how to use a lever, a panther can follow his prey by its tracks, and in these and all human examples, experience, knowledge and a mixture of subjective and objective factors are involved. The analysis of such factors is the laborious task of epistemology, which Spengler has chosen to do without, since it would undoubtedly restrict the free flight of his thoughts. Musil insists that facts are facts and must be mastered, not ignored: 'I attack him where he is typical. Where he is superficial. By attacking Spengler one attacks the age which produced him and approves of him, for his errors are the errors of the age'.[48] Thinkers who claim to represent 'the spirit' deride empiricism and the central function of experience, while ignoring the steady growth of scientific thinking since the eighteenth century throughout the civilised world.

On the other hand, where it is not a question of factual knowledge, different methods of thinking are appropriate. Once again, Musil elucidates the distinction between rational and non-rational thinking already set out in his 1918 essay on the creative writer. The works of Emerson, Maeterlinck, Novalis, Nietzsche or Rudolf Kassner stimulate the reader to intense spiritual and mental activity, but this cannot be called 'knowing' in the empirical sense. Understanding, in all these cases, involves an individual experience and recollection of similar ones; feelings, impressions and other imponderable aspects play their part, and the result is personal and unique. Such writings nevertheless contain much that is rational, and Musil protests against the baleful misunderstanding opposing spirit to reason; humanity would be much better served by undertaking systematic research in the field of irrational experience, to aid comprehension of its processes. The distinction between 'dead' and 'living' thinking depends ultimately on the emphasis of the particular purpose in each case. Rational ideas and concepts are, in a sense, dead; but they can possess an independent existence. In the realm of feeling, art and personal relationships however, words and ideas are individual and alive.

Musil then goes on to consider the question of intuition, and condemns the uncritical use of this word by writers incapable of logical thought. He points out that intuition exists even in rational areas: where methodical preparation has taken place, the crucial idea leaps suddenly into the conscious mind. In the non-rational sphere the effect is all the more striking, for this type of thinking depends on the vitality of the words, 'the cloud of thought and feeling surrounding the insignificant nucleus of concept'.[49] Musil quotes Spengler's definition of intuition and adds that it may occur at many levels, from those accessible to the believer and the lover, to the great visions of the saints; he also refers to some associated pathological conditions. Anticipating the rejoinder that intuition cannot be analysed, only experienced, he demonstrates in a few moving sentences that he knows very well what is meant by the 'other condition'. He points out, however, that most of those who so glibly use the word 'intuition' do not believe in it anyway: they defy reason by appealing to another, secret authority locked away in a casket. 'That is the treasure chest Intuition. Why not open it at last and see what it contains? Perhaps it is a new world.'[50]

With a bitterness that reveals his personal involvement, Musil then sums up his main arguments against Spengler: that according to the latter, the most important areas of human life can never be discussed in a rational manner, since they come under the heading of intuition; that he is ultra-sceptical of everything to do with reason, yet highly credulous of his own random ideas; and that in spite of all his protestations, he compares and combines facts like an empiricist, but without any regard for accuracy or truth.

Finally, Musil discusses Spengler's theories concerning the rise and fall of cultures. In his view the doctrine that cultures eventually collapse from inner exhaustion is plausible without recourse to metaphysics, and may be deduced by analogy with the lives of individuals. Musil points out that cultures always begin as small societies and expand over generations both in numbers and space. During this process the vital ideas of a culture are subjected to constant change, while the forms in which they were originally expressed persist. Thus there is usually a discrepancy between older forms and newer ideas, until a point is reached where 'the centre cannot hold' and the culture collapses.

Looking at his own period however, Musil rejects Spengler's explanation of this historical process. For he regards the society of his time as a 'civilisation', defining this as a later, diffuse form of a culture, with greatly increased numbers, but also an amalgam of old and new ideas. The large numbers in his opinion pose a special problem of communication. In Musil's view, the greatest need of the age is to put an end to the fatal division between the representatives of reason and of the spirit, and to work together for a greater understanding of society and mankind. Philosophy, the transmission of ideas, education, research and all the activities connected with the spirit need to be reorganised if anything is to be achieved, if indeed the civilisation is to be saved. Rational and non-rational aspects of life, instead of opposing one another, must be combined, and science and literature must work together for a common future.

In the two following essays Musil continues his analysis of the contemporary situation. 'The Nation as Ideal and as Reality' (1921) is essentially an indictment of outdated concepts of nationhood; Musil examines the relationship of the individual to the state, and seeks to produce some realistic suggestions for clearer thinking and positive action.[51] Any political and philosophical discussion in 1921 is of course bound to start with the First World War. What was it? Its beginning was felt by all as an overwhelming, irrational experience; at its end, thousands cherished apocalyptic hopes for a renewal of life, whose fulfilment was at least partly vitiated by the punitive Treaty of Versailles. Three years later, Musil finds a general feeling of disillusionment, a spiritual vacuum, and a readiness on the part of the individual to blame anyone but himself for the horrors of the war. He argues that this self-deception has no basis in fact, but can be explained by the individual's feeling of impotence in the face of decisions taken by remote authority. Yet a people is made up of the sum of its individuals, plus their organi-sational form, and at a time when renewal is so vitally needed, the nature of that organisation must be clearly understood.[52]

Musil then examines in turn the concepts of a nation as a racial entity, a state, and a national spirit. What he has to say about racialist attitudes is based on his reading of Paul de Lagarde, Houston Stewart Chamberlain and other writers. He condemns such tendencies as highly dangerous and spells out the inevitable consequences: by being told that he belongs to a race endowed with all the virtues, the individual is relieved of moral responsibility for his own actions and develops a sinister apathy in moral decisions. Musil connects this with the philosophy of idealism which, according to his definition, consists in referring every idea back to older, so-called eternal verities, instead of thinking it through to its logical conclusion. This results in prejudice, distortion of values and corruption of the moral sense, which are bound to inflict fatal damage on the fabric of the nation. In this connection it is worth noting Musil's correspondence with the literary historian Josef Nadler, who had sent him a presentation copy of his *History of German Literature*, arranged according to the separate tribal areas of the German-speaking nations. Even in his letter of thanks Musil felt bound to distance himself from Nadler's point of view, and in spite of two more letters did not seek a closer acquaintance.[53]

The concept of the nation as identical with the state, accepted in the Communist Soviet Union as much as in the old Austrian empire, is examined by Musil with considerable scepticism. Again he points to the dangers arising from the sheer numbers involved: the state is too big, communication is impossible except in one's own immediate circle, the individual feels alienated and impotent, and therefore allows things to be done in his name which he would not support on a personal level. This passivity is complemented by the workings of the bureaucratic machine, depersonalising every aspect of life. At the same time business and intellectual circles, as well as personal life in all its forms, ignore the bureaucracy wherever they can, and from time to time the development of the state is subjected to almost imperceptible, yet vital, alterations emanating from these spheres.[54]

Turning thirdly to the concept of the nation as embodied in a national spirit, Musil demolishes this in few words, and points out that, except in wartime, a German farmer, for instance, has more in common with a French farmer than with a German city-dweller. The idea of the nation ultimately exists only in the imagination. At a time when the German nation was suffering blame and punishment, it might well have been objected that such demoralising conclusions should have not been openly expressed; on the contrary, Musil says that he finds it more than ever necessary to analyse the concept of the nation with a view to reformulating it for practical use. The outdated idealisation of the state has led to rigidity and lack of progress in the development of moral ideas appropriate to the present age, he says. As the war has shown, mankind is capable of anything, but while scientific thinking advances, for example by adopting the concepts of function theory, in the moral sphere thinking has stood still for far too long. In the year after the founding of the League of Nations Musil pleads with considerable urgency for the abolition of the ideals of nation and state, in favour of some kind of international organisation representing, not separate countries, but interests shared across national boundaries by economic, intellectual and other groups.[55]

Whereas Musil's pre-war work concentrated on the individual, emphasising the non-rational aspects of life, after the war he became increasingly conscious of the social dimension. On two occasions he noted how war service had changed his outlook: firstly by the experience of 'an ecstasy of altruism', where he was aware for the first time of a feeling of community with all other Germans; secondly when he, highly-educated and a member of an upper-class family, found himself living and working with the 'average man', with people who never in their lives read anything more than a newspaper.[56] Musil's increased social awareness showed itself in his support for the Activist group of intellectuals and writers led by Kurt Hiller, a group which, while not itself belonging to a political party, was committed to the renewal of mankind and of society. He signed their manifesto in 1918 and was also sympathetic to a secret society with similar aims calling itself Catacomb, and led by his friend Robert Müller.[57]

Musil's essays and notebooks of these years reflect his conviction that if the individual's conditions of life are to be improved, it is society which must be changed. His conclusion that many of the inadequacies of the German situation apply with equal force elsewhere leads him to entitle his next essay, published in 1922, 'The Helplessness of Europe'.[58] Referring to the course of the war, he affirms that many of the essential decisions of the conflict might well have gone another way, in other words that history is not, *pace* Spengler, governed by immutable laws. Similarly, a theory of historical epochs as closed systems is shown not to correspond to the known facts; for example, oriental elements affected ancient Greece, and Greek influence on the modern world is discernible even today. If human nature endures throughout, any changes must be due to circumstances; but human nature is not constant, and the demand from many quarters for steadiness, immutability and 'character' is based on premisses refuted both by the evidence of psychology and by simple experience of life. Human beings are as capable of cannibalism as of writing the *Critique of Pure Reason*; Musil does not, of course, deny the differences between primitive and developed societies, but points out that changes in the course of human development are often due to chance, and so gradual that they are barely perceived. To those who would accuse him of cynicism in these opinions, he retorts that, on the contrary, they demonstrate unbounded optimism, since they affirm that we ourselves can will an improvement in our condition, a confident outlook which had been lacking since the eighteenth century.[59]

The reasons for the prevailing lack of confidence, he thinks, are to be found in the oppressive weight of historical knowledge accumulated during the nineteenth century, and in the attempt to make the historian undertake the task of interpreting the world, which the philosophers have failed to do. On the other hand, Musil declares, the scientific and technological approach to life, despised by German writers, is central to modern civilisation, and not only in science. Pragmatism and positivism, understood in the widest sense as an attitude of mind, imply a realistic view of the world, a respect for facts and a confidence in one's own senses. To those who complain that the modern age has no philosophy, Musil commends a book by Wolfgang Köhler, one of the founders of *Gestalt* psychology, as demonstrating that such a work, starting from a factual basis, is able to suggest solutions to ancient metaphysical problems.[60] The same respect for facts, he goes on, sustains the varied activities of the businessman and the politician, and in *The Man without Qualities*, on which he was working at the same period, Musil shows typical representatives of these and other sectors of society interacting with one another.

Returning to his central and urgent problem, how to make sense of the present state of Western society in order to bring about fundamental reforms, Musil finds no philosophy adequate to unite the three disparate areas of our inheritance from the past, our separate fields of knowledge and the phenomena of daily life. Such philosophical discussion as takes place relies either on remnants of an unfounded belief in progress, or on the obsolete fetishes of epoch, nation, race and so forth. No-one has the courage to form judgements or to create new ideas. Modern society is a tower of Babel with a thousand conflicting voices; no wonder the individual is affected by this anarchy. Yet in the cellar of this madhouse, the ancient will to create is hammering away: age-old dreams are being fulfilled, such as the ability to fly, seven league boots, machines to enable us to see through solid bodies, and countless others. But the age that creates these marvels has at the same time lost all sense of wonder at its own achievements.[61]

The war broke out as a sickness in this society. It was a crisis of European culture, characterised by passivity, not only in the relationship of educated citizens towards the executive powers of the state, but also in the lack of political awareness of the various ideologies. Musil compares pre-war attitudes to those of railway passengers in a sleeping-car, fast asleep up to the very moment of collision. The manner in which signs of the approaching catastrophe were ignored is for him another symptom of a lack of concern with real issues. The rapid and phenomenal spread of the conflagration shows that people were longing for earthquakes, fires and upheaval: the war was a rejection of bourgeois life, a leap into adventure, a flight from peace.[62] Only a few years later, he finds renewed signs of dangerous passivity, not only in Germany, but also in France.

Never again will a culture arise spontaneously in the white world; therefore, says Musil, we must work with all the powers at our disposal for a change in the society we have. Yet those who should undertake the responsibility for organising this new society, for organising debate, research and education, are not even aware of the need. Rather, they blame reason and the intellect for social decay, failing to realise that all societies decay eventually, but that counter-measures cannot be left to chance. It is not true that the intellect destroys values; if they are destroyed, they must already have begun to break down. 'It is not the case that we have too much reason and not enough soul; we do not use reason enough in matters concerning the soul . . . *we do not think and take action with regard to our own nature.*'[63] In this area objectivity is inappropriate.

Musil then considers what might be done, pointing out that care must be taken to distinguish between 'impersonal' morality and 'personal' ethics, just as theology must be distinguished from religion. Whereas theology and morality are intellectual areas and contain rational, static knowledge, true religion and mysticism are the sphere of vitality, feelings and love; the same vitality is to be found in the writings of the non-mystical sages, from Confucius to Emerson and beyond. In the modern world, real ethics, where it is found at all, lives in the arts, in essays and in private relationships, although Musil's comments on the contemporary state of the arts show little confidence in their ethical function. He ends with a plea for a radical change in the teaching of literature, for an end to the method by which Goethe and other great writers are merely held up as examples to be imitated; not only their lives and achievements, but above all their values and ideas should be discussed, compared and analysed, for it is from them that most is to be learned. Studies of this kind put reason to work in the service of the soul and the spirit, producing a survey of causes, of connections, and of the fluctuating significance of human motives and actions — an interpretation of life. An age that has failed to undertake such work or train itself in such a discipline will never be able to solve the vast organisational problems of its time.[64]

The three essays discussed here constitute, in the main, an analysis of, and protest against, obsolete attitudes and institutions, against intellectual confusion and lack of remedial action. Yet Musil also deals elsewhere with possible reforms in education as a necessary condition for reforming society. While working in the education department of the War Ministry in Vienna, he had to give lectures on the aims of education, and to train army officers in educational methods. They were to be shown how to deal with their men according to democratic principles, a new concept for most of them; to develop managerial skills and win the soldiers' confidence. Theoretical, physical and craft instruction were to be combined with military training. The three main political parties each appointed a consultant for this purpose; Musil, as the fourth and only non-political one, had the task of co-ordinating the opinions of the other three. In July 1922 he was invited to Berlin to discuss the uses of applied psychology in the army with the corresponding specialist at the German War Ministry. He remained there until the end of August and during his stay probably visited Ernst Rowohlt, who became his publisher the following year.[65]

In October 1923 Musil reviewed a collection of studies on the sociology of education under the heading 'An Important Book'.[66] Right at the start he declares that the future depends entirely on a positive approach to the problems of education, interest in which is wholly lacking except in those immediately involved. He criticises the present state of education in the German-speaking countries as backward-looking, sluggish and fragmented, and links its failures with the moral and cultural decay of the pre-war years. Repeating his call for a new approach to the organisation of spiritual and intellectual matters, he stresses that in a situation where the individual is faced by multifarious and conflicting ideas and ideals, the solution lies not in imposing a single *Weltanschauung*, but in improving the general capacity to grasp and digest the central issues. He especially praises the book under review for presenting the problems clearly, and revealing the links between education and other cultural institutions. Nothing, he finishes, is more urgently needed, for the involuntary isolation of each group of specialists in the modern world has a disastrous effect on the growth of informed public opinion.

In the following year Musil returned to what he described as the crisis in education, in an essay on the theatre. He knew Schiller's essay on the theatre as a moral institution and was writing in the context of keen public awareness of the theatre, of dramatists, actors and producers. H. F. Garten writes: 'In Germany drama may be said to take first place among literary forms . . . Moreover, the number of theatres showing a first-rate repertory is far greater than in the (other) Western countries . . . Since the middle of the eighteenth century . . . the theatre has come to be regarded not so much as a place of entertainment but . . . a platform where the vital ideas of the day, as well as the timeless issues of human destiny are presented.'[67] Thus Musil could count on his theatre criticism being read by a public with an active interest in these matters, and in two essays of 1922–3, he discussed the theatre as a symptom of the age. A third essay in this series was entitled 'The "Decay" in the Theatre' (1924), and in it he first considers what other commentators have described as a crisis in the theatre, before linking it with the crisis in education.[68] Once again he draws attention to a dangerous confusion in the intellectual situation of the period, and a lack of confidence among those who should be responsible for taking action. In an illuminating survey of the history of the concept of education in German-speaking countries he traces the successive meanings attached to the word *Bildung*, showing that Herder's eighteenth-century interpretation of education as an imitation of antiquity, especially of Ancient Greece, still persists in the grammar schools. Quoting Herder's definition of *Bildung*, Musil comments bitterly that 'we stand with our backs to the future' and equip tens of thousands of young people every year with an education which makes it impossible for them to succeed in life. The capacity to assimilate new ideas has utterly failed to keep up with the development of such ideas and with increases in population; the institutions which ought to promote progress in education, schools, political bodies and the church, in fact resist change. No wonder that the thin educated layer of the population has lost all confidence, all the more so since the chief developments in the world at large have been in science and technology, while the dominant concept of education is still based on Herder's one-sided definition. Goethe, it is true, was a scientist as well as a great writer, but his outlook was inevitably limited by the age in which he lived. Musil finds the greatest cause for concern in the split down the middle of educated society, dividing it into backward-looking teachers, lawyers and church dignitaries on the one hand, and forward-looking scientists, technologists and businessmen on the other. He points to the division even of the German grammar schools into institutions with a 'classical' or a 'realistic' bias, and asks how the vital synthesis in the intellectual and cultural life of the age can possibly be achieved while this division persists.[69]

German writers had voiced criticism of the national education system in literature long before Musil wrote this essay; works that come to mind include Wedekind's *Spring's Awakening* (1891) and Musil's own *Young Törless* (1906). In the same decade books on this theme were written by Hermann Hesse and the brothers Thomas and Heinrich Mann. The father-son conflict was a central theme of German expressionism, and criticism of parental authority often implied criticism of military and educational institutions, but these works expressed the revolt of the younger generation, rather than offering any constructive suggestions for change. Musil's achievement in his penetrating essays is to show by analysis how the shortcomings of society at large and of its constituent parts relate to one another, and the backward-looking, divided education system is seen to bear a heavy responsibility for the failure of those in authority to give a lead in solving society's problems. His courageous stand against Spengler's political philosophy, highly popular in some circles, and his warnings against warped moral standards, read like a prophecy of later events. Above all, his pragmatic approach, his efforts to turn the attention of thinking citizens from a preoccupation with national problems towards an international outlook and an awareness of the major areas of twentieth-century thought, are still relevant for us today. It is perhaps not without significance that one of the leaders of Austria's recovery since the Second World War, Dr Bruno Kreisky, is devoted to Musil's work and, when forced to flee from the Nazi invasion of Austria, chose *The Man without Qualities* as the only book to take with him into exile.[70]

In the writing of *Young Törless* during the first decade of the century, one of Musil's principal themes was perception of the unconscious and the possibility of expressing what is perceived. Seeking to win greater recognition for the function of the unconscious, he examined the spheres of life where words are or are not appropriate, drawing attention to the vital role of intuition in human life. Twenty years later he is finding that intuition has become a catchword adopted by those wishing to avoid mental effort; he therefore makes it his business to include in his analysis of the cultural situation a renewed attempt to define what intuition is. In the essay on Spengler, and in a later one published in 1925, he attempts to establish the nature of intuition, to delimit areas of life where it occurs, and to separate, if possible, areas where one may depend on intuition alone from others where this is inappropriate. As we have seen, Musil insists on clear thinking in the factual sphere, not only in the physical sciences but also in the sociological field, where facts are available for anyone willing to take the trouble of finding them. The other side of life, the sphere of personal relationships, feelings, religion and art, is equally essential, but while the two aspects are combined in the individual, each of them functions in a different way and must not be confused with one another.

The essay 'Towards a New Theory of Aesthetics' (1925) was inspired by a book on the art of film by the Hungarian writer and critic Béla Balázs, a friend of Musil's and librettist of Bartók's opera *Bluebeard's Castle*.[71] Musil's high regard for Balázs was shown in 1924 when, in response to a request for information from Josef Nadler, he quoted a few lines by the Hungarian writer to sum up the essence of his own work: these describe the loneliness of Musil's characters as a symptom of their indignation at the false relationships of modern society.[72] Musil is concerned to restore authenticity and truth to human life by bringing about greater awareness of the essential function of the 'other condition'. In the first section of the essay he states that many of Balázs's remarks on the art of film may also be applied to the other arts. Pointing out how the beginnings of art are rooted in very ancient times, he advocates further study of the anthropological background, and recommends a book on *The Thinking of Primitive Societies* by the French writer Lévy-Bruhl. At the same time, he sees much scope for a psychological approach, and mentions Ernst Kretschmer's *Medical Psychology* as a valuable aid to the study of the psychology of feeling.[73] In following Musil's arguments we should remember that he was writing of silent films; sound films were not shown in public until 1927. He quotes a comment by Balázs pointing out how, in silent films, inanimate objects acquire a 'symbolic' significance which they lack in normal life. Since both actors and objects are mute, the effect is to raise the objects almost to the same level of significance as the human beings in the film, thus allowing the spectator to sense the 'frontier between two worlds' usually hidden from all but the most sensitive. This leads

Musil to his view of the two states of mind of human beings. The active, calculating side has made men what they are by enabling them, through countless ages, to overcome obstacles and outwit their enemies; this is the normal state of mind of daily life and of all external activities. Yet the 'other condition' is just as ancient and central to all human beings: it is the state of love, of goodness, of contemplation, and fundamental to the religion, mysticism and ethics of all societies throughout history. In this state each thing becomes not an object of action, but a wordless experience, and in this respect, what occurs in silent films is true of all art: the bounds of normality are suddenly broken and we become aware of another world, and in that world we are mysteriously at one with things and with other people.[74]

Looking back over the most recent decades, Musil traces the growth of attempts to 'liberate' the soul from the intellect; among the authors of this movement he names the German Romantics, Emerson and Maeterlinck. Revolt against the increasing mechanisation of life was usually said to be the cause of these tendencies, which only later became associated with the term expressionism. But deep down they were the result of a widespread longing for the 'other condition', no longer satisfied by the institutionalised forms of religion and art. The decisive error in all this, however, was — and still is — to regard 'thinking' as the factor to be eliminated; again Musil stresses the importance of seeing the issues clearly. Drawing on his knowledge of the psychology of perception, he shows how even the most basic activities of the senses, like seeing and hearing, depend to some degree on the intellect, so that the relationship between concepts and experience may be likened to a constant process of mutual adaptation, as between a liquid and a flexible container, producing an equilibrium without a firm foundation which has never yet been properly described. Not thinking as such, but the purposeful thinking of normal life may be eliminated from art; but then we enter the dark area of the 'other condition', in which for the time being everything ceases.

After this, Musil analyses the relationship of thought to art, the nature of aesthetic perception and of artistic expression. Art as form limits and arranges the content of normal life; it enriches normality, but remains linked with it. The half-tones and nuances of the different arts, and in particular the irrational effect in literature of words irradiating one another, break open our jaded mental images of everyday life; just as in an old painting, when it is varnished, previously invisible details emerge. But an art that lacks any kind of link with reality soon approaches a state of chaos, and this is where contemporary efforts to liberate art from the intellect at all costs are bound to lead.

Musil investigates the potential of the different arts, but particularly of film and literature, as means of artistic expression, and points out, long before McLuhan, that the possibilities of expression condition the thoughts and feelings to be expressed. He also speaks of the different stages of the individual's reception of a work of art, showing how these can vary not only between, say, music and literature, but between one poem and another. The actual aesthetic experience is perhaps no more important than its after-effects and the process of assimilation during readjustment to normal life. On the other hand it may be said that every work of art offers an individual, unique and unrepeatable experience, never to be added to the person's store of *knowledge*, but existing in a different dimension altogether. In ethics and religion the same immediate experience is possible, different in kind from moral codes, or theology. The 'other condition', the 'frontier between two worlds' does not relate to any outer purpose; it is an inner state in which we are moved and transformed, and may take the form of human love, of artistic or mystical experience. Every time an object is perceived with 'creative' eyes, it is transformed by the feelings associated with the creative state, whether of the artist or the recipient. In a footnote, Musil suggests that a psychological approach to the study of intuition may well show it to be a normal state, but one that is usually hidden, except in the context of mysticism. Yet unlike mysticism, art never quite loses contact with normal behaviour; it is not separated from reality but, rising from the ground, curves away in an arch, as if supported by an abutment in the imagination.[75]

The choice of the bridge image for creative thought at the conclusion of this essay links it with two others from Musil's earliest writings. In Notebook 24 he speaks of the literary imagination constructing, as in music, an edifice on invisible pillars, connected with us like a fourth dimension; and in his first novel, Törless expresses the idea of imaginary numbers in the image of a bridge whose central span is missing.[76] We have seen how Musil employs spatial images throughout his work: doors, gates, architectural details, containers of all kinds, with spheres of glass used to indicate relationships or describe processes in the mind. The psychology of feeling is explored at length in draft chapters of *The Man without Qualities* and in later essays. One other public statement by Musil of his conception of literature was the address given in Berlin in 1927, in memory of Rainer Maria Rilke, who had died the previous year.[77] After commenting on the muted public reaction to the poet's death, he surveys the development of German literature since the age of Goethe, Novalis and Hölderlin, and arrives at an assessment of the contemporary literary scene that can hardly be called flattering. In a period when mediocrity was dominant, he says, Rilke's poetry raised the German lyric to a state of perfection never seen before. Musil finds the distinguishing marks of Rilke's work in his uniform high level of achievement, that produces in the reader an impression of high and unabated tension, a crystal-clear stillness at the heart of never-ending movement. Instead of tracing Rilke's growth as a writer, Musil seeks out the most characteristic elements of his art. Listing some of the themes of individual poems, he declares that the essence of each lies not in its themes or form, but in the 'incomprehensible juxtaposition and invisible web' of the ideas and objects contained in it. Not only do stones or trees change into human beings, 'but also human beings change into things or nameless creatures and only thus gain their final . . . humanity'.[78] The different categories of beings, kept separate in normal thinking, seem to be united in Rilke within a single sphere. Whenever he says one thing is like another, it immediately appears to be, and have been, that other since the world began. In his use of imagery Rilke interweaves things as in a tapestry: they seem to be separate, but are united by the background; then their appearance changes, and strange relationships evolve.

Musil ends the address by restating his doctrine of constant flux in the world and in human beings, what he calls elsewhere 'the theorem of human formlessness'.[79] The normal view is that of a solid world in which the emotions alone are unstable and changeable, but history shows this to be a fallacy. Nothing is stable, and the emotions are far more central than is generally admitted. There are poems that amount to nothing more than decoration, or at best an interruption of the world of solid reality; but Rilke's poetry expresses the ferment, the mutability of life; it embodies the emotion on which the world rests like an island. Rilke was perhaps the most religious poet since Novalis; he saw differently, in a new inner way, and will be recognised one day as having taught others how to see.

Musil's condemnation of the German press for its failure to honour Rilke may be linked with his own position at this time. As the decade progressed he became increasingly bitter at being ignored by the public, while authors he considered inferior to himself such as Franz Werfel, Stefan Zweig and Josef Roth enjoyed popular acclaim. Towards Thomas Mann, more frequently mentioned in the notebooks than any other contemporary writer, he reacted in a manner which has been described as a rivalry complex.[80] He reproached Mann with doing nothing but articulate the prejudices of his readers, whereas he himself was trying to educate them. Only in his last years, in exile, when Mann joined with other writers in attempting to give Musil some practical help, did the latter acknowledge that he had often been unjust to him.

During the years from 1924 until the publication of Book I of *The Man without Qualities* in 1930, Musil was working on the novel almost without pause. Rowohlt, his publisher, continued to make advance payments as agreed, but the relationship was not improved by Musil's method of writing. He was determined to incorporate ideas, reflections and all the intellectual material originally intended for the long essay 'The German as a Symptom'; at the same time the novel was an epic narrative with a constantly changing plot, the changes being dictated by the problem of giving form to the ideas. The third factor in the situation was his meticulous attention to style and his untiring search for the best, most precise way of expressing what he wanted to say. All this work, accompanied by excessive smoking and constant financial worries arising both from lack of any regular salary and the inflation of the time, led to a nervous breakdown in early 1929. He consulted Dr Hugo Lukács, a pupil of Alfred Adler, founder of individual psychology; Lukács was able to gain Musil's confidence and help him overcome the inhibitions that had held up progress on the final stages of Book I.[81] In the autumn of 1929 Musil was awarded the Gerhart Hauptmann Prize, but was informed that the fund to pay the money associated with the honour was bankrupt. Later, in January 1930, the publisher S. Fischer advanced a token amount of 250 Marks towards the prize; nevertheless, at this stage Musil and his wife had only enough money left for the coming few weeks, and this insecurity lasted throughout the year. Despite these pressures, work on the novel continued, and in November 1930 the first book was finally published. Musil was fifty years old.

Notes

1. Dinklage, LWW, p. 239.
2. Musil, *Die Schwärmer*; 'The Visionaries', GW II, pp. 309–407.
3. Dinklage, LWW, p. 234.
4. K. Otten, 'Eindrücke von Robert Musil', LWW, pp. 357–63, p. 362.
5. GW II, p. 356.
6. Ibid., p. 311.
7. Ibid., p. 334.
8. Ibid., p. 400.
9. Ibid., pp. 342–3.
10. Letter to J. v. Allesch, 1 November 1947, LWW, p. 321.
11. Berghahn, p. 82.
12. GW II, p. 310.
13. Ibid., pp. 1444–7.
14. TB I, p. 493.
15. GW II, p. 1029. See also Chapter 4.
16. Ibid., pp. 333–4.
17. Ibid., p. 350.
18. H. Hickman, ' "Lebende Gedanken" und Emersons *Kreise*', in: *Robert Musil, Untersuchungen*, 1980, pp. 139–51. See also Chapters 6 and 7.
19. Ibid., pp. 148–9. See also Nachlassmappe 7/11, sheets 111, 112, quoted from R. W. Emerson, 'Circles', *Works* II, *Essays, First Series*, pp. 299–322, p. 317. German translation 1902, p. 112.
20. TB I, pp. 134–5: Notebook 24, 1904–5. Quoted from Maeterlinck, *Le Trésor des Humbles*, 1896, pp. 108–9; German translation 1898. Musil also mentions a German edition of Plotinus, *Enneads*, 1878–80.
21. Musil, *Vinzenz und die Freundin bedeutender Männer*; 'Vincent and the Mistress of Important Men', GW II, pp. 409–52.
22. E. Naganowski, ' "Vinzenz" oder der Sinn des sinnvollen Unsinns', *Musil Studien*, 4, 1973, pp. 89–122, p. 121.
23. TB I, p. 631.
24. GW II, p. 420.
25. Ibid., p. 441.
26. Ibid., pp. 1615–17.
27. Naganowski, pp. 93–4, 106–7.
28. GW II, p. 412.
29. Ibid, p. 417.
30. Ibid., pp. 420–1.
31. *Briefe* 1981, pp. 340–1.
32. TB I, pp. 629–30, 911.
33. LWW, pp. 242, 288–90.
34. GW II, pp. 1687–1705.
35. TB I, p. 644.
36. Ibid., p. 354.
37. Musil, 'Der deutsche Mensch als Symptom'; 'The German as a Symptom', GW II, pp. 1,353–1,400.
38. Musil means First *Book* etc. The First Book (chapters 1–123) was published in 1930. See A. Reniers, 'Drei Briefe', *Studien*, 1970, pp. 288, 291, 293. Cf. *Briefe* 1981.
39. Musil, 'Geist und Erfahrung'; 'Spirit and Experience', GW II, pp. 1042–59, publ. in *Der Neue Merkur* 1921. H. Kohn, *The Mind of Germany*, 1961, pp. 330, 333–6, 340–1.
40. Kohn, p. 330.

41. Ibid., p. 335, Cf. Pascal 1973, pp. 57, 89.

42. Ibid., p. 336.

43. H. Holborn, quoted by Kohn, p. 152. Cf. H. Holborn, *A History of Modern Germany, 1840–1945*, 1969, Chapter 12.

44. H. Trevor-Roper, 'Thomas Carlyle's historical philosophy', *TLS*, no. 4082, 26 June 1981, pp. 731–4, p. 734. Bismarck wrote to Carlyle for his 80th birthday, praising his *Frederick the Great* (1858–65), cf. O. v. Bismarck, *Werke in Auswahl*, ed. G. A. Rein *et al..*, vol. 5, 1973, p. 614. Hitler and Goebbels knew Carlyle's book well and re-read it in 1945 in Berlin while awaiting defeat, cf. H. R. Trevor-Roper, *The Last Days of Hitler*, 5th edn, 1978, pp. 109–10, 254.

45. Kohn, pp. 340–1.

46. GW II, p. 1044.

47. R. B. Farrell, *Dictionary of German Synonyms*, 1962, pp. 224–5.

48. GW II, pp. 1047–8.

49. Ibid., p. 1053.

50. Ibid., p. 1054.

51. Musil, 'Die Nation als Ideal und als Wirklichkeit'; 'The Nation as Ideal and as Reality', GW II, pp. 1059–75, publ. in *Die Neue Rundschau* 1921.

52. Ibid., p. 1063.

53. A. Reniers, 'Drei Briefe', 1970, pp. 285, 288–9, 292.

54. GW II, pp. 1068–9.

55. Ibid., pp. 1069–75.

56. TB I, pp. 544, 945.

57. See Marie-Louise Roth, 1972, pp. 115–18.

58. Musil, 'Das Hilflose Europa'; 'The Helplessness of Europe', GW II, pp. 1075–94, publ. in *Ganymed*, 1922.

59. Ibid., pp. 1075–82.

60. Ibid., p. 1085. W. Köhler, *Die physischen Gestalten . . .*, 1920.

61. GW II, pp. 1082–8.

62. Ibid., pp. 1089, 1071.

63. Ibid., p. 1092. Emphasis in the original.

64. Ibid., pp. 1091–4.

65. Dinklage, LWW, pp. 236–8.

66. Musil, 'Ein Wichtiges Buch'; 'An Important Book', GW II, pp. 1622–5. *Soziologie des Volksbildungswesens*, ed. L. v. Wiese, 1921. Cf. excerpts from this work in TB I, pp. 653–8.

67. H. F. Garten, *Modern German Drama*, 1964, p. 11.

68. Musil, 'Symptomen-Theater I'; 'The Theatre of Symptoms', GW II, pp. 1094–1103; 'Symptomen-Theater II', ibid., pp. 1103–11. Publ. in DNM 1922; 1922/1923. (III) 'Der "Untergang" des Theaters'; 'The "Decay" of the Theatre', ibid., pp. 1116–31 (DNM 1924), Section 3: 'Bildungskrisis'; 'Crisis in Education', pp. 1121–26.

69. Ibid., III. Cf. GW II, pp. 1385–6. For information on recent reforms in the German school system see *Facts about Germany*, 1979, pp. 304–5.

70. Personal information from Professor Karl Dinklage. Cf. the statement by Dr Kreisky at the foundation of the Intern. R. Musil Society, *Musil-Forum*, 1-1975-1, pp. 67–8, also in *Robert Musil*, Cahiers de l'Herne, ed. Marie-Louise Roth and R. Olmi, 1981, p. 293 (in French).

71. Musil 'Ansätze zu neuer Ästhetik'; 'Towards a new Theory of Aesthetics', GW II, pp. 1137–54. Published in DNM 1925. Béla Balázs, *Der sichtbare Mensch*, 1924.

72. Reniers, 'Drei Briefe', 1970, pp. 287, 292.

73. GW II, p. 1141. L. Lévy-Bruhl, *Les fonctions mentales dans les sociétés inférieures*, 1910, German translation 1921, E. Kretschmer, 1922.

74. GW II, pp. 1138–45.

75. Ibid., pp. 1145–54. Cf. 'Literat und Literatur'; 'The Writer and Literature' (1931) on the relationship of content and form in literature, especially in poetry, GW II, pp. 1203–24.

76. TB I, p. 118; GW II, p. 74. See also Chapter 2.

77. Musil, 'Rede zur Rilke-Feier'; 'Rilke Memorial Address', GW II, pp. 1229–42, given in Berlin, 16 January 1927. *Briefe* 1981 includes two letters from Musil to Rilke, pp. 104, 361–5.

78. Ibid., p. 1237.

79. Ibid., p. 1371.

80. Berghahn, p. 106. Cf. Chapter 7 of this book.

81. TB I, pp. 681 ff.; II, pp. 496, 1182–3.

6 THE TURNING-POINT: *THE MAN WITHOUT QUALITIES*

The action of *The Man without Qualities* is set in the twelve months leading to the outbreak of the First World War. Although Musil often dismisses factual detail in literature as unimportant, there can be no doubt that the novel as published arises from the same deep concern for the crisis in Europe and the future of the 'civilised' nations that informs the essays discussed in Chapter 5. The whole work, but especially Book I, is to be seen as a portrait of a society moving inexorably towards war, like the passengers fast asleep in the train on course for collision. This inevitable outcome casts a shadow of irony over the entire narrative, as the various characters, each one a representative figure of the time, pursue their own concerns and seek their own salvation. Only Ulrich, the man without qualities, is clear-sighted enough to perceive the sickness at the heart of civilisation, but his efforts to alert those in positions of power to the dangers ahead meet with almost total lack of comprehension. Eventually he undertakes a personal attempt, together with his sister, to find a way of life devoted only to the 'other' dimension of human beings, to a life of imagination, feeling and mysticism. The author's plans up to the year 1936 show that Ulrich's and Agathe's personal venture was also destined to fail, that the work would end with the outbreak of the First World War and with Ulrich volunteering for military service. During Musil's last years, he wrote several versions of the later chapters of the novel in his search for the most fitting conclusion; some of these will be considered in Chapter 7. Although the work was not completed by the time he died in April 1942, a notice written in January of that year lists ideas for a final section, including comments on political and social developments during the Second World War; these show that even then he was still concerned with the wider issues.[1]

The first outline of *The Man without Qualities* appeared in 1926. Musil's friend Oskar Maurus Fontana relates that the author had been invited by the editor of the Berlin weekly *Die Literarische Welt* to speak about his work, but had declined the offer. Early in 1926, however, the journal printed an interview between Fontana and Thomas Mann, whereupon Musil, realising that such a public statement of work in progress might after all have its uses, asked Fontana if he would conduct a similar literary interview with him, and this was published in April of that year.[2] At the beginning of the conversation the title of the novel is give as *Die Zwillingsschwester* (*The Twin Sister*), but by the time of publication in 1930 it had been changed to its present one. Having stated that the book concludes with the outbreak of war, Musil immediately contradicts any assumption that he might be writing an historical novel. His interest, he declares firmly, is not directed towards facts as such, but towards the underlying, typical, even uncanny aspect of events.

Before going into detail, Musil sets the scene. The ironic framework for the action of the novel is provided by the long-standing rivalry between Austria-Hungary and Germany. The year 1918 was to have marked the jubilee celebrations of two emperors: by that year Francis Joseph I of Austria would have reigned for seventy years and William II of Germany for thirty. In the event, as Musil's readers know, by the end of 1918 Francis Joseph was dead, Karl, his successor, and William had both abdicated, and both empires had collapsed in ruin and defeat. In the first book of the novel Musil chronicles the imaginary efforts of Austrian patriots at the highest levels of society to promote the idea of a Glorious Austria. Their activities are intended to rival similar preparations in Berlin to celebrate the image of Germany, and for this reason the Austrian efforts are referred to as the collateral campaign. It emphasises the world mission of Austria-Hungary as an example of the peaceful co-existence of many different peoples, at a time when nationalist groupings threaten its cohesion on every side, in the year before the assassination of the Austrian Crown Prince at Sarajevo. The Austrian patriots portrayed by Musil intend to stage jubilee festivities of historic significance, outshining anything Germany can do in spite of her technological and manufacturing superiority.

During the course of his conversation with Fontana, Musil summarises various aspects of the novel. Ulrich, the protagonist, a young man trained in mathematics, physics and technology, finds to his astonishment that 'real' life as it is lived today lags at least a hundred years behind advances in scientific thinking. Musil emphasises that when he says 'today' he means 1926, the date of the interview, just as much as the pre-war period of the narrative. This phase difference between thought and life, repeatedly noted in Musil's essays, forms the basis for one of the central themes of the work: how should a person rooted in the life of the mind and spirit relate to the 'real' world?[3] Ulrich soon encounters a man described as his opposite pole, a wealthy and influential industrialist, combining in one person business acumen and the ability to write. In the meantime, the collateral campaign has begun its work under the chairmanship of the wife of an Austrian diplomat; the lady, whom Ulrich names the 'second Diotima' on account of her reputed wisdom, is related to his family, and as a result he is drawn into the campaign. As the action proceeds, Diotima and Arnheim, the industrialist, fall in love, but their relationship, based largely on pretence, comes to nothing.

The second main theme is given by Ulrich's meeting with his long forgotten sister, Agathe. In the interview, Musil describes the Utopian ideal of a twin sister as 'the idea of oneself made manifest', and for Ulrich the idea becomes a living being. He and Agathe withdraw from the frenzied activity of the campaign to live out their lives in a state of mystic goodness, or at least attempt to do so; it emerges that such a life is impossible. The author comments that the world cannot endure without evil, for evil produces movement; goodness alone leads to rigidity. A further strand of the action is associated with the figure of Clarisse, a young woman married to Ulrich's friend Walter. During the course of the novel she becomes more and more unbalanced, and is finally declared insane. This figure, with her obsessions, plays a significant role in the work; at the same time both Clarisse and the murderer Moosbrugger, not mentioned in the interview, are discussed in a way which calls into question the usual definitions of reality.

The author then describes how the money intended for the collateral campaign is fought over by representatives of various interests, but eventually appropriated by the delegate of the War Ministry and spent on armaments. After further adventures, Ulrich's desire to participate in the shaping of events, never very strong, is abandoned. All the rivalries and contradictions of society finally lead to the horror of war, when, for Ulrich as for the other characters of the novel, personal choices are no longer possible.

When the interviewer points out that this scheme surely runs the risk of becoming too theoretical, Musil agrees, explaining how he hopes to meet the danger: firstly by means of an ironic approach, not as a gesture of superiority, but employing irony as a weapon, a means to an end; and secondly by the writing of lively, convincing scenes. In conclusion, Fontana asks whether Musil's fundamental attitude is one of pessimism. On the contrary, Musil replies, Mankind needs a new morality to match its tremendous achievements in our time. His aim is to provide material for such a new morality through the medium of his novel, which he describes as being simultaneously an attempt to dissolve the existing world and to chart a possible new synthesis of its elements.

*   *   *

The reader embarking on the first chapter of *The Man without Qualities* might be forgiven for supposing that he had, by mistake, opened a meteorological report. Highs and lows, temperatures and humidity, isotherms and isotheres all combine to yield, at last, the information that it was a fine day in August 1913. There follows a graphic account of the traffic of a modern city, described in terms of light and darkness, pulse and vibrations, and metaphors of noise drawn from the science of metallurgy. We are told that the city is Vienna, but immediately reminded that this fact is of small importance. The author deliberately introduces us to an anonymous scene, as if we had arrived there, at that time, purely by chance. Like the movement of clouds in the sky, the affairs of men, in Musil's view, depend to a large extent on a random coincidence of facts, and the opening chapter is intended as a symbolic statement of this truth.[4]

The two characters who now move into view are similarly treated in an impersonal manner. They are described as a man and a woman belonging to the upper classes; their identity is suggested only to be denied, and they are seen walking confidently along one of the main streets of the city. Suddenly the peace of the seemingly normal street scene is shattered; a crowd gathers, and at its centre something like a deep hole appears. A careless pedestrian has been knocked over and injured by a heavy lorry. The passers-by are shocked and concerned for the man's safety; as soon as an ambulance arrives, however, and its crew begin their efficient ministrations, the onlookers proceed on their way, relieved that they need no longer feel obliged to act. In the same way, according to Musil, the surface of civilisation may suddenly collapse into unsuspected depths; but afterwards, most people are only too ready to walk away, without considering whether they themselves might be able to help prevent such a catastrophe occurring in the future.

In Ulrich, the man without qualities, Musil shows a man engaged

in a serious quest, trying to find out who he is and what his function in life and place in society should be; in the process the author
discusses and illuminates some of the central dilemmas of the
twentieth century. In his youth Ulrich was fired with admiration of
Napoleon, and made up his mind to become a Great Man. Following in the steps of his hero, he joined the army, but soon discovered
that becoming a famous general was likely to take somewhat longer
than he had imagined. His second attempt to achieve greatness led
him to train as an engineer, a profession widely regarded at the turn
of the century as possessing the key to the future. Throughout the
nineteenth century, science and technology had progressed from
one discovery to the next, and those working in this area of
apparently unlimited potential looked down with ill-concealed
impatience upon artists, philosophers and other people foolish
enough to waste their time on unquantifiable matters such as
beauty or morality. All the world's problems, so it seemed, could
be solved with the aid of a slide rule: 'If you possess a slide rule,
and someone comes along with large claims or great emotions, you
say: Excuse me a moment, first of all we'll calculate the margins of
error and the probability value of all that!'[5] The works of Emerson,
so Ulrich thought, were full of possible watchwords for engineers,
and a saying such as 'Men walk as prophecies of the next age' ought
to hang on the wall of every workshop.[6] Unfortunately, Ulrich was
soon forced to acknowledge that most engineers, while they were
bold and innovative in their professional activities, failed to extend
this fearless mode of thought to their private lives, where they
might be as obtuse and old-fashioned as anybody else. At this point
disillusionment set in, and he rapidly left the profession.

For Ulrich's third and last attempt to find a rewarding career he
turned to mathematics. The mathematical sciences, in Musil's view,
represent the spirit of the modern age and the basis of the vast and
fundamental changes that distinguish it from preceding centuries.
The aeroplane, the motor-car, the submarine, the telephone, the
gramophone and countless other inventions are all made possible
by mathematics, the realisation of ancient dreams, not so much
science as magic, the revelation of the secrets of God. Admittedly,
a price has to be paid: 'We have won reality and lost our dreams'.[7]
Many people, says Musil, are only too ready to blame mathematics
for the inner emptiness, the loss of sense of direction, and the crisis
of culture in our time. Ulrich, for his part, loved mathematics out
of opposition to those who hated it. He was passionately convinced

that scientific thinking would indeed usher in a new age: if only human beings could be taught to think in new ways, they would discover a new way of life.

A few years later, however, despite undoubted success in this demanding field, Ulrich was still not satisfied, and his seemingly innate restlessness was closely linked with a characteristic described as a 'sense of possibilities', as opposed to a sense of reality. Even as a child he had shocked his teachers by suggesting in an essay that God makes the world, but thinks, as he does so, that it might just as well be completely different.[8] As Ulrich advanced in years, this free-thinking outlook, instead of giving way to solid realism, had grown ever stronger. What some would call useless dreaming, the author describes as 'conscious Utopianism', and in this spirit Ulrich regarded the existing world not as finite, but as a challenge. The possibilities inherent in the world had, for him, equal validity with so-called real facts; he regarded them as divinely inspired and potentially unlimited. A man with such an outlook will naturally take the 'real' world less seriously than it takes itself; he may well be unpredictable in his dealings with others, and inclined, for example, to ascribe blame for a crime not to the wickedness of the criminal, but to the faults of society.[9] Moreover he will probably extend this unorthodox attitude to himself, refusing to give even his own person the benefit of unquestioning allegiance. Ulrich's scientific training had led him to work hard in his profession, but over and above the demands of his research he looked on himself, in Nietzsche's terms, as an explorer of the spirit, working for the future. A day came, however, when he recognised that he was as far away from any goal as ever, and meanwhile the stupidity of the outside world had apparently reached the stage where even a race-horse could be described as a genius. Taking stock, Ulrich saw that he possessed all the abilities and qualities prized by his age, but had lost the will to make use of them, at least in any way the outside world was likely to accept. He seemed to have been born with a talent for which, at present, a use did not exist. Having reached this conclusion, Ulrich abandoned his research and decided to take a year's leave from his life, to become, temporarily, a man without any qualities at all, in order to seek a suitable application for his talents.[10]

The action of Musil's novel is set in a country he calls Kakania, a name made up from the double letter K associated with the Dual Monarchy of Austria-Hungary: *kaiserlich* (imperial) and *königlich* (royal). In an early notebook entry he describes the background of his projected novel thus: '. . . the capital city of a country in decline, full of party disputes . . . a city like Madrid or Vienna, where the needs of society in general can no longer be met, while the development of the individual and of high society has reached its peak.'[11] This description provides a thumbnail sketch of Viennese society as Ulrich encounters it. While it is evident that the author sets great store by the 'sense of possibilities' so vital to his protagonist, it should not be thought that the setting of the novel is therefore in any way abstract or imaginary. On the contrary, it is precisely because the declining empire and society constitute an all-too-solid reality which also claims to be the only one, that Musil is so concerned to show that this is not necessarily so.

The description of Kakania in Chapter 8 of the novel is preceded by a sketch of its opposite, an exaggerated portrait of an ultra-modern city with its skyscrapers, lifts and underground trains, where everyone is rushing around to little purpose: a portrait clearly intended by the author as a caricature of the future, but which strikes us in the 1980s as uncomfortably familiar. Some denizens of this mad universe may eventually be seized with an irrepressible desire to escape, to cry, in the words of the title: 'Stop the world, I want to get off!' In the good old days when the Austrian empire was still in being, one could, indeed, do so, and return home to Kakania. This was the land at the centre of Europe, where the axes of the old world intersect, a huge country stretching from glaciers down to the sea, still highly conscious of its historic role as the heir to the medieval Holy Roman Empire, and embracing within its boundaries a vast number of different peoples. Largely self-sufficient, the empire had little ambition for world power, whether economic or political. It was ruled under the emperor by the best bureaucracy in Europe; although nominally democratic, its seats of power were still, as in feudal times, occupied with few exceptions by members of the aristocracy. 'Before the law all citizens were equal, but then, not everyone was a citizen.'[12] In Musil's view, the collapse of the empire was to a large extent due to a combination of feudal attitudes with an insufficient understanding of the nature of a state containing so many different nationalities. Since 1867 Hungary had once again possessed a separate parliament and was therefore entitled to regard herself politically as Austria's equal. For this very reason however, Austria, or in other words, the rest of the Dual Monarchy, consisting of Czechs, Germans, Poles, Italians, Slovenes, Serbs and many others, became a structure impossible to manage, whose citizens, unable to envisage it as an entity, naturally preferred to think of themselves as Czechs, Germans and so on. Every aspect of the life of the nation suffered from this lack of cohesion, while the various groups within it, regarding each other with permanent suspicion, behaved like the limbs of a creature all pulling different ways, to prevent it assuming any recognisable shape whatsoever.[13]

It follows that this background was likely to have an adverse effect on the development of a young man such as Ulrich, inclined by his very nature to observe and analyse rather than to throw himself wholeheartedly into a demanding career. Recent criticism has pointed out with some force that Ulrich's position as a voluntary outsider was only possible because, for some unspecified reason, he was under no obligation to earn a living. Be that as it may, the author leaves us in no doubt of the connection between political stagnation and a lack of positive thinking in the state, and the dissatisfaction and disorientation of the protagonist. In a country suffering from a fateful division between the ideas that people believed in and the things they actually did, a profound lack of self-confidence was bound to be felt by at least some members of the population. Musil's Kakania is described with affectionate irony, but also with sadness, as the most advanced state in this regard, the state whose life was prolonged by sheer inertia, without inner conviction, until at last the general feeling that there was insufficient reason for its further existence was translated into historical fact.[14]

In Chapter 15 of the novel Musil gives a vivid account of the cultural and intellectual climate in Austria at the turn of the century; the title of the chapter, 'Intellectual revolution', sums up the underlying spirit of those years. During the last two decades of the nineteenth century, considerable progress in technology, research and commerce had been accompanied by a marked lack of originality in architecture and the other arts. Suddenly, or so it seemed, change was in the air throughout Europe, and everywhere people rose up to fight against tradition:[15]

> The Superman was adored, and the Subman was adored; health and the sun were worshipped, and the delicacy of consumptive girls was worshipped . . . one had faith and was sceptical, one was naturalistic and precious, robust and morbid; one dreamed

of ancient castles and shady avenues, autumnal gardens, glassy ponds, jewels, hashish, disease and demonism, but also of prairies, vast horizons, forges and rolling-mills, naked wrestlers, the uprisings of the slaves of toil, man and woman in the primeval Garden, and the destruction of society.

No one could be sure what was being born, whether it was a new art, a new man, a new morality or a restructuring of society. The plethora of fervent passions and contradictory ideas had only one thing in common: the expectation that the 'magic date' of the new century would indeed usher in a new age.

Yet within a comparatively short space of time, perhaps ten or twelve years, the fervour had abated. It seemed to Ulrich (Chapter 16) that in spite of as much external activity as ever, a sense of disillusionment had set in. What then had been lost? Something hard to define. It was like iron filings in disarray after being released by a magnet; like threads falling out of a neat ball of wool; like an orchestra playing out of tune. All boundaries and distinctions had become blurred; dubious ideas were taken seriously; persons rose to prominence who would formerly not have been considered. And suddenly all positions of power in matters of the mind and spirit were occupied by such people, and all decisions were made by them. A mysterious sickness pervaded all aspects of cultural life. To free himself from the despondency caused by these reflections, Ulrich concluded that the sickness was nothing more than common stupidity, which as he saw it, is adept at assuming manifold disguises in order to displace truth wherever possible. It was at this point that Ulrich became so conscious of his own lack of sympathy with the age in which he lived that he despaired of finding any useful place within it.

After his return to Vienna, Ulrich had chosen a home symbolic of the layers of history that constituted Austria in the year 1913. The original owner in the seventeenth century had built it as a country house, perhaps a hunting lodge, and each succeeding age had left its mark on the exterior. Faced with the problem of furnishing the inside, Ulrich had tried to choose a consistent style, but, finding himself baffled by the conflicting claims of Art Nouveau, functionalism and various other fashions, eventually entrusted the task to a firm of interior decorators. The result was delightful, but in many ways was as alien to himself as the rest of his life at that time.[16]

Some weeks after moving into his new home Ulrich acquired a new mistress. This lady, who might have stepped straight out of the pages of Schnitzler, is referred to in the novel as Bonadea, the Good Goddess, after a Roman goddess of chastity whose temple became notorious for the excesses that took place there. Like the goddess, Bonadea led a double life. She was the wife of a well-known lawyer and the devoted mother of two small boys; but at the same time was dominated by her senses to an extent that could only be described as nymphomania. Her affair with Ulrich began late one evening when, driving home, she had noticed the young man lying in the gutter. He had been attacked and robbed; Bonadea's coachman lifted him into her carriage and drove him to his house. The next morning she called to enquire after his health, whereupon the visit rapidly evolved into a closer acquaintance.[17]

Since his return to the capital, Ulrich had renewed his friendship with Walter and Clarisse. Walter, his friend since school and student days, was an artist, also at various times a musician, teacher, critic and now some kind of official in an art institute. Although undoubtedly gifted he did not seem to achieve very much; even worse, now that he held a position which allowed him to paint, the great works expected by all his friends failed to materialise. Instead of painting he spent much of his time at the piano, playing Wagner, whose music he had formerly branded as decadent, but to which he was now addicted. Long before their marriage Clarisse had believed Walter to be a potential genius. Her thinking was dominated by the ideas of Nietzsche, with the result that she regarded it as Walter's vocation to become a genius, a goal that in her view could be attained simply through willpower. As Clarisse began to realise that her husband would never achieve any kind of greatness, she saw this more and more as a personal betrayal, and although they still played piano duets together, the rest of their married life was increasingly filled with tension.

The figures of Walter and Clarisse, as well as of some other principal characters in the novel, are based on real people known to Musil, and their shaping to his literary purpose may be traced in the notebooks. Yet it should be remembered that in all these cases the author is never drawing a portrait of the original person as such, but using them as a model, often with a good deal of poetic licence, to establish the character for his own particular purposes.[18]

The models for Walter and Clarisse, Gustav and Alice Donath, are discussed at length in Musil's first extant notebooks, beginning about 1904—5. In September 1910 he records that Alice was taken to a mental hospital. This personal acquaintance with a woman who gradually loses her mental balance no doubt reinforced his interest in the questions of personality, stability or disintegration evident in all Musil's fiction and drama. The chief protagonists, whether Törless, Homo or Ulrich, are of course modelled on aspects of the author, and in the major novel Musil lays bare the alienation of the central figure from his society and the consequent disorientation in himself that is also so eloquently depicted in the tortured portraits of Egon Schiele. Musil's friendship with some of the *Gestalt* psychologists intensified his interest in these matters, while his own breakdown in 1929 and his treatment by the Adlerian Dr Hugo Lukács gave him experience of another approach to the study of personality. The notebooks contain innumerable brief comments on people he met in daily life, from the humble to the eminent; these single out one aspect or another of a personality. In the novel he shows the interplay of many different personalities with one another, and with Ulrich. In Ulrich's reflections on other figures, on himself and on the state of society, his main concern is always with the balance between the factors that make up human personality and character, particularly the balance between intellect and emotion. The second book of *The Man without Qualities* centres on the debate regarding the role of emotion in human life, and in the first book Ulrich returns to such questions time and again, not only during committee meetings of the collateral campaign, but even, somewhat tactlessly, during his encounters with Bonadea.

At the furthest extreme from cold reason stands the spectre of madness, and, not content with chronicling Clarisse's gradual descent into insanity, Musil introduces early in the novel the figure of Moosbrugger, the psychopath. Moosbrugger, a big man with enormous strength, but mentally subnormal, had murdered a prostitute in a horrifying manner. In the longest chapter of his introduction, Musil traces in some detail the previous life of this man, on first encounter apparently a decent, good-natured workman like any other, who had already committed a number of crimes. Whether he was or was not responsible for his actions was a question even the psychiatrists seemed unable to decide. The author writes as if from inside the mind of Moosbrugger, who had led a wandering life as a carpenter's apprentice, had never settled, was always short of money and so was unable to approach any woman except by force. On the night of the crime, the murdered prostitute had in fact approached him, had begged, cajoled and followed him until at last he had stabbed her, just to make her keep quiet. At the trial, Ulrich was struck by the differing attitudes of the participants. Moosbrugger, intent on his dignity, refused to have his defence counsel imply diminished responsibility; on the other hand, when the judge, citing numerous previous convictions, sought to prove murder with malice aforethought, Moosbrugger also disputed this interpretation. In his simple mind there was no connection between the successive incidents of his lonely life, and he was utterly incapable of understanding the arguments put forward by the judge. But the judge for his part, in Ulrich's view, brought to the case legal and moral principles that were inappropriate and out of date. When the death penalty was pronounced, Moosbrugger called out in a loud voice that he was content, but wished to confess that he was insane! Ulrich was fascinated by this incoherent behaviour; clear evidence, he thought, of insanity, but at the same time no more than a distortion of the elements of normal life. At that moment he was certain that the connection between himself and Moosbrugger was much closer than anyone might suspect. At the end of the trial the defence counsel gave notice of appeal, thus ensuring that Moosbrugger would reappear later in the novel.[19]

*   *   *

Ulrich's father, unlike his son, was a man with qualities. From modest beginnings as a lawyer he had risen to a university chair of jurisprudence; in addition, he assiduously cultivated the aristocratic connections formed while he was a young tutor in great families, becoming not only the trusted confidant of court dignitaries, but also being ennobled and nominated to membership of the upper chamber of Parliament. One day Ulrich received a letter from his father outlining the plans for the emperor's jubilee in the year 1918. He urged his son, whose failure to settle down had caused him bitter disappointment, to make contact with a friend of his, a senior official at court, who had promised to find a place for Ulrich on the jubilee committee. Ulrich was also invited to lose no time in calling upon a distant relative, wife of Herr Tuzzi of the Ministry of External Affairs, who was herself closely involved in the jubilee preparations.[20] This letter forms the prelude to Ulrich's participation in the collateral campaign and thus to the main body of Book I of *The Man without Qualities*. The overall title at the head of this section is a short phrase bound to give any translator a headache. I would suggest two possible equivalents: 'History repeats itself' or 'There's nothing new under the sun'. The author uses the same title for Chapter 83, adding for good measure: '. . . or why not invent history?' By this time it will be apparent that the collateral campaign attracts the full force of Musil's satire. The committee meetings, petitions, deliberations, postponements, and a variety of social events, adding up in the last resort to nothing at all, are described with a sharp and observant wit, and transmuted now and then into high comedy.

The leading figures of the campaign were Diotima Tuzzi and Count Leinsdorf. In spite of his years, the count, owner of vast estates, was keen to play an active part in the life of the nation. Like the emperor himself, aged eighty-three in 1913, Leinsdorf belonged to another age and ruled his peasants with benevolent despotism. A fervent patriot, he took upon himself the ultimate responsibility for the jubilee preparations, while being content to leave the organisation in the capable hands of Diotima. When Ulrich made the acquaintance of his cousin, he found she was beautiful, charming and, to his surprise, relatively young. Her husband, though not of noble birth, occupied a high place in the Kakanian Foreign Office and was reputed to be the minister's right hand man, one of the few men with real power in European affairs. Thanks to his influential position and Diotima's aptitude in learning and deploying impressive phrases, her home had become known as a salon, a meeting-place of the rich and the great, and thus the obvious centre for the proceedings of the campaign.[21]

Despite Count Leinsdorf's patronage and her responsible position, Diotima was not happy, and the reason was to be found in her marriage. As usual at this period, it was a marriage based on prudence as much as love. Her husband was considerably older than herself and, while he encouraged her cultural activities, well aware of their potential advantages for himself, he was not prepared to take them in the least seriously. Having no children, she was free to read a great deal; her favourite authors were Maeterlinck, Novalis and other writers concerned, above all, with the soul. One day Diotima received a visit from Dr Paul Arnheim, a wealthy and powerful Prussian industrialist who had arrived in Vienna, so he said, to recuperate from the pressures of business, confident that the baroque charm of Austrian culture would restore his mind and soul. She had already learnt that, in addition to his responsibilities in the family firm, he had written books advocating a much greater use of ideas in business, diplomacy and all spheres of power. When this important man proved to be not only responsive to her person, but equally impressed by her mind, she was enchanted, and immediately had a brilliant idea.[22]

Diotima's idea was that the great man should undertake the leadership of the campaign. The fact that he was a Prussian and that the campaign had originated from rivalry against Prussia did not, in her elated mood, present an insuperable obstacle. Count Leinsdorf, on the other hand, was adamant that leadership was out of the question, though he eventually allowed Arnheim to join the committee. He declared that the only man he would consider for the post of honorary secretary of the campaign was Ulrich, and soon the man without qualities found himself appointed whether he liked it or not.[23] Arnheim remained in Vienna for some time, and the affair between him and Diotima developed along unusual lines. There was undoubted attraction on either side, but after prolonged hesitation, caution at last prevailed, so that in the end the relationship amounted to little more than the exchange of high-flown phrases quoted from Maeterlinck. A parallel affair between Diotima's pretty Jewish maid, Rachel, and Arnheim's young Negro servant, Soliman, followed a more predictable course. Perhaps the chief justification for bringing Arnheim into the plot lies in his use as a foil to Ulrich. The character is based on Walther Rathenau, whom Musil had encountered in 1914 in Berlin; he was an industrialist and writer, and later Foreign Minister of the Weimar Republic.[24] In the novel, Arnheim's presence in Vienna is not so innocent as he likes to pretend, as he has commercial motives. He is first and foremost a realist, and therefore the antithesis of Ulrich, involved in the business world, concerned with money for its own sake and for the power it confers, and yet claiming the right to pronounce at length on matters in which, according to Ulrich, he can only be considered an amateur. The tension between these two men reaches its climax in Chapter 121.

To complete the panorama of Viennese society the author introduces a number of figures, for example General Stumm von Bordwehr of the Ministry of War. He is presumably intended as a representative of the forces of evil, but emerges as an old friend of Ulrich's from his army days, plump and down-to-earth, with a homely turn of phrase that makes a pleasant change after the quasi-philosophical utterances of some other characters. Another minor but significant figure is the Jewish banker Leo Fischel with his Gentile wife Klementine, whose daughter Gerda is caught not only in the crossfire of parental disagreements, but also in the friction between old and new views of a woman's role in life. In her determination to show her independence, to break away from the stereotype of the elegant young lady waiting at home for a husband to appear, Gerda becomes involved in the German Nationalist movement, a precursor of National Socialism which was gaining ground in German-speaking areas of the empire at this time. The movement is represented in the novel by an unprepossessing young man called Hans Sepp, with whom Gerda enters into a frustrating Platonic relationship, made all the more difficult by his tendency to expound his irrational and frequently anti-Semitic theories in her father's house.[25] To balance Hans Sepp's Nationalist views, Musil also planned to include a young Socialist revolutionary called Schmeisser, whose name contains a suggestion of 'overthrow'; but this figure does not appear in the final text.

It is in the plenary sessions of the collateral campaign that Musil's gift for comedy finds greatest scope. Diotima's salon had long been known as the place where one could meet the rich, the powerful and the cream of society, together with those noted as world authorities in some specialism or other that one had never heard of. Thanks to Count Leinsdorf's action in designating the Tuzzi residence as official centre of the collateral campaign, Diotima's cultural evenings acquired even greater brilliance. She had decided to set up a special committee in order to formulate a guiding resolution for the emperor's jubilee celebrations; the members of this group were to be drawn from the fields of art, literature and scholarship, and joined by others invited merely as observers. On the occasion of their first meeting, each guest was graciously welcomed by the lady of the house with a few well-chosen words concerning his latest work, an admirable achievement only made possible by the assistance of Arnheim's private secretary who had prepared a collection of suitable excerpts. The interconnecting rooms of the apartment had been emptied of furniture except for a large bookcase against the end wall, and as the distinguished guests drifted through the crowd, each one could be observed examining the books on display with selfless curiosity until at last, having located his own works, he assumed an air of quiet satisfaction.[26]

Surprisingly enough it was General Stumm who, in his admiration for Diotima and desire to assist in her investigations, took upon himself the task of putting the thoughts of the modern age into some kind of order. The confusing interplay of multifarious ideas and ideologies, new directions in art, science and politics, expressionism, socialism, Marxism, psychoanalysis and half a dozen others, all of which were represented at the gatherings in Diotima's home, had somehow failed to yield the one saving idea she had hoped to find. The general decided, therefore, to take action. Never a man to do things by halves, he made straight for the Imperial Court Library where, he thought, he would surely be able to discover the greatest idea of modern times. His original plan had been to read his way through the accumulated material at the rate of a book a day, but by the time he had worked out that this would require ten thousand years, he was obliged to change his tactics. The librarian acting as his guide was perplexed by the general's lack of precision regarding the object of his search. When he led Stumm into the central catalogue room and handed him the bibliography of bibliographies, in the hope that this would solve the problem, the general, perhaps understandably, was panic-stricken, and when he explained that he could only keep these millions of books in order by never reading a single one himself, Stumm was dumbfounded. In the end it was left to an old porter to come to Stumm's aid, which he did by finding for him all the books Diotima herself read on her regular visits to the library, much to the general's delight.[27]

Musil's ironic view of the professional librarian may be traced back to his own employment in the library of the Technological University of Vienna from 1911 to 1914. At the end of Chapter 100, General Stumm's entertaining account of his expedition to the library suddenly takes on a more serious note when he reflects on the concept of order as such. Order is necessary, order is good; but, whether in the realm of ideas, politics or morality, a system of universal order without exceptions, where every single thing functions according to the rules, may end by killing the thing it aims to preserve. As the system itself becomes paramount, rigid and bereft of life, everything within it must eventually freeze to death. This concept of order as potential death forms one side of the dichotomy to which Ulrich constantly returns, and the imagery associated with it usually focuses on the contrast between rigidity, ossification and rigor mortis, and the abundance, even luxuriance of uncontrolled plant life as a metaphor for imagination and feelings. One of the first occasions where Musil makes this contrast in a published work is in the important essay on the nature and functioning of the creative writer's mind, and there, as later, the opposition between rigidity and movement carries vital significance.[28]

In Ulrich's opinion, a striking example of ossification in thought and practice was to be found in the attitude of the law towards the psychopath Moosbrugger. Although at the trial the psychiatrists were largely agreed that he was insane, their reluctance as scientists to make exaggerated claims on the basis of the available evidence prevented them from challenging the verdict of the lawyers. According to long-established legal criteria Moosbrugger was therefore declared responsible for his actions and thus guilty of murder. The trial led Ulrich to reflect that the division between psychiatrists and lawyers could be seen as merely one instance of the widespread division in daily life between, on the one hand, scientists and other workers whose activities were based on facts and empirical evidence, and on the other, philosophers, lawyers and writers, whose professional sphere was that of values. He observed that the rationalists were quite prepared to leave vital decisions in the field of beauty, justice, love and belief to their wives, or failing that, to the other group of men who regarded values as their professional domain. Even stranger was the fact that those who in their work were dedicated champions of factual truth would allow the opposite camp to lay down the law in matters which after all affected everyone, without believing a word they said and without considering whether things might not be managed differently. Now one side was in the ascendant, now the other. Quite recently opinion had turned against the scientific outlook, and now it was the opposite mentality which dominated public life, decrying exact knowledge and calling fervently for a new belief in man, the soul and eternal values.[29]

Ulrich for his part declined to take such attitudes seriously. His outlook, since his earliest years, had been formed by a view of life as a hypothesis: nothing is definite, all things in the world, including human beings themselves, are engaged in an invisible but constant process of change, the possibilities are unlimited, and from time to time one may briefly glimpse the intense flame of truth. It is an outlook akin to Emerson's: 'Very few of our race can be said to be yet finished men'.[30] Musil made excerpts from Emerson's essay 'Circles' while working on *The Visionaries* and early sections of the novel, and in these notes he uses the phrase 'dynamic morality' to denote an open view of life and a belief in the possibility of improvement. Musil's indebtedness to thinkers like Emerson is clearly shown in Chapter 62, one of the most explicit statements in the novel of Ulrich's personal beliefs. With increasing maturity Ulrich had given up the idea of a hypothesis as a basic approach to life, and now preferred to regard the world and his own existence in a manner not unlike that of an essay, considering now this, now that aspect in turn, in order to gain as full and complete a picture as possible. This outlook however retained the essential flexibility of the earlier approach, being linked with a view of morality in which the value of an action or a quality, or even its very nature, depended on the attendant circumstances or on the whole of which they formed a part. One may see this as an extension of *Gestalt* theory into the realm of morality: in such a view the moral significance of an action was conditional upon the 'field of force' or the 'constellation' of the circumstances, so that a murder, for example, could be regarded as a crime or, in different circumstances, as the action of a hero.[31]

Chapter 62 sets out Ulrich's view of man as the 'embodiment of his possibilites, the potential man', in contrast with the traditional view of man as a solid reality or a stable character. The disquieting corollary of such an understanding of human nature was of course that Ulrich felt capable of every virtue and every vice. He looked upon morality in the usual sense as a system exhausted by age, whereas, he thought, in the modern world human beings should constantly create their own vital morality through deliberate reform of underlying assumptions, having regard to the particular facts and circumstances. Such an existentialist understanding of morality would interpret it no longer as a set of rigid rules, but as a finely poised balance, requiring unceasing effort for its constant renewal. It seemed to Ulrich that many isolated developments in recent years pointed towards the possible recognition of this new approach. He thought it would require above all a combination of exactitude and passion, of the mathematical and the emotional elements in human beings — yet not in the shape of systematic philosophy which he, like many of his contemporaries, regarded with suspicion. Experience had taught him that philosophers tended to imprison ideas within a system, while his own search for enlightenment was fired by the hope that truth could be known without recourse to systems and their inevitable rigidity. Here again it was the concept of the literary essay which came to Ulrich's aid, a form understood as the unique expression of the inner life of a thinker at a particular moment. The writers of such essays, 'masters of an inner life in balance', were for him men of true wisdom, saints with and without religion; and although no names are given, the author in his own essays often refers to Novalis, Emerson, Nietzsche and Maeterlinck in such a context.[32] Ulrich was nevertheless convinced that any attempt to extract and codify the teachings of these masters was doomed to failure: once separated from their living, appropriate form, they could not hope to survive, any more than the delicate, iridescent body of a jellyfish lifted out of the water on to dry sand. The emotional atmosphere of their writing was as essential as the knowledge embodied within it, and in considering this apparent paradox Ulrich found himself caught in the opposition between the emotional and logical halves of his own being.

Logic versus emotion — was this the real reason for abandoning his mathematical research? What had been the original driving force behind his work? The quest for the just life; but what was that, and when had he expected to attain it? Ulrich suddenly realised that in his efforts to know before he would allow himself to feel, in his determination to exclude emotion from his life altogether, he had for years lived against himself. He longed for something unexpected to occur, to resolve the conflict between his own heart and mind. Six months had now gone by since his decision to take a year's leave from life, and what had he achieved? Apart from his meaningless participation in the campaign, nothing. He was waiting; waiting behind his own person, and his quiet despair, held back like water behind a dam, rose higher with every day that passed. It was the deepest crisis of his life, and he despised himself for the things he had left undone. All that remained was a kind of dogged persistence, a grim determination to hold on, in the hope that the future would bring a resolution of his problems.

In the meantime, the activities of the collateral campaign continued much as usual. In addition to officiating as Count Leinsdorf's secretary, Ulrich found himself called upon by various other people who hoped to profit from his influential position. Leo and Klementine Fischel thought it would be an excellent idea to revive Ulrich's former interest in their daughter Gerda and so rescue her from her unfortunate association with Hans Sepp. Ulrich's father, the eminent jurist, wrote him a long letter on the vexed question of defining a state of diminished responsibility; he was most anxious that in the revised version of the criminal law then being drafted his own interpretation should prevail over that of his rival Professor Schwung.[33] Moosbrugger remained in prison waiting to be re-examined by the psychiatrists. Between Walter and Clarisse, as between Diotima and Arnheim, tension was mounting, and in both cases Ulrich was somehow involved.

When the organising committee of the collateral campaign met once more, its members reported a dispiriting lack of progress in the choice of a guiding theme for the emperor's jubilee year. Nothing so far put forward had met with unconditional approval, and new ideas were scarce. Perhaps The Defence of the Realm, in other words, new armaments? suggested the general. This led to much debate, in the course of which it emerged that a demonstration against the campaign was being planned in German Nationalist circles, who regarded it as inimical to German interests. Finally Count Leinsdorf, exasperated by the endless stream of words around a vacuum, announced slowly and firmly: 'Something must be done!' Asked what he had in mind, he was unable to be more specific, but insisted again that something must indeed be done, with all the force at his command.[34]

Ulrich was present, but his mind was elsewhere; once again he was preoccupied with his own problems. On the morning after his sudden realisation that half a year's freedom had not brought him any nearer a solution of his difficulties, he had received a visit from Bonadea. Determined not to become emotionally entangled this time, Ulrich engaged her in conversation, during which she attempted, for reasons of her own, to interest him in the possibility of saving Moosbrugger from the death penalty. Ulrich evaded both this question and Bonadea's other obvious intentions, but eventually his mind began once more to brood over a highly unflattering mental picture of himself. What was left of him now? A man who imagined that for the sake of his inner freedom he could disregard most of the laws of society. Yet inner freedom consisted in knowing, in every human situation, why one need not be bound by it, and at the same time never finding anything by which one would wish to be bound! The ability to see both sides of every question was nothing more than moral ambivalence, a predisposition shared by most of his contemporaries. His relations with the world had become pale, shadowy and negative, based on a resounding inner emptiness.[35] Ulrich's anguish at this point may be linked with the older Törless briefly delineated towards the end of Musil's first novel; freedom from moral constraints, ironically predicted for Törless, had turned in Ulrich's life to ashes and bitter disillusionment.

On the day of the latest committee meeting, Ulrich's mind was moving in a more positive direction, for he was beginning to see that, to find salvation, he would somehow have to restore the balance in himself between intellect and emotion. It was only to be expected that a man like Ulrich should think of emotion in terms of love, but the remarkable fact was that with one significant exception all his sexual encounters had lacked real involvement on his part. His affair with Bonadea meant passion of a kind, resisted rather than sought by him, and in his dealings with Diotima, Clarisse and Gerda he was certainly aware of their feminine qualities. Yet only once, as a very young officer, had he truly been swept off his feet, by love for an older woman, the wife of a major in his regiment, and even then he soon felt compelled to escape from an impossible situation to a distant island. Lying alone between ocean, rocks and sky, he had thought of his beloved; but a greater feeling overwhelmed him, a sensation of oneness with the world, a falling away of cause and purpose, a clarity and intensity such as he had never known before, another condition of life.[36]

Now, much later, it was becoming clear to him that it was this 'other condition' that he must somehow recover if he were to regain true health. Should he therefore abandon the intellect? That was no solution, even had he been capable of doing so. As he sat in the meeting, half-aware of what was being said, yet intent on clarifying his own thoughts, it flashed into Ulrich's mind that the whole of creation, as well as his own nature, could be summed up in the concepts of power and love. He imagined his own being divided into two trees, each of which grew and flourished but was separated from the other. The tree of power contained the intellect, logic, a certain tendency to violence, a desire to attack and dominate life shown even in his youthful Napoleonic plans; but also his detachment from people and events, his sense of possibilities, his call for a new, dynamic morality, and all his other demands, whose purpose was nothing less than transformation of the real world. The other tree, the other half of his own life, was more difficult to perceive, since much of it lay in dreams and shadows. It held memories of an early, childlike relationship with the world, one of trust and openness, and since then, a longing for a state of 'love' not restricted to its usual sense, but as 'another condition' in which all things are changed and glow with intensity. His only attempt to develop this side of his being had been the affair of the major's wife, but since that time the tree of emotion had remained hidden from sight, and its continued existence was only to be inferred from the leaves and twigs drifting about on the surface. Perhaps the clearest indication of its survival lay in Ulrich's awareness that whatever was undertaken by his active half, he could not escape a sense of all his efforts being provisional and possibly worthless. His life had been divided into two tracks, one lying in the light of day, the other in darkness; therefore the feeling of stalemate that had oppressed him for so long must be due to the fact that he had never succeeded in uniting them with one another.[37]

At this point Ulrich recognised that what he had discovered held a far greater significance than merely its application to his own problems. Since the beginning of history two fundamental attitudes could be traced in the affairs of mankind. Clear, unambiguous thinking is common to logical argument and effective action in any sphere, and arises from the sheer necessity to survive. The dreamlike associations of the imagination, on the other hand, the 'unfettered logic of the soul', belong to art and religion, but also to affective relationships of every kind. Musil sets out his ideas with a plethora of examples and allusions, many of which apply to life at the end of the twentieth century as much as to the year 1913. Ulrich, following his ideas through to their application for mankind, came to the conclusion that if his life had any meaning at all, it must be to demonstrate how the two fundamental spheres of humanity were divided and opposed to each other within himself. And how were they to be reunited? He could not tell; he only knew that to undertake this task on his own lay beyond his powers.

Gradually Ulrich's mind returned to the other people in the room, still engaged as they were in fruitless discussion. He felt very lonely, with a premonition that he would soon be called upon, for the first time in his life, to make a real decision; all the same, he wanted to contribute what he could to the debate. Turning to Count Leinsdorf, Ulrich suggested that they devote themselves to the 'only worthwhile' enterprise: to draw up an inventory of the mind and spirit. 'What if the Day of Judgement were to fall in the year 1918, when the old spirit would be at an end, and a higher one about to begin?' He proposed that they establish, in the emperor's name, a World Secretariat for Exactitude and the Soul, since without such a body all other tasks would be insoluble. The reaction of the committee may be imagined. Oddly enough it was Count Leinsdorf himself, the aged aristocrat, who best understood Ulrich's intention; but after a while the meeting broke up without reaching agreement, as usual.

The next four chapters turn from words to action, being concerned with passion and the threat of violence. After a chapter recounting the climax of the affair between Rachel and Soliman, the author describes a tense scene between Walter and Clarisse, in which her obsession with Nietzsche, his jealousy of Ulrich, and her refusal to bear Walter's child all played a part. In Chapter 119, yet another sexual encounter, Ulrich was himself involved: Gerda visited him alone at his home, whereupon he reluctantly assumed that she wanted to be seduced; at the very last moment, however, she began to scream in a fit of hysteria. At this, Ulrich tried desperately to comfort and reassure the girl, but at the same time found himself tempted to stop her screams by smothering her with pillows, a reaction not so different from that of Moosbrugger to the prostitute he had murdered. Finally, the expected demonstration against the collateral campaign took place: Chapter 120 describes an outbreak of mass hysteria which Musil, like other European writers of his time, had had ample opportunity to observe. The crowd marched on Count Leinsdorf's palace, but to everyone's relief, violence was averted.

On his way home from this event (Chapter 122) Ulrich was accosted by a prostitute, gave her money to avoid further involvement and then, continuing alone, remembered Moosbrugger on the night of the murder. By a strange inversion he felt for a moment that even Moosbrugger's diseased compulsion to act might be preferable to his own endless inaction. 'All that has to be decided!' he said with unaccustomed force. At his home he found a telegram announcing the death of his father, but was also met by Clarisse, whereupon another extraordinary scene ensued. Ulrich spent the night writing letters and packing, since he had to leave for the funeral by an early train.[38] He sensed that he stood at a turning-point. In the hours before dawn, over-tired yet oddly awake, his mind was filled with fragments of his past life: places, melodies, smells, the insignificant and unregarded details of many years, now the only reality he had left. And, even more strangely, the light streaming from the lamps still alight wrought a subtle change between himself and his surroundings. The tension in his body and mind gave way; it was a loosening effect, as if a tightly knotted thread had come undone. The space around him and his relationship with it seemed to be altered, yet he did not know how or why: it was a different mode of being in him, and, therefore, in the things around him. All their proportions were somehow changed, and the emotion on which senses and intellect were normally based seemed itself to be in a state of flux.

After some time Ulrich realised that this was the 'other condition' he had last experienced long ago, when he had fled from his involvement with the major's wife to a lonely island. Was it a sign? He did not know. It passed, and soon he dressed and left for the station.

*   *   *

The publication in 1930 of Book I of *The Man without Qualities* was greeted by enthusiastic reviews in Germany, Austria and Czechoslovakia. The critics praised Musil's fearless analytical approach and acute observation, combined with his awareness of the deepest levels of the human psyche. The author himself, in a letter of 1931 to Johannes von Allesch, confessed his surprise that in Ulrich he had apparently created a representative figure of the age.[39] Yet Musil's personal situation remained as precarious as ever, and he was obliged once again to write miscellaneous articles and essays in order to earn money. In addition, his health deteriorated, and in February 1931 he had to undergo a gall-bladder operation.[40] As a result of the Depression, Musil's publisher, Rowohlt, was himself in financial difficulties, but was eventually persauded in September 1931 to extend his support for Musil for a further six months. Musil and his wife then moved to Berlin, partly because he was assured of help by a group of admirers led by Kurt Glaser, Director of the National Library of Art. A further reason for the move was his wish to gain greater objectivity by distancing himself from Vienna, with its echoes of the Austro-Hungarian empire, the world at the centre of the novel. In Berlin, he believed, he would be closer to contemporary events. Among his friends in the German capital were Wolfdietrich Rasch and the mathematician Richard von Mises.[41]

By 1933, however, Rowohlt began to insist on the publication of at least part of the second book of the novel. Experience of Musil's method of work led him to fear that by the time the whole book was ready, public interest would have evaporated; consequently the author reluctantly agreed to publish the first thirty-eight chapters in March 1933. This was also the month in which the new National Socialist regime set the Reichstag on fire and announced emergency decrees to abolish the Communist and Socialist parties in Germany. As an eye-witness of these events, Musil recorded them in Note-book 30 with comments on the Nazi leaders, the party's activities and the reactions of the public.[42] The Musil Society, consisting for the most part of Jews or opponents of the Nazi regime, was dissolved, and with it, Musil's financial support in Berlin. He returned, therefore, to Vienna, where he still had an apartment.

Since the first thirty-eight chapters of the second book complete that part of *The Man without Qualities* published in the author's lifetime, and since this is also the extent of the present English translation, this section of the work will be considered here; the remaining chapters of the book and the problems of completing the novel will be briefly discussed in Chapter 7.

The overall title of Book II is 'To the Millennium', with a subtitle in parentheses, 'The Criminals'. These two apparently contra-dictory titles make sense when understood in the light of Ulrich's reflections in Book I. He had come to the conclusion that while he had devoted much effort to developing his intellect, logical faculty and willpower, he had, by the same token, neglected the other fundamental area of human life, that of the emotions, imagination and religion. The function in the novel of Ulrich's sister Agathe, based partly, like some women characters in earlier works, on Musil's wife Martha, is to represent this 'other' aspect of human nature. She complements Ulrich as his *alter ego*, or, in Jungian terms, his *anima*. As we have seen, Musil had long been pre-occupied with the nature of the emotions and the almost unlimited areas of life in which they play a part. In Book I the irrational is represented by the figures of Clarisse, with her gradual descent into insanity, and by Moosbrugger the psychopath. In Book II the author concentrates on other aspects of the irrational, the areas of love and mysticism. Yet even here there is an element of anti-social behaviour culminating in at least one criminal act, as if to emphasise that those who live by emotion, even if outwardly normal, are not likely to conform to the norms of society. In this way Ulrich and Agathe, engaged in seeking the millennium, the realm of God here on earth, also become criminals by transgressing the law of the land.

When Ulrich arrived in the provincial town where he had grown up, he was met by his father's old servant, who informed him that his sister was already at the house. Ulrich had almost forgotten Agathe since the time when, following their mother's early death, they had been sent to different boarding schools. He recalled that she had married for love very young, that her equally young husband had tragically died within their first year of marriage, and that eventually she had married again. At the wedding, Ulrich had formed a less than favourable impression of her second husband, Hagauer, although (or because?) the latter was in every respect a worthy citizen and even a noted educationist. Ulrich guessed that his sister must now be about twenty-seven years old.

During the two weeks it took to clear up the family home after the funeral, Ulrich and Agathe came to learn a great deal about one another. Agathe had decided on the spur of the moment not to return to Hagauer, whom she had never loved and had only married to please her father. She was discontented not only with her marriage, but also with her entire previous life: lacking all self-confidence, she described herself as stupid and lazy, although her conversation was lively and intelligent and she possessed a remarkable memory. Her sense of worthlessness stemmed from her failure to achieve success either in her marriage, largely vitiated by her secret devotion to her first husband, or in any personal activity such as a career. She could not even find fulfilment in children; indeed it is curious that in a novel set at a time when all women were expected to marry and produce children, no children in fact appear. Of all Musil's central women characters, only the lady from Portugal is shown as being actively involved with her children. Whether this aspect of Musil's work is to be attributed to his particular outlook, or whether it has any connection with a general feeling of sterility underlying the age in which he lived, is a question yet to be clarified.

From the moment of their very first meeting Ulrich sensed an affinity between himself and Agathe as close as that between a pair of twins. Throughout the funeral period they spent much time simply talking to one another and discovering that in many things they thought alike, even though his approach was more intellectual, hers more emotional. He was reminded of the ancient belief in a masculine and a feminine principle at work in all human experience. The author underlines Ulrich's growing awareness of Agathe's significance by describing how she transformed the rigidly formal drawing room of the house to suit herself, arranging a luxuriant houseplant and an oriental rug around the divan where she lay reading by the light of a single lamp. Thus she created a personal domain filled with the untrammelled lines and patterns of the forest, of nature, symbols of the imagination in wilful contrast to the rational purity of the neo-classical drawing room.[43]

Agathe for her part was fascinated and delighted to discover that like herself, Ulrich was essentially a rebel against the traditional, authoritarian society represented by their father and by Hagauer. Many of Ulrich's sayings struck her as in some way familiar, as if she had thought the same without being able to put it into words. 'The virtues of society are vices of the saint' he quoted from Emerson, to illustrate his own outlook; but the impression such remarks made on Agathe was far deeper than he supposed.[44] One fundamental difference between the siblings soon showed itself. Ulrich's mind was filled with knowledge, yet he hesitated over the simplest action and at times longed desperately, like Törless in Musil's first novel, to become involved in events — senseless, even criminal events, just so long as they were real. Agathe on the other hand, lacking any intellectual training, yet endowed with the intuitive capacity to understand human beings, tended to embark impulsively on a course of action which she then defended with all the powers at her command. Thus she had not only resolved to break with Hagauer, but was also adamant that he should not inherit a penny of her father's money, even though for this purpose it was necessary to alter the will by means of a forged document. When Ulrich attempted to restrain her from imitating their father's handwriting, she retorted that he himself had described good and evil as relative concepts, saying that rigid rules were contrary to the innermost spirit of morality. Ulrich was obliged to admit that he had not only said all these things and more, but had aided and abetted his sister's plans by lying to Hagauer on the day of the funeral.[45]

Ulrich returned to Vienna, where Agathe soon joined him. After some time Hagauer realised that instead of returning home, she was seeking a divorce; the later course of this part of the novel, involving legal action, flight and possible incest, was left undecided at the time of the author's death. Meanwhile, the business of the collateral campaign continued as before, but Ulrich let it be known that he wished as soon as possible to withdraw from any further part in its affairs. It was clear to him that his experiment of living as a detached observer had failed, and he intended from then on to devote all his energies to a new experiment together with his sister, a way of life sustained by love, imagination and mysticism. Agathe and Ulrich lived quietly, avoiding social contacts whenever they could, talking together and reading the works of the great essayists and mystics. Musil knew Martin Buber's collection of personal accounts of mystical experiences, and some of these are quoted in the novel by Ulrich or Agathe.[46] They also spent a great deal of time discussing the nature of good and evil, the extent to which their interpretation of morality coincided with the world's understanding of this term, or the relationship between reason and imagination. Musil had already expressed many of these ideas in his great essays, beginning with the essay on the writer, but in the novel he puts his own theories to the test by placing them in the mouth of two fictional characters who then make a serious attempt to live by them. Ulrich and Agathe are explicitly described as not religious, as inhabitants of *this* world, not the one beyond; yet the author stresses that they too are capable of having visions, of knowing the life of the imagination and of dreams. Their life together is a quest, a voyage 'to the edge of the possible' which may not altogether avoid the dangers that this implies. It is a 'borderline case' of two people, both of whom have so far failed to find fulfilment, prepared to stake everything on an intense and desperate search for their own vision of the truth.[47]

The last chapters of this section of Book II underline the irrational aspect of human affairs from two further angles. Chapters 32 and 33 describe a visit to the mental hospital where Moosbrugger was awaiting a decision on his case. Clarisse, having made up her mind to save him from the death penalty, had somehow obtained permission to visit the hospital, with several others, including Ulrich. The author's detailed account of various categories of mental patients and their behaviour is based on his own visit in 1913 to the Municipal Mental Hospital of Rome, recorded in Notebook 7.[48] Finally, Chapters 34–8 describe the last reception of the collateral campaign attended by Ulrich, an occasion that might be summed up as a cacophony of opposing opinions, a deafening noise behind which, unheard and unseen, the spectre of war advances step by step.

*   *   *

The Man without Qualities is a great and complex work, but its central ideas are already developed in Musil's earlier writings: the theoretical basis of Book I rests largely on the essays published after the First World War, while the chief fictional characters also have a long pedigree. The author himself stated that the novel might well be approached via *Törless* and *The Visionaries*,[49] and it is possible to draw a straight line from Törless and Thomas/ Anselm to Ulrich, from Regine to Agathe, and from Josef to Hagauer. The links between Ulrich and Törless show how consistently Musil treated the same themes throughout his life as a writer. Both the schoolboy and the adult have problems in accepting current definitions of reality; both of them are certain that other kinds of reality are also valid, but have the greatest difficulty in convincing anyone else that this is so. Such an outlook is likely to have particular consequences. One is a preoccupation with identity: without knowing what is real, how can one know who one is? Moreover, a person who does not know who he is will find it almost impossible to take decisions and to act. This is a fundamental weakness in the boy Törless, and in the major novel Ulrich progressively withdraws from all situations requiring him to act, until it is left to Agathe to take any positive action at all, and then it is a criminal one. However, while it seems that Ulrich's preoccupation with words and ideas prevents him from taking outward action, conversely, words may impose order upon chaos, and this in itself may be counted as action of a different kind. Finally, as in the first novel, so in the later one the theme of the balance between reason and emotion, intellect and imagination touches upon every part of the whole. Perhaps one of the chief differences between the early and the later work lies in the much broader spectrum, the way in which the central themes are explored in a much greater number of figures and situations, and with a considerably enlarged range of reference. One theme developed at some depth in *The Man without Qualities*, showing Musil's increased social awareness after his war service, is that of responsibility or action in a social context. At first glance it seems to be connected only with the case of Moosbrugger, but reflection shows that many figures in the novel, and particularly Ulrich and Agathe, are examined in the light of responsibility for their actions or lack of action, while the hair-splitting and seemingly irrelevant legal dispute on this subject is held up to ridicule.

Some of the influences that helped to shape Musil's mind in youth are still at work in *The Man without Qualities*, even though the mature writer approaches them with greater objectivity. There can be little doubt that it was Nietzsche who had affected him — and indeed his whole generation — most profoundly. According to Karl Löwith, Nietzsche's significance as a critic of his age was as crucial as that of Rousseau in the eighteenth century, an opinion shared by Thomas Mann and other contemporaries.[50] In Musil's major novel, the most immediate connection with Nietzsche is seen in the figure of Clarisse, obsessed by the concept of genius. Ulrich had given her the works of Nietzsche as a wedding present, and she naïvely attempts thereafter to follow the master's teachings as a literal guide to life, even reciting them to her husband, to prove that he does not deserve a child. As time goes by, the discrepancy between what she regards as her mission and what she is able to achieve completely deranges her unstable personality. Ulrich himself has learnt by experience that in the twentieth century one cannot live by adherence to Nietzsche's brilliant flights of rhetoric; yet the very characteristics that make him a man without qualities, namely scepticism, logic, fearlessness and the passionate search for a new morality, recall Nietzsche's heroic attitudes and his eulogy of 'free spirits' (see Chapter 1). Nietzsche praises the 'immoralists' who understand, rather than condemn, and Ulrich seeks to understand the murderer Moosbrugger, with whom he feels an inexplicable affinity. It has been pointed out that in one of the earliest *M. le vivisecteur* sketches there appears 'a fool . . . a poet . . . the murderer of young women, who was hanged yesterday' showing that originally Musil saw the figures of the scientific researcher, the writer and the psychopath as one and the same man.[51]

The influence of Maeterlinck on the young Musil had been considerable, but in *The Man without Qualities* he distances himself from this writer, no doubt because he feels that those who constantly quote Maeterlinck on 'the soul' are the same as those who decry the value of exact and purposeful thinking in any sphere. As was shown in Chapter 5, Musil's essay on Spengler (1921) shows his alarm at this tendency, which threatened, especially in Germany, to undermine advances in modern thought by an inappropriate and dangerous emphasis on emotion in the public and political domain. In the novel it is Diotima and Arnheim, in a relationship largely sustained by their often unconscious borrowings from Maeterlinck, who evoke Musil's satire. Yet in discussing what he means by the 'other condition' Musil refers to the Belgian writer in a different tone, and it is significant that the unexpected and dramatic reunion of Ulrich with his sister, on the occasion of their father's funeral, is prefigured almost word for word in a Maeterlinck essay: 'One must learn to see in order to learn to love. "I had lived for more than twenty years at my sister's side, a friend . . . said to me, and I *saw her* for the first time at the moment of our mother's death." ' The association in Musil's mind between Agathe as the representative of the 'other condition' and the Belgian writer, is supported by a remark in Notebook 8, where he remembers the latter's view of women as being nearer the primitive state and therefore more perceptive and closer to nature. Describing Agathe reading Maeterlinck, he writes: 'She reads him not . . . as a poet, but as a messenger from her native land.'[52]

Musil's almost unique position as a writer of the twentieth century stems from the fact that by nature and training he was able to bridge the gulf between the 'two cultures', between science and the humanities. One thinker whose influence certainly endured throughout his life was Ernst Mach (see Chapter I). While Musil declined to accept all Mach's theories, he was full of praise for the methods developed by the physicist and philosopher: observation of facts, formulation of appropriate hypotheses, comparison and analogy, in other words, experimental methods; but Musil then suggested extending their use beyond the scientific field. One critic has seen here the basis of Musil's 'sense of possibilities', although it would probably be truer to say that knowledge of Mach reinforced a natural tendency of his mind.[53] Another element of Musil's thought that may be connected with this source is his view of space and time as relative, rather than absolute, values, enabling him to focus attention on the 'underlying, typical, even uncanny aspect of events' that he claimed as a central interest in *The Man without Qualities*.[54] The mathematical concepts of function theory, also emphasised by Mach, are similarly used by Musil to argue that natural phenomena and even human behaviour are often too complex to be explained simply in terms of causality. Thus he advocates the abolition of the rigid divisions and absolute characterisations of conventional morality and the criminal law, in favour of efforts to understand the social and psychological causes of behaviour, whether 'normal' or 'criminal'; in the novel these efforts are associated with the case of Moosbrugger.

Further connections between *The Man without Qualities* and the ideas of the age have been explored in a number of studies; space does not allow wider discussion here, but selected titles are listed in the bibliography. Since the publication of the new edition of the *Notebooks* and *Collected Works*, some facts have come to light regarding Musil's study of Emerson while writing the novel. As most of the relevant material is to be found among the papers left unpublished at the author's death, it will be discussed in the next chapter, together with the problem of the ending of the work.

Notes

1. GW I, p. 1943.
2. O. M. Fontana, 'Erinnerungen an Robert Musil', LWW, pp. 325–44, 337–41; also in GW II, pp. 939–42. *Die Literarische Welt*, 30 April 1926.
3. GW II, p. 940.
4. Cf. GW II, p. 1,374 in 'Der deutsche Mensch als Symptom'.
5. Musil, *Der Mann ohne Eigenschaften*, GW I, p. 37; *The Man without Qualities*, vol. 1, p. 72.
6. Ibid., p. 38; MwQ 1, p. 72. Cf. R. W. Emerson II, 'Circles', pp. 299–322, p. 305. See also Chapter 7.
7. GW I, p. 39; MwQ 1, p. 74.
8. Ibid., p. 19; ibid., p. 50.
9. Ibid., p. 17; ibid.; p. 49.
10. Ibid., pp. 45–7, 60; ibid., pp. 81–3, 97.
11. TB I, pp. 88–9 (not later than 1906).
12. GW I, p. 33; MwQ, p. 67.
13. Ibid., pp. 450–1; MwQ 2, pp. 180–1. Cf. GW II, pp. 1037–9, 'Der Anschluss an Deutschland' (see Chapter 4).
14. GW I, pp. 34–5; MwQ 1, pp. 68–9.
15. Ibid., p. 55; ibid., p. 92.
16. Chapters 2 and 5.
17. Chapter 7.
18. Chapter 14.
19. Chapter 18.
20. Chapters 3 and 19.
21. Chapters 21–3.
22. Chapters 23, 25–7.
23. Chapter 40.
24. TB I, p. 295, II, p. 173. Musil reviewed Rathenau's book *Zur Mechanik des Geistes* in 1913: GW II, pp. 1015–19, 1806. Rathenau was assassinated in 1922.
25. Chapters 51, 73 and 113.
26. Book I, Chapters 24, 42, 44, 71, Book II, Chapters 34–8. With regard to Musil's trenchant observation of the social scene, it may be noted that he thought highly of Stendhal, knew Dickens, and read Thackeray's *Vanity Fair* at least twice,

TB I, pp. 953, 988.

27. Chapters 85 and 100.
28. GW II, pp. 1027–8. See also Chapter 4.
29. Chapters 60–2.
30. Emerson VI, 'Culture', pp. 129–66, p. 165.
31. GW I, p. 250; MwQ 1, p. 315.
32. E.g. GW II, pp. 1049, 1337, 1451.
33. Chapters 74 and 111.
34. Chapter 116.
35. Chapter 63.
36. Chapter 32.
37. Chapter 116.
38. Chapter 123.
39. Letter to J. v. Allesch, 15 March 1931, LWW, pp. 301 ff., also in *Briefe* 1981, I, pp. 503–5.
40. Cf. TB I, p. 846; II, pp. 632–3, information from O. Rosenthal.
41. Berghahn, pp. 116–18; cf. W. Rasch, 'Erinnerung an Robert Musil', LWW, pp. 364–76.
42. TB I, pp. 722 ff.
43. GW I, p. 717; MwQ 3, pp. 71–72.
44. Ibid., p. 696; ibid., p. 46. Cf. Emerson II, 'Circles', pp. 299–322, pp. 316–17.
45. GW I and MwQ 3, Book II, Chapter 15; also p. 738; p. 95
46. M. Buber, ed., *Ekstatische Konfessionen*, 1909. Cf. 'Die Bedeutung der Formel "Mann ohne Eigenschaften" ', D. Goltschnigg, *Musil-Studien*, 4, 1973, pp. 325–47, pp. 339 ff.
47. GW I, p. 761; MwQ 3, pp. 121–2.
48. TB I, pp. 278–81.
49. Quoted by Martha Musil in a letter of 1 November 1947, LWW, p. 321.
50. I. Frenzel, *Friedrich Nietzsche in Selbstzeugnissen und Bilddokumenten*, 1966, pp. 136–8.
51. TB I, p. 7; cf. R. Olmi, 'La présence de Nietzsche', in *L'Herne*, 1981, pp. 153–66, pp. 155.
52. M. Maeterlinck, *Le Trésor des Humbles*, 1896, 'La Vie Profonde', pp. 253–82, p. 275. Emphasis in the original. Cf. TB I, p. 390.
53. H. Arvon, *Studien*, 1970, pp. 200–13.
54. GW II, p. 939.

7 VALIANT FOR TRUTH: *LEGACY IN MY LIFETIME,* SPEECHES AND THE FINAL CHAPTERS

Anyone reading the vast amount of material for Book II of *The Man without Qualities*, on which Musil was working from 1930 until his death in 1942, must be daunted by the sheer size of the task he had set himself. 'It is a great mistake to be bound by what one has written'[1] is a salutary maxim for any who ever set pen to paper, but although Musil regularly issued such challenges to himself, he seemed unable to live by them. The tensions of his life are revealed in letters to friends, some reprinted in LWW, many now available in the new edition of the *Notebooks* and the separate new edition of the *Letters* (1981). To Franz Blei, for example, he writes in May 1930 that he notes that Rowohlt has sent Blei the proofs of Book I of the novel. He hopes his friend has gained a favourable impression of the work, parts of which were written under severe pressure. Musil also mentions his immense relief at receiving some money after all from the foundation responsible for the Hauptmann prize, awarded to him the previous year: 'When I heard that the money would be paid, I slept three nights in succession, the first time in a long while . . .' Yet he is obsessed by the fear that, while correcting the proofs, he will come across 'some dreadful things'. Musil recognises that much of this anxiety is due to nervous exhaustion, after a year in which he has been greatly overburdened; no wonder that, much as he would like to read Blei's recent book, he cannot find the energy to do so. Finally he asks for suggestions regarding another project: Rowohlt has asked him to produce, after the appearance of *The Man without Qualities*, a greatly shortened version of the work, suitable for serial publication in a newspaper; Musil confesses that he has not the slightest idea how this adaptation might be done.[2] This project was in fact never carried out, although isolated portions of Book II were published in 1931–2.[3]

Such letters, read in conjunction with the multitude of working papers for completing the novel, create the impression of a lonely man engaged in a single-minded struggle to finish his *magnum opus* in spite of financial insecurity, variable health, the commercial considerations urged by his publisher, the deteriorating political situation, and ultimately, in spite of his own perfectionism. This impression is only partly true. The last seven notebooks, covering the period from 1928–41, reveal, as do the earlier ones, a man of the widest possible range of interests. Musil was, for example, a founder member of an Austrian society (established in 1936) to promote understanding of the cinema, and his interest in film as an art form is documented in the essay inspired by Béla Balázs's book on the subject.[4] He enjoyed films, particularly those of Fred Astaire and Ginger Rogers, and the cinema provided one of the few relaxations he allowed himself. Musil's reading during these years also continued to cover a wide field. Notebook 30, for instance, lists among books read: André Gide, Georges Bernanos, Goethe, Thomas Carlyle, Clare Sheridan, Gerhart Hauptmann; a life of Baudelaire, the speeches of Clemenceau, a life of Abraham Lincoln, and many others.

Notebook 30 runs from 1929 to 1941, and thus overlaps with all the other late notebooks. While it is not always easy to gain a clear picture of the sequence of events, the editor's detailed notes and the letters quoted provide much useful information. As regards daily life, Musil and his wife set great store by a regular afternoon walk, and some of their favourite walks are briefly described. Social evenings at the homes of friends or at a café, visits to the cinema or to art exhibitions, evoke detailed descriptions of the people or works encountered. Even a painful operation for a dental abscess is analysed as objectively as possible, with Musil noting not only his own psychological reactions as a patient, but also the personality of the dental surgeon, as well as external particulars.[5] In the years after Musil moved to Switzerland, especially while he and his wife lived in a garden apartment in Geneva, he devoted much space to descriptions of trees, colours, light at different times of day, and changing aspects of the mountains surrounding the city, showing his pleasure at being able to observe all these things at close range, while in other respects life often seemed hopeless.

Notebook 33 (1937–41) consists of a series of notes for a projected autobiography. In these entries Musil gives much background material concerning his parents and his own youth; other entries also illuminate the social and political changes he had experienced in his lifetime. In Notebook 32, begun in 1939, he then undertakes a detailed examination of the relationship between politics and *Geist* (mind and spirit); by this term he refers chiefly to literature and creative writers, but Machiavelli and the Greek philosophers are also discussed, in addition to predominantly contemporary examples. His aim is to analyse the political situation in Germany and Austria, the failure of democracy and the rise of National Socialism, comparing these countries with Italy, Great Britain and France as examples of democracy, and with the Soviet Union as a Communist state. In earlier essays, as we have seen, Musil had already attempted to analyse and understand political developments in Austria and Germany before and after the First World War (see Chapters 3, 4 and 5). Notebook 32 represents a further, more intense effort to find a connection between contemporary political developments and the personal characteristics both of politicians and the people, interpreted with the eye of the novelist. In carrying out this analysis Musil is also seeking to justify to himself his view of the function of the writer in such an age, as being no mere entertainer but, at the deepest level, an interpreter of life.[6] Notebooks 30, 31 and 34 contain other references to the National Socialist leaders, although their names are always disguised, for fear of the books falling into the wrong hands. Hitler is often referred to simply as H.; sometimes Musil uses the letter C, or the name 'Carlyle' to denote either Hitler or dictatorship in general.[7] On several occasions Musil alludes to *Young Törless*, and also to the military boarding school where he himself had been a pupil, and the two bullies, whose real names were Reising and Boineburg. In a reference to himself as a flea, 'a German flea', he comments: '. . . he has known today's dictators since their schooldays'.[8]

After leaving Berlin in 1933, Robert and Martha Musil returned to Vienna. For almost a year they possessed no regular source of income, but in 1934 Bruno Fürst and other friends established an Austrian fund to support Musil and the work on his great novel.[9] Life in Austria was still overshadowed by the defeat of 1918 and the collapse of the empire, together with the world-wide economic Depression. In Austrian politics, the Social Democratic party, National Socialist elements, and the ruling Christian Socialist party were all engaged in a struggle for power that was to pave the way for the *Anschluss*. Engelbert Dollfuss, Federal Chancellor since 1932, was assassinated in 1934. His successor, Kurt Schuschnigg, was eventually summoned by Hitler, early in 1938, to a meeting in Berchtesgaden that ended with the Austrian Chancellor being forced to make humiliating concessions. Four weeks later, on 12 March 1938, Hitler's troops marched into Austria.[10]

During all this time Musil continued to work in Austria, and his notebooks and letters provide an unrivalled inside view of the National Socialist period. Not the least poignant aspect of his personal record of the age is the list of names of friends or acquaintances emigrating to France, Switzerland or overseas — the uprooting of almost an entire generation of writers, musicians and intellectuals. While Hitler's concentration camps were being set up, while Thomas Mann, Hermann Broch, Arnold Schönberg, Albert Einstein and Kurt Lewin were, sooner or later, able to continue their work in the United States of America, and while Musil's friends Bruno Fürst and Otto Pächt emigrated to England and Ireland, Musil lived in Austria and then in Switzerland, and followed events closely. Nothing could be further from the truth than to see in Musil a writer in his ivory tower, without contact with the outside world. The notebooks prove that he was very much aware of all that was going on, and this may well be one of the major reasons why his progress on Book II of the novel was so painfully slow. His constant concern was to make the novel relevant to contemporary events as well as to the world of 1913; but the more life around him diverged from the 'normal', the more his original plans needed to be adapted to changed circumstances.

In December 1934 Musil was invited to address the Society of German Writers in Austria, whose Vice-President he had been for five years, on the occasion of the twentieth anniversary of its foundation; he chose the title 'The Writer in Our Time'.[11] The fundamental ideas expressed in this speech may be linked with his essays written during the 1920s; by 1934 however, the helplessness of Europe that he had diagnosed in 1922 had given way, in Germany at least, to a highly purposeful dictatorship, supported in Austria, so that it required courage for Musil to speak at all. In the first place, he outlines his view of the present political situation, of the nature of collectivism as a political philosophy and its consequences for the individual. This leads to consideration of ideas such as humanitarianism, freedom and objectivity, all of them essential to literature, all now regarded as obsolete. Despite the prevailing view, Musil emphasises the international and timeless character of true art, although he does not hesitate to point out that in the field of writing, many works claiming to be 'literature' do not deserve the name. Even more serious, in his view, is the fact that in Germany and Austria political considerations have infiltrated all areas of life and culture, so that many find it impossible to envisage any kind of activity free from politics: yet for literature to be created, such freedom is essential. At the end, in a reference that none of his hearers will have misunderstood, Musil recalls the burning of the great library of the ancient world, at Alexandria. Inimical attitudes translated into political power can destroy the spirit; nevertheless, he hopes, a time may come when a true European culture will once again arise.

This address was enthusiastically received, not only by the audience but also by the critics. Musil was invited to repeat it, to publish and translate the text; it seems, however, that he chose not to do so. Less successful was his appearance in Paris at the International Congress of Writers for the Defence of Culture, in July 1935.[12] Taking part in this were André Malraux, André Gide, Henri Barbusse, Heinrich Mann, E. M. Forster, Aldous Huxley and many others; the meeting was intended as a demonstration against Fascism, and a number of the participants were active Communists. Although one eyewitness commented later that Musil's very presence, since he came from Austria, showed great courage, his speech aroused anger: it followed the lines of his address in Vienna, but sounded to his audience in Paris too abstract and too impartial. The hall contained a number of refugee writers from Nazi Germany, and when Musil spoke of Bolshevism and Fascism in the same breath, they hissed. Musil was upset by what he regarded as a series of misunderstandings, especially after a critical report of his speech appeared. He prepared a reply, but before it could be printed, the journal concerned ceased publication.[13]

Once a year Musil used to read from his works in a College of Adult Education in Vienna. In November 1935 he was invited to visit Switzerland, where he gave a reading in Zürich, followed by two in Basel. Harry Goldschmidt, who had taken the initiative in arranging the tour, relates that he had asked Thomas Mann, then living in exile near Zürich, to introduce Musil. Mann declined this invitation, but was present, and afterwards the two writers sat next to one another, in friendly conversation.[14] This is the only occasion, so far as I know, when these two men, two of the greatest German writers of the twentieth century, actually met face to face. Musil's notebooks show that he read and appreciated Mann's works, but was jealous of his much greater success, compared with his own. In January 1933, Thomas Mann for his part took the initiative, together with his brother Heinrich and the poet Gottfried Benn, in arranging some financial support for Musil from the

German Academy of Writers. Later, in 1939, Mann also joined in an appeal, organised by Rudolf Olden under the auspices of the British PEN Club, which was intended to help Musil, possibly enabling him to move to England. Unfortunately, nothing came of it.[15]

During 1935 Musil's friends in Vienna became increasingly troubled by the seemingly hopeless situation in which he found himself. The more the external circumstances of his life deteriorated, the slower was his progress on Book II of the novel. Above all, beyond financial problems, was the feeling that he had lost contact with the reading public; this oppressed him and made him bitter. To alleviate this state of affairs, his friend Otto Pächt arranged to publish a selection of the many prose sketches that had previously appeared in newspapers. Musil called the small volume which came out at Christmas 1935 *Legacy in My Lifetime*,[16] a title explained with typical self-irony in the Preface (see also above, Chapter 3). The first group of sketches, under the heading 'Pictures', consists of short pieces, poems in prose, often with a touch of irony, all of them revealing unknown, uncanny aspects of the world. This is followed by 'Unkind Reflections', a number of pieces devoted to the discussion of cultural questions, apparently light-hearted in tone, but wickedly pointed in attack. The third section, 'Unreal Stories', contains four fables that illuminate, from different points of view, the vast area of character and morality. Finally Musil included a longer story, 'The Blackbird', originally published in 1928.

Musil's interest in animal psychology, already mentioned in Chapter 2 as an essential ingredient of *Young Törless*, is again evident in many of these sketches. A number of the original drafts for the pieces published in 1936 are found in the notebooks, and one of these, from the period of Musil's army service, contains a list of titles for a projected 'Book of Animals'.[17] A somewhat later sketch, first published in 1923, is 'Catastrophe with a Hare', a masterly piece barely two pages long, set on a holiday island, in which the author describes an encounter between a fox terrier and a young hare. The owner of the terrier is an elegantly-dressed lady, and the narrator himself seems to belong to a fairly exclusive group of holiday visitors. The dog, however, has caught a scent; his instincts take over, and he chases and kills the hare. In the space of a few seconds the human spectators, too, are caught up in primitive blood lust, like the members of the class torturing the boy Basini in

Törless; the island becomes a wild, lonely expanse, and not all the fashionable clothes in the world can disguise the humans' underlying nature.

At the beginning of the final story in the volume, the author explains that it is told by a man he calls A-Two to his old friend A-One; the reader is reminded of Musil's predilection for presenting opposite aspects of a character as two separate persons.[18] A-Two proceeds to relate a story in three parts, linked by the image of the blackbird. The central episode tells of a day during the war when, fighting in the mountains, he felt the elation of danger, seeing himself as a small feather in the plumage of the Bird of Death. Soon afterwards, during an air attack, he escaped death as if by a miracle; the certainty of death, combined with his miraculous deliverance, lifted him into a state of exaltation. The first and last episodes show A-Two withdrawing from normal life, firstly to follow the blackbird and its magic song wherever it may lead, even though this means abandoning his wife. In the final episode he returns to his family home after the death of his parents, and becomes more and more engrossed by rediscovered objects from his childhood. A blackbird flies into the room and claims to be his mother, and it seems that A-Two will stay there with her for ever. What is the significance of this story? The blackbird draws him away from normal life to 'another condition'; but how are we to interpret the ending? One might see it as a return to a state of innocence, or alternatively, as a regression into childhood, a culpable withdrawal from social responsibility. 'If I knew the meaning,' says A-Two, 'I should not need to tell you all this,' and we, too, are expected to choose our own interpretation.[19]

If 'The Blackbird' presents the reader with an enigma, the collection as a whole contains superb examples of Musil's art, and was warmly welcomed. But in the meantime, the constant pressure of work and worry exacerbated his tendency to high blood pressure. Being accustomed to systematic daily exercise, he hoped to counteract this condition by energetic swimming; unfortunately he overexerted himself and suffered a slight stroke early in 1936. From then on he had to take great care.

In March 1937 Musil gave a public address in Vienna under the title 'On Stupidity'. With great subtlety he examined the concept of stupidity from all angles, linking it with vanity, with violence and sadism, and distinguishing between simple-mindedness and the far more dangerous attitudes of those who, in the mass, perpetrate deeds that are forbidden to the individual. An address that, to the superficial listener, appeared as nothing but a harmless academic discourse, succeeded in identifying and condemning the beliefs and actions of the National Socialist leaders and their supporters in Austria as well as Germany. This speech evoked such a response that it had to be repeated the following week, and Musil's new publisher printed the text the same year.[20] In the summer of 1937, he arranged with Rowohlt to sell his publisher's rights in *The Man without Qualities* to the house of Bermann-Fischer, now established in Vienna. Bermann-Fischer was anxious to remind the reading public of Musil's existence, and the author agreed to publish a further twenty chapters of Book II; when these were already in proof, however, he decided to withdraw them and rework them up to the end of the novel. At this stage he was overtaken by events. Immediately after the *Anschluss* in March 1938, Bermann-Fischer fled to Sweden, and the Jewish-owned publishing house was placed under National Socialist management.[21] It became clear to Musil that his only hope of survival as a writer lay in emigration. His wife, being Jewish, was in immediate danger, and it was inconceivable that he should remain in Austria without her; but even if this possibility had entered his mind, a writer of his fearless honesty could not have continued to work under a Fascist dictatorship. In August 1938 Robert and Martha Musil left Vienna, ostensibly for a holiday, although their apartment, filled with books and manuscripts, was still held in his name. After a short stay at Edolo in Italy they moved to Zürich to begin their exile.

*   *   *

From 1938 until his death in 1942 Musil and his wife lived first in Zürich and then in Geneva. These were insecure and dangerous years for millions, especially, in many ways, for writers, dependent on publications and a readership in their own language. Stefan Zweig and Carl Zuckmayer, to name only two, have left in their memoirs moving accounts of the period. Switzerland was becoming crowded with refugees, many of them without sufficient funds for their needs. For more than a year Musil received regular support from the Swiss Committee for Aid to Refugee Intellectuals, and its secretary, Dr Nellie Seidl, helped him to find other contacts and sources of help. Another loyal friend was Pastor Robert Lejeune of Zürich, who was genuinely interested in Musil's work and did much to provide him with a minimum income. Other regular help came from an American couple, Henry Hall Church and his wife Barbara, whom Musil had known for some time; they lived in France and were engaged in literary activities of various kinds. Barbara Church produced the first French translation of two chapters of *The Man without Qualities*, in 1935.[22]

After moving to Switzerland, Musil continued to revise the twenty chapters of Book II withdrawn from publication at the proof stage; according to notes found in the working papers, he hoped to lighten their tone and redress the balance in them between theory and narrative action.[23] The emphasis in Book II as a whole lies on the 'other condition', on feeling and imagination rather than reason and intellect. On the one hand Musil wished to show Ulrich and Agathe living through the 'experiment' of a life that would allow full rein to feeling and imagination without being fettered and suppressed by external considerations, although he was sceptical about the long-term prospects of such an existence. On the other hand, as a truthful interpreter of human beings and contemporary society, he continued in Book II as in Book I to show typical personalities of the age in their interactions with one another and with the two central figures, and especially the extent to which the emotions played a vital but unacknowledged part in private and public life.

The closing session of the collateral campaign, described in Book II Chapters 34–8, presents an ironic, and at the same time tragic, picture of a fragmented culture on the point of collapse. The rich and the great, those who had influence as well as those who merely sought it, were all there, but in addition, there were representatives of the law, the army, high finance, politics, scholarship, old and new trends in art and literature, and many more. Even Ulrich and his sister had been persuaded to attend. There were arguments in plenty. General Stumm was puzzled by a dispute between a Marxist and a psychoanalyst as to whether human beings were conditioned more by economic or instinctive factors, the general being prepared to concede that the masses would always follow their instincts, while not accepting this in individuals. The Minister for War was deep in discussion with the poet Feuermaul, whose guiding principle appeared to be that man is essentially good, and that all problems may be solved by love. A recent study has shown that the figure of Feuermaul is a composite of all those contemporary writers who, in Musil's opinion, achieved easy and undeserved success, and therefore aroused in him both envy and scorn; the notebooks contain a number of references in this vein to Franz Werfel, Anton Wildgans, Leonhard Frank and others.[24] In the novel, Feuermaul represents an outlook which Musil had already castigated in his essay on Spengler and elsewhere, an attitude which, in rejecting the positivism of the nineteenth century, threw out with it reason and exact thinking of any kind, choosing to rely instead on intuition and emotion alone.

In Chapter 38 Feuermaul, the apostle of love and goodness, and Hans Sepp, the champion of purity and strong leadership, began by hurling insults at one another, but ended by making common cause in a resolution against war. When the general, greatly alarmed, asked Ulrich how this could have happened, the latter expounded his ideas on the ominous neglect of emotion as a force in human affairs, by those in positions of power. While matters pertaining to reason were kept in order, irrational feelings, central to all areas of public as well as private life, were not officially acknowledged to have any significance and were therefore allowed to run riot. From generation to generation the rubble of futile emotion had mounted higher and higher. So, Ulrich concluded wryly, the War Ministry could set its mind at rest: the next collective disaster would certainly take place.

At this point the author comments: 'Ulrich was prophesying the fate of Europe, though he did not realise it. Indeed, he was not concerned with real events at all; he was fighting for his own salvation.'[25] Before returning briefly to Ulrich and Agathe, we may perhaps recall that by the time this novel was written, the attitudes of a fictional Feuermaul or Hans Sepp, or an actual Werfel or Hitler, had been evolving for some decades. In the early years of the century, as we saw above, the protest of Musil's generation against the exclusive domination of the intellect had developed, in many writers and artists, into an expressionist concentration on the soul and the inner man. The writings of Freud, Jung and Adler further emphasised the significance of emotion; yet these discoveries had little impact on the thinking of political leaders or others in positions of public responsibility. In the same period, however, the centrifugal tendencies of the Austro-Hungarian empire, as well as the anti-liberal politics of the German empire established by Bismarck, had encouraged the growth of fervent nationalism. After the humiliating defeat of both Austria and Germany in 1918, exponents of this irrational nationalism such as

Spengler and Moeller van den Bruck found a ready audience. The politically unstable solution was exacerbated by the economic Depression. Yet even in 1931 Werfel, one of the foremost expressionist writers, declared in a speech that the ideal of a 'new man' was more important than the solution of social problems.[26] Thus Musil would have had little difficulty in finding models for his portrayal of contemporary attitudes. He was trying to alert his readers to the dangers of a situation in which society and its leaders behaved as they had always done, while irrational undercurrents weakened the ground beneath their feet. If in the last resort military interests gained the upper hand and war broke out, that, as he knew from personal experience, would be the most irrational reaction of all. In conversations with Wolfdietrich Rasch in Berlin, while Book II was being written, the author confirmed that at each stage of writing the novel he was thinking as much of the contemporary scene as of the fictional one, and in 1932 more than ever before he felt this to be justified.[27] Seen in this light, Musil's analysis of the prevailing ideologies in Book II, published in Germany at the moment the National Socialist government came to power, must be seen as an act of considerable courage.

Ulrich and his sister were resolved to have nothing more to do with the collateral campaign. The tranquillity of their life together was, however, disturbed by the arrival of an angry letter from Hagauer, Agathe's husband, accusing her in measured terms not only of failure in her duty towards himself, but of 'social failure' in every respect. This letter affected her deeply. The elation she had felt for weeks suddenly evaporated into a sober and profoundly depressing appraisal of herself, which made her long for reassurance; but Ulrich, as so often, did nothing but talk. In the end she could bear it no longer, rushed out of the house and thought of suicide (Book II, Chapters 29–31). In her distress, Agathe encountered a man who, unlike her brother, seemed anxious to help her survive what he recognised as a crisis. This kindly stranger was a teacher and university lecturer named Lindner, and in several of the unpublished chapters of Book II the author develops this figure and Agathe's relationship with him in some detail. Lindner saw himself as a responsible educationist. He regarded the whole of life as a moral challenge, quoting Goethe at every turn, though he was convinced that the moral decay of the age was at least partly due to an over-indulgence in cultural pursuits. He was religious, in the sense that he was *for* religion but not *in* it (Chapter 56). All these worthy characteristics are nevertheless set in perspective by his pedantry and the neurotic obsessions evident in his personal habits (Chapter 40). The author's unmerciful ridicule of both Lindner and Hagauer reveals a deep scepticism regarding the ability of professional pedagogues to bring about appropriate and lasting reforms in the educational system. Musil has little faith in the theoretical pronouncements of educators who show themselves in private life to be petty and unimaginative. Both these figures are contrasted with Agathe, the personification of feeling and imagination.[28]

Most of the other completed chapters of Book II describe the life of Ulrich and Agathe and their quest to understand and experience the 'other condition' of emotion and mysticism. As the days passed, a deep sympathy grew up between them, so that each sensed what the other was feeling, often without need of words. At times they moved as if in a dream, one of being separate and yet united. Everything within and outside them seemed to impel them towards physical union, yet as brother and sister they knew this was a boundary they must not cross.[29] On one occasion, when the tension became almost unbearable, Agathe decided to visit Lindner and ask his advice about her divorce. She was intrigued by her encounter with this representative of the outside world; but the recognition that Lindner was himself vulnerable in certain ways restored her own self-confidence.[30]

Chapters 45 and 46 recount the further adventures of Ulrich and Agathe. In poetic language the author describes the intensity of feeling between them; this relationship forms a climax for both these people who, although previously involved with partners of the opposite sex, had only briefly known real love. By a wordless agreement they continued to avoid physical fulfilment, not so much out of respect for convention as by their own choice. They began to be aware of their surroundings with a greater and deeper sensitivity. Light and shadows, colours and many other details acquired unaccustomed meaning, first at a window by the light of the moon, but also the following morning in an atmosphere of 'daylight mysticism'. In the spring sunshine they reclined in deckchairs in the garden, and Ulrich found a fascination quite new to him in seeing plants and flowers as if for the first time. Agathe read to him out of a book from his own library, a collection of the sayings of mystics through the ages; reflecting on these, Ulrich began to think about God and his own attitude to religion, something he had not done for a very long time.

From Chapter 47 onwards the reader has a choice of versions. In 1943, after Musil's death, his widow published a selection of material under the title *The Man without Qualities* Book III, stating in her introduction that the author had made important changes in some of the 1938 material before he died. It thus appears justified to regard these variant or improved chapters as preferred by the author to the earlier, 1938 proof versions; the completed variant chapters are Book II Chapters 47–52, printed on pp. 1204–39 of the 1978 edition.[31] These last six chapters continue the description of Ulrich's and Agathe's life together. Avoiding their former friends, they stayed at home, although occasionally venturing into the city, drifting with the crowd and content simply to be part of humanity. In Chapter 51 they began a discussion of emotion, arising out of their particular situation but extending to a review of the psychology of emotion in general. This discussion had originally occupied six chapters of the group withdrawn in 1938; indeed it was clearly one of the chief reasons for Musil's decision to delay publication, since this material was far too theoretical in tone for a novel. For the sake of completeness, however, these earlier psychology chapters are reprinted in the 1978 edition, and provide evidence of his continuing interest in psychology, especially in psychiatry and the work of the *Gestalt* school of psychologists he had known in Berlin.[32] With regard to Freud, Jung and Klages Musil's attitude was more reserved. He was prepared to give the psychoanalysts much credit for making it possible to discuss sexuality openly, yet he distrusted their methods of work. He himself had been trained in experimental psychology, but in his capacity as a writer regarded Freud and others like him as 'pseudo-writers', trespassing on his own territory. The extent to which Musil knew and made use of psychoanalytical theory has been discussed by Corino and others.[33]

In the course of surveying Musil's work we have seen that the concept of the 'other condition' had fascinated him from the beginning. Non-rational experience, as he called it in preference to 'irrational', is generally acknowledged to exist for artists and mystics, and for the rest of mankind perhaps in the sphere of love; but he was convinced that the 'civilised' nations should assign far greater importance to it than hitherto, in order to counterbalance their excessive concentration on the intellect. In *Törless* and his shorter fiction, in the two plays and the essays, Musil had pointed to the significance of feeling; in the major novel Ulrich had proposed a World Secretariat for Exactitude and the Soul before embarking on his own experimental relationship in love with Agathe. In 1922 Musil had been pleased to find in Kretschmer's *Medical Psychology* a definition of a personality like that of Ulrich, evenly divided between logical and non-rational ways of experiencing the world, together with a description of the nature of immediate non-logical experience corresponding to his own idea of the 'other condition'.[34] At about the same period Musil returned to the work of Emerson, making a number of excerpts from his essay 'Circles'; these quotations, some of which, with Musil's comments, were recently transcribed, may be seen to have played a vital role in the development of *The Man without Qualities*. They form part of a series of papers identified by the letter 'E' (= Emerson), all concerned with aspects of intuition and feeling. Several of them return to the theme of words or ideas as living or dead according to circumstances, one found again and again in *Törless* and the early notebooks; the Emerson quotations are annotated along similar lines. The 1978 edition of the major novel reprints drafts from the 1920s which describe tensions in the relationship of Ulrich and Agathe, and form the basis of their later conversations on feeling and mysticism; in these drafts Musil lists statements from Emerson's essay, together with related material from other sources. Many of the statements have to do with immediate, non-intellectual experience in religion, in love or simply in human communication:[35]

In common hours, society sits cold and statuesque. We all stand waiting, empty, — knowing, possibly, that we can be full, surrounded by mighty symbols which are not symbols to us, but prose and trivial toys. Then cometh the god, and converts the statues into fiery men, and by a flash of his eye burns up the veil which shrouded all things, and the meaning of the very furniture . . . is manifest. The facts which loomed so large in the fogs of yesterday . . . have strangely changed their proportions. All that we reckoned settled shakes and rattles . . .

Living words, living ideas breathe new life into human beings, break up old habits and fossilised attitudes and reveal the world in a new light. Musil adds: 'Did not Van Gogh paint . . . like this?'

The echoes of this passage and others like it reverberate wherever Musil speaks of creative thinking or the 'other condition', both in *The Man without Qualities* and, as already mentioned in Chapter 5, in *The Visionaries*.

Another aspect of the same essay that he finds attractive concerns the idea of 'dynamic morality'. Men and women who are truly alive and creative will not remain content with a society in which history simply repeats itself, but will seek to change it: 'Our culture is the predominance of an idea which draws after it . . . cities and institutions. Let us rise into another idea; they will disappear.'[36] Such challenging views appeal to Musil's experimental turn of mind, and find expression in Ulrich's concept of life as a hypothesis (see Chapter 6). Even in the notes, however, he is critical of Emerson's boundless optimism: the hopeful outlook of early nineteenth-century America cannot be transferred unaltered to a Europe suffering the traumatic consequences of the First World War. Nevertheless, he continues to have faith in the power of 'living thoughts', and a detailed working paper for Book II of the novel, compiled about ten years after the excerpts were made, still contains many of Emerson's ideas.[37]

The final completed chapter of the novel begins with a lyrical description of the garden, where sunshine, the young green of the leaves and the soundless drift of blossom from the trees combined to create an atmosphere of timeless peace. As on the day when Agathe read the words of the mystics, she felt again that she had reached the millennium: the world seemed to be transfigured. She summoned all her energies to make herself worthy of the divine presence, to experience in herself the meeting of inner and outer reality; yet after a while found that she could not maintain the necessary concentration. From here onwards the discussion of the nature of emotion continues until the end of the chapter. Ulrich had already stated (p. 1219) that there were two ways of experiencing reality. Long before, he had envisaged his own life irrevocably divided into two trees, the tree of power and the tree of emotion; his seeming inability to reunite the separated halves of his being had then caused him much distress. At the point he had now reached, he recognised a basic duality inherent in all human beings, with one side or the other predominating in two different kinds of people. Yet even in the same person, one side or the other might predominate at different times, with every emotion, in addition, possessing two contrasting aspects, one active and another better described as 'mood'. The difference between the active and the contemplative outlook is expressed in this part of the work by means of animal and plant imagery, while the two people still see the symbolic drift of blossom in their mind's eye: 'For in every human being is a hunger like that of a ravenous beast, and also no hunger, but something that, free from greed and fullness, ripens tenderly like grapes in the autumn sun.'[38] Thus the author reaffirms the connection already seen in *Törless* between animal imagery and the active, expressive side of life, but also that between plant imagery and the contemplative, perceptive side. Ulrich and Agathe conclude that human beings may experience life either in a state of serene contemplation or in purposeful activity, meaning not only external activity but also creative thought and expression of any kind. As we have seen, Musil often uses animal imagery for the unconscious sphere, but here this is widened to include the effects of the unconscious. After Ulrich's and Agathe's mystical experiences, the former speaks of the positive achievements due to animal instincts in man, to counterbalance the blame so often attached to them for their destructive effects. Action, creativity and progress in the worldly as in the artistic sphere are all ascribed to this source; thus the link between animal imagery and action or expression in Musil becomes explicit. Ulrich does not deny that animal instincts in man often lead to confusion and disorder, but insists that they produce as many positive results as negative ones, and that they should be accepted, not condemned.

Thus Ulrich recognises at last that his 'exact' and 'emotional' halves need not imply a schizophrenic split in his personality, but may coexist peacefully, side by side. This vision of a possible balance between the separated halves of his being is realised together with Agathe, when they accept that contemplation and activity both have a place in human life. He and she have both known periods of activity, but also others when the contemplative side was dominant: for a rounded personality, a balanced life, both are needed.

This was the last chapter Musil was able to complete. What of the ending? According to the plan described in 1926, the action of the novel was to consist of three related strands developed simultaneously: the wider area of the collateral campaign, the personal area, the relationship between Ulrich and Agathe, and the area of insanity and crime in which the figures of Clarisse and Moosbrugger were eventually to meet. Musil's wish to produce something of real value in the discussions of emotional experience between Ulrich and Agathe led him to devote much more time to this section than he had foreseen, but the broad outline of the original plan still held: 'Greatest problem: war / . . . The Collateral Campaign leads to war . . . / The religious element at the outbreak of war. Action, feeling and "other condition" coincide / . . . This . . . is the great Idea, now discovered / . . . U: It is the same as we have done: flight (from peace) . . . / U at the end: understand, work, believe . . . but does not avoid mobilisation. . . .'[39]

These notes date from 1936, but later ones largely confirm this outline as remaining valid, although the personal and religious element was afterwards given much more emphasis. It is this aspect which led Ernst Kaiser and Eithne Wilkins, the English translators of the novel, to suggest that Musil finally abandoned his plan to let the relationship between brother and sister founder after the incest episode, and to make Ulrich enlist for war. In their view, Musil had decided to end the novel with the tranquil beauty of the garden scene, in a 'mystical union' of Ulrich and Agathe far removed from the real world.[40] However, the author still referred to the incest episode in notes written in 1940, and in a letter of April 1942, a few days before his death, described the central theme of the last section of the novel as 'the story of an unusual passion, whose eventual collapse coincides with that of culture . . .'[41] The study by Kaiser and Wilkins illuminates Musil's writings from many different angles, but their underlying theme that his work should primarily be regarded as an attempt to heal his own neuroses has a limiting effect. A more recent study approaches Musil from a Marxist position, maintaining that his isolation and often bewildered response to political and social developments after 1918 spring from his own essentially bourgeois nature. Hartmut Böhme implies that had Musil been able to overcome the handicap of his background and upbringing, the result might have been very different: but in the circumstances he was precluded from working out a satisfactory ending for the novel. While this challenging analysis provides valuable insights, it runs the risk of surveying Musil's work ultimately from a one-sided and negative point of view.[42]

Notes for the final version of the last chapter (52) show that the author hoped until a late stage to round off all three strands of the plot, but eventually decided to 'finish off somehow' and summarise his last thoughts in an epilogue for Ulrich. Karl Dinklage traces the

development of his ideas by detailed study of the latest manuscripts, and quotes the plan for this epilogue dated January 1942:
the themes listed include the future role of China, the confronta-
tion between Russia and the West, Musil's renewed interest in
Dostoevsky, and Ulrich, during the Second World War, considering his own story and its meaning for the present and the future.
Finally, there are two areas given for further reading: Lao-tse, and
Sufism. The planned epilogue demonstrates that any attempt to
interpret Musil in his last years as mentally withdrawing from the
world has little foundation in fact.[43]

In Geneva, Musil and his wife lived for eighteen months in a
ground floor apartment situated in the garden of a home for
mothers and babies. He was fascinated by the seasonal changes in
the trees and bushes outside his study window; never before, in a
lifetime spent in city apartments of one sort or another, had he
enjoyed the opportunity to observe colours, shapes and the play of
light upon them in such detail and over such a continuous period of
time. He was also intrigued by the various cats to be seen in the
garden, whose personalities and relationships he recorded with
sardonic humour. A close neighbour and friend was the Austrian
sculptor Fritz Wotruba, also a refugee, who lived nearby with his
wife, and sometimes provided the Musil family's only social
contact for weeks at a time. The two men had known each other in
Vienna, and in 1939 Fritz Wotruba made a portrait bust of the
author. In April 1941 Musil became alarmed at the prospect of a
noisy family moving into the apartment above his own, and was
fortunately able to find a tiny house surrounded by a garden on the
southern edge of Geneva, where he and Martha were able to live by
themselves.

Musil's life in Switzerland was only made possible by the support
of a number of friends and charitable organisations. The help given
by Mr and Mrs Church, Pastor Lejeune and Dr Seidl has already
been mentioned. The musician Rolf Langnese, an exiled member of
the Viennese Musil Society, sent money from time to time, and in
1939 the American Guild for Cultural Freedom awarded him a
stipend for six months. The apartment in Vienna had to be given up
in 1942 and its contents transferred to a warehouse; this, however,
was destroyed by bombing in 1945. Apart from the unsuccessful
attempts to arrange Musil's emigration to Great Britain, the
possibility of emigration to the United States was seriously

considered, with the encouragement of Hermann Broch, Albert Einstein, Thomas Mann and others, but it came to nothing.[44] In the meantime Musil heard that *The Man without Qualities* had been placed on the list of books banned in Germany and Austria; although independent evidence for this edict can no longer be found, he was convinced of its truth, and the news depressed him profoundly. When he applied to the police authorities in Zürich for an extension of his residence permit, Musil pointed out that in the circumstances it was impossible for him to return home, since the prohibition meant that his only possible source of income, from sales of his work, was now denied him.[45]

For a long time Musil's attitude to organised religion had been reserved; his parents had been atheists, and he had seen no reason to become involved with the church. Yet during his last years, the kindness received from a few loyal friends made him think anew about the basis of true Christianity, and above all Pastor Lejeune by his steadfast friendship aroused Musil's interest in religious questions; he noted some ideas for a 'layman's theology'. Study of the mystics, in preparation for writing on the 'other condition' had confirmed his view, so often expressed in earlier works, that genuine action and genuine belief must be infused by emotion to have any worth. Near the end of his life he was more willing than before to see God in personal terms, as a creator who cares how human beings live, and despite the hopelessness of his own situation, wrote in Notebook 30: 'If God wishes to create and develop the spirit through human beings, if there is any value in the individual's spiritual contribution, then suicide is a mortal sin; it is disobedience towards God the creator.'[46]

Although Musil's health had not been particularly good, he had hoped to continue working for many years. On 15 April 1942 he spent the morning completing the final revision of Chapter 52 of Book II of the novel, and then told his wife he would take a bath before lunch. When she went to call him, he was lying dead on the floor, killed by a stroke. At first she thought he was teasing her, as he had sometimes done; but this time death was real. The funeral took place two days later in the crematorium at Geneva. Pastor Lejeune came from Zürich to give the address; in it he called Musil the greatest writer of our time in the German language. Another friend in exile, Harald Baruschke, singled out the three guiding principles of Musil's life and work: honesty, truthfulness and a refusal to compromise. There were only eight mourners. After the war Martha Musil scattered her husband's ashes in a wood near Geneva.

Soon after Musil's death, his widow collected subscriptions for a posthumous volume of *The Man without Qualities* which she published herself in 1943. She died in 1949, and her last years were devoted to making her husband's work more widely known; since her death these efforts have been carried on by many others. Musil's *Collected Works, Notebooks* and *Letters* have appeared in scholarly editions prepared by Adolf Frisé, and research centres for Musil studies have been established in Klagenfurt, Saarbrücken and Vienna. Ernst Kaiser and Eithne Wilkins established a Robert Musil Research Unit at the University of Reading, and their extensive collection of Musil papers is now kept in the university archives.

Honesty, truthfulness and a refusal to compromise are the qualities of a fighter. When Musil wrote: 'I am the man without qualities, but people do not realise it', he was doing himself an injustice.[47] Ulrich, the figure he created, is indeed a man totally detached from the life around him, who finds that analysis without commitment only produces sterility, and whose sincere but desperate attempts to remedy this situation are destined to fail. Musil, the writer, by contrast, was committed to interpreting for his readers the meaning of life. In his major essays and speeches he was able to make his points directly, and even here a telling image often illuminates hidden meanings. At times, especially when outward difficulties crowded in upon him, he was tempted to think it might have been wiser to avoid creative writing, to confine himself to theoretical work. But then he remembered that constructive irony was his special gift; by the incomparable use of this gift he became a modern moralist in the truest sense.[48] By analysing the modern world, its inherited and newly-created problems, together with its representative types, from high society, politics and other walks of life, he was following in the tradition of the medieval *Everyman* and of Bunyan's *Pilgrim's Progress*. Yet the world in which Musil grew up was no longer a world of coherent religious belief, particularly in the wake of the scientific advances of the nineteenth century and the widespread acceptance of Darwin's theory of evolution. Nietzsche had called for greater attention to the role of instincts in human life; Emerson had preached that within every human being, every society lie unsuspected possibilities for renewal and improvement. Musil's concern was always to strive for balance. Whether by virtue of the mathematical and philosophical elements in his early training or, at a deeper level, by the nature of his own mind, he constantly saw and presented ideas and persons as opposed pairs, striving for enlightenment through the union of opposites. Perception versus expression, contemplation versus action; or, to reverse the order, intellect versus feeling, exactitude versus imagination: 'Rationalism and mysticism are the two poles of the age.'[49] Because Musil experienced these dichotomies as real conflicts in his personal life, he was able to present them convincingly for his readers.

The empirical outlook of the scientist shows itself in Musil's central characters, in their refusal to take anything for granted. Törless, Ulrich and Agathe are not satisfied with ready-made answers to their questions: they must test the validity of any theory, however widely accepted, for their own situation, the alternative being that dangerous world of half-truths attacked so bitingly in the essay on Spengler and elsewhere. At the beginning of his writing career Musil had shown in the figure of Beineberg, and in the implied criticism of his and Törless's parents, that using the ideas and words of others uncritically as a basis for one's own existence might produce the most dangerous distortions. Later, at a time when truthfulness required real courage, Musil was not afraid to portray the age as he saw it.

Yet Musil the writer also knew that words possess magic properties known since ancient times. Poetry and creative writing interpret life.[50] So how are the factual and imaginative functions of language to be reconciled? Musil expresses this dilemma and a possible solution in the central passage of *The Man without Qualities*, where Ulrich becomes fully aware of the division between his active and contemplative halves, seeing them as two trees or two paths, one in daylight, the other in darkness. In Ulrich's thoughts the two realms of the rational and the non-rational are explicitly linked with the uses of language, logical and imaginative, and the connection between the two kinds of experience is shown in the example of a poetic image. The 'exact' side of life finds expression in logical discourse, the side of feeling in dreams and art; yet words may be used to fulfil both functions. They contain truth and untruth, and it is through the imaginative use of words, through imagery, that the two sides may be joined together:[51]

A metaphor contains a truth and a falsehood, which are inextricably interlocked in one's emotions. If one takes it as it is and forms it with one's senses, giving it the shape of reality, what arises is dreams and art; but between these two and real, full life there is a glass wall. If one takes it up with one's intellect, separating whatever does not accord from the elements that are in perfect concord, what arises is truth and knowledge, but emotion is destroyed. In the same way that certain species of bacteria split an organic substance into two parts, the human species by its way of living splits the original vital state of the metaphor into the solid matter of reality and truth, on the one hand, and, on the other, the glassy atmosphere of premonition, faith, and artefacts. It seems that between these two there is no third possibility. And yet how often something uncertain does come to a desired end if one only sets about it without taking too much thought!

It is this third possibility, the synthesis of the two opposing areas, which Ulrich seeks to discover and Agathe helps him to realise. Just as the same words may have two different but related functions, so, Musil seems to be saying, human beings may themselves achieve a synthesis between intellect and feeling, exactitude and imagination, action and contemplation, a true synthesis to serve as the foundation of a better life. Such a conception of mankind may seem Utopian, but every individual has the power to work for such a balance in himself. On a larger scale, a society which consciously aims for such a goal, unfettered by outworn systems or rigid ideologies, will indeed make it possible for men and women to fulfil their true potential.

Notes

1. GW I, p. 1911.
2. TB II, pp. 1184–5.
3. Ibid., p. 1188, note c.
4. GW II, pp. 1137–54, cf. Chapter V. Cf. TB I, p. 924; II, pp. 692, 810, 1245.
5. TB I, pp. 717–20.
6. Ibid., pp. 967, 969.
7. Ibid., pp. 740, 907; TB II, p. 537. A. Frisé suggests the name 'Carlyle' may refer to the latter's book *On Heroes, Hero-Worship and the Heroic in History*, 1841; elsewhere the letter C may stand for Caesar = Dictator.
8. TB I, pp. 893; 834, 914, 955.

9. TB II, p. 576.

10. Ibid., p. 750.

11. Musil, 'Der Dichter in dieser Zeit'; 'The Writer in Our Time', GW II, pp. 1243–56.

12. Musil, Speech in Paris: no title, 2 versions, GW II, pp. 1259–65 and 1266–9; 1829; cf. TB II, pp. 741–4.

13. Cf. TB II, pp. 742, 1255–61.

14. Ibid., pp. 580–3. Thomas Mann published an enthusiastic review of Book I, *The Man without Qualities*, in *Das Tagebuch*, 3 December 1932. Reprinted (in French) in *L'Herne*, 1981, pp. 271–2.

15. TB II, pp. 690–1, 786–7, 1275–80; TB I, p. 1003.

16. Musil, *Nachlass zu Lebzeiten*; Legacy in My Lifetime, GW II, pp. 473–562.

17. TB I, p. 340.

18. GW II, pp. 548–62.

19. The third episode of 'The Blackbird' may also be regarded as significant for a psychoanalytical interpretation of Musil, cf. K. Corino, *Musil-Studien* 4, 1973, pp. 123–235, pp. 209–10.

20. Musil, 'Über die Dummheit'; 'On Stupidity', GW II, pp. 1270–91.

21. Cf. TB II, pp. 751–4; GW I, pp. 2047 ff.

22. TB II, pp. 782–5, 561–2, 586–8.

23. GW I, p. 1910.

24. J. Strutz, *Politik und Literatur in Musils "Mann ohne Eigenschaften". Am Beispiel des Dichters Feuermaul*, 1981.

25. GW I, p. 1038; MwQ, vol. 3, p. 442.

26. F. Werfel, 'Realismus und Innerlichkeit', quoted by Strutz, p. 23.

27. W. Rasch, LWW, pp. 364–76, p. 375, quoted by Strutz, p. 14.

28. Cf. TB I, pp. 572–6.

29. GW I, pp. 1060–2.

30. Ibid., p. 1081.

31. Cf., ibid., pp. 2047 ff.

32. Cf. references in TB I and II to K. Lewin, M. Scheler, E. Bleuler, E. Kretschmer, E. v. Hornbostel, M. Wertheimer and W. Köhler. Musil's unpublished papers also contain excerpts from works by K. Lewin, K. Koffka, S. Freud (Mappe 6/1); E. Bleuler (Mappe 4/3); R. Wilhelm and C. G. Jung, P. Janet (Mappe 7/13) *et al.* Cf. also R. v. Heydebrand, 1966, E. v. Büren, 1970 and M.-L. Roth, 1972.

33. Cf. GW II, p. 832; TB I, p. 787 and *passim*; K. Corino 1973 and 1974; also Chapters 2 and 3.

34. E. Kretschmer 1922, pp. 65 ff. Cf. TB I, p. 785, II, p. 565.

35. Emerson II, 'Circles', pp. 299–322, p. 311. Quoted (in German) in Nachlass-Mappe 7/11/105 (= E2r). Cf. GW I, pp. 1640, 1645, 1648–51. See also H. Hickman, *Untersuchungen*, 1980, pp. 139–51, pp. 141–2, 145, 148.

36. Emerson, ibid., p. 302. Quoted by Musil, Mappe 7/11/109. Cf. Heydebrand for further discussion of Musil's links with Emerson and others.

37. GW I, pp. 1831–5, especially pp. 1834–5 (= Nachlass-Mappe 2/04/039). Date c. 1931.

38. GW I, p. 1236.

39. Ibid., p. 1902.

40. E. Kaiser and E. Wilkins, *Robert Musil. Eine Einführung in das Werk*, 1962, Chapters 7–10.

41. TB I, pp. 1010–11, II, pp. 789–90. Letter to H. H. Church, *Briefe*, 1981, I, pp. 1418–22.

42. H. Böhme, *Anomie und Entfremdung. Literatursoziologische Untersuchungen zu den Essays Robert Musils und seinem Roman "Der Mann ohne Eigenschaften"*, 1974, e.g. pp. 379–82.

43. K. Dinklage, 'Musils Definition des Mannes ohne Eigenschaften und das Ende seines Romans', *Studien*, 1970, pp. 112–23. Cf. GW I, p. 1943.

44. TB II, pp. 577–80; 1225–6. Cf. *Briefe* 1981.

45. Ibid., pp. 751–3; LWW, p. 317.

46. TB I, p. 811.

47. Nachlass-Mappe 2/4/120, quoted by Dinklage 1970, p. 112.

48. GW I, p. 1939; TB I, pp. 972–3.

49. TB I, p. 389.

50. GW II, p. 970.

51. GW I, pp. 581–2; MwQ, vol. 2, p. 339.

1880	Robert Musil born, November 6, in Klagenfurt, Carinthia, Austria, son of Alfred Musil, engineer, and his wife Hermine, née Bergauer. The father's family is Austrian, the mother's family Bohemian.
1881–91	The family moves first to Komotau (Bohemia), then to Steyr (Upper Austria). First years at school.
1891	Move to Brünn (Brno).
1892–4	Junior military boarding school at Eisenstadt.
1894–7	Senior military boarding school at Mährisch-Weisskirchen (Hranice).
1897	Military Academy of Technology, Vienna.
1898–1901	Gives up training as an army officer to study machine construction at the Technological University, Brünn, where his father is a professor.
1901	Degree in engineering.
1901–2	One year of military service in an infantry regiment stationed in Brünn. Meets Herma Dietz.
1902–3	Assistant at the Technological University, Stuttgart.
1903–8	Move to Berlin, to study philosophy, mathematics, physics and experimental psychology at the University of Berlin. Friendship with Johannes von Allesch and other *Gestalt* psychologists; many literary contacts.
1906	First novel published: *Young Törless*. Musil constructs a chromatometer for use in testing colour perception.
1907	Meets Martha Marcovaldi.
1908	Degree of Doctor of Philosophy. Thesis: *A Contribution to the Assessment of Mach's Theories*. Declines academic post offered at the University of Graz.
1908–10	Literary activities in Berlin. Death of Herma Dietz.
1910–14	Move to Vienna: librarian at the Technological University.
1911	Marriage to Martha Marcovaldi. Publication of *Unions*.

1911–14   Visits to Italy. Contributor to leading periodicals, including *Die Neue Rundschau*, Berlin. First essay published: 'Obscenity and Disease in Art'.

1914   Return to Berlin. Editorial post with *Die Neue Rundschau*.

1914–18   The First World War. Musil serves as an officer of the Austrian army.

1916–17   Editor of army newspaper. Award of various military decorations.

1917   Musil's father is elevated to the nobility; his title is hereditary.

1918   Musil returns to writing. Essay: 'The Mind of the Writer'.

1919–20   Clerical post in the Austrian Foreign Office.

1920   April–July: Berlin. Meets Ernst Rowohlt, who is to become his publisher in 1923.

1920–22   Educational consultant at the Austrian War Ministry.

1921–31   Theatre critic and writer, mainly in Vienna. Major essays. Work on the novel *The Man without Qualities*.

1921   Drama *The Visionaries* published.

1923–9   Vice-President and committee member of Society of German Writers in Austria; contact with Hugo von Hofmannsthal, President of the society.

1923   Awarded the Kleist Prize for *The Visionaries*. Farce *Vincent and the Mistress of Important Men* published, and performed in Berlin.

1924   Musil's parents die within months of one another. Literature Prize of the city of Vienna. Publication of *Three Women*.

1927   Memorial address for Rainer Maria Rilke in Berlin.

1929   Musil suffers a nervous breakdown and is treated by Dr Hugo Lukács. First performance of *The Visionaries* in Berlin in a shortened and unauthorised version, despite Musil's protest in a Berlin newspaper. Award of Gerhart Hauptmann Prize.

1930   *The Man without Qualities, Book I* is published and acclaimed by critics. Musil's financial position still precarious.

1931–3   Move to Berlin. Work on the novel continues. Establishment of a Musil Society in Berlin by Kurt Glaser and others, with the aim of supporting the author during his work on the novel.

1933   The National Socialist Party takes over the government of Germany. Publication of *The Man without Qualities, Book II*, Chapters 1–38. Musil returns to Vienna.

1934–8   After the dissolution of the Musil Society in Berlin, a similar society is formed by the author's friends in Vienna.

1935–6   Musil speaks at the International Congress of Writers for the Defence of Culture in Paris. Reading tour of Switzerland. Meeting with Thomas Mann. Publication of *Legacy in My Lifetime*. Musil suffers a stroke.

1938   The *Anschluss*: the German National Socialists invade Austria and take control of the government. Musil and his wife visit Italy, then emigrate to Zürich in Switzerland. Musil's works are placed on the list of books prohibited in Germany and Austria.

1939   Beginning of the Second World War. Musil moves to Geneva. Work on the novel continues despite financial insecurity and lack of contact with the reading public. Support from the Swiss Commitee for Aid to Refugee Intellectuals, Pastor Robert Lejeune, Barbara and Henry Hall Church, and others. Attempts to emigrate first to Great Britain, then to the United States are supported by Thomas Mann, Hermann Broch and Albert Einstein, but remain unsuccessful.

1942   Death of Robert Musil on April 15 in Geneva.

BIBLIOGRAPHY

Texts by Robert Musil

Gesammelte Werke, ed. Adolf Frisé, 2 vols., Reinbek, 1978. (GW I and II)
Tagebücher, ed. Adolf Frisé, 2 vols., Reinbek, 1976. (TB I and II)
Briefe 1901–1942, ed. Adolf Frisé with Murray G. Hall, 2 vols., Reinbek, 1981. (*Briefe* 1981)
Beitrag zur Beurteilung der Lehren Machs, Berlin, 1908. Reprint, ed. Adolf Frisé, Reinbek, 1980.
Nachlass. Unpublished papers in the National Library of Austria, Vienna.

English translations of Musil's works, all by Ernst Kaiser and Eithne Wilkins

The Man without Qualities, 3 vols., London, 1968. (MwQ)
Young Törless, London, 1971. (YT)
Tonka and other stories, London, 1965. Includes *Unions* and *Three Women*. (*Tonka* . . .)

Secondary Literature

a) *in German*

Anthologies

Robert Musil. Leben, Werk, Wirkung, ed. Karl Dinklage, Vienna-Reinbek, 1960. (LWW).
Robert Musil. Studien zu seinem Werk, ed. Karl Dinklage et al., Reinbek, 1970. (*Studien* 1970).
Musil-Studien, ed. Karl Dinklage and Karl Corino, Vol. 4: *Vom Törless zum Mann ohne Eigenschaften*, ed. Uwe Baur and Dietmar Goltschnigg, Munich- Salzburg, 1973.
Robert Musil. Untersuchungen, ed. Uwe Baur and Elisabeth Castex, Königstein, 1980.
Sprachästhetische Sinnvermittlung (1980), ed. Dieter Farda and Ulrich Karthaus, Frankfurt a/M-Berne, 1982.

ARVON, Henri	'Robert Musil und der Positivismus', *Studien* 1970, pp. 200–13.
BAUR, Uwe	'Zeit- und Gesellschaftskritik in Robert Musils Roman "Die Verwirrungen des Zöglings Törless" ', *Musil-Studien* 4, 1973, pp. 19–45.
BERGHAHN, Wilfried	*Robert Musil in Selbstzeugnissen und Bilddokumenten*, rowohlts monographien, 81, Reinbek, 1969.
BOHME, Hartmut	*Anomie und Entfremdung. Literatursoziologische Untersuchungen zu den Essays Robert Musils und seinem Roman "Der Mann ohne Eigenschaften"*, Skripten Literaturwissenschaft, 9, Kronberg, 1974.

BÜREN, Erhard von — *Zur Bedeutung der Psychologie im Werk Robert Musils*, Zürich and Freiburg, 1970.

CORINO, Karl — 'Törless ignotus', *Text und Kritik*, 21/22, December 1968, pp. 18–25.

—— — 'Ödipus oder Orest? Robert Musil und die Psychoanalyse', *Musil-Studien* 4, 1973, pp. 123–235.

—— — *Robert Musils "Vereinigungen". Studien zu einer historisch- kritischen Ausgabe, Musil-Studien 5*, Munich-Salzburg, 1974.

DINKLAGE, Karl — 'Musils Herkunft und Lebensgeschichte', LWW, pp. 187–264.

—— — 'Musils Definition des Mannes ohne Eigenschaften und das Ende seines Romans', *Studien 1970*, pp. 112–23.

FONTANA, Oskar M. — 'Erinnerungen an Robert Musil', LWW, pp. 325–44.

GOLTSCHNIGG, Dietmar — 'Die Bedeutung der Formel "Mann ohne Eigenschaften"', *Musil-Studien* 4, 1973, pp. 325–47.

HEYDEBRAND, Renate von — *Die Reflexionen Ulrichs in Robert Musils "Der Mann ohne Eigenschaften". Ihr Zusammenhang mit dem zeitgenössischen Denken*, Münster, 1966.

HICKMAN, Hannah — 'Der junge Musil und R. W. Emerson', *Musil-Forum* 6, 1980, 1, pp. 3–13.

—— — '"Lebende Gedanken" und Emerson *Kreise*', in: *Robert Musil, Untersuchungen*, 1980, pp. 139–51.

KAISER, Ernst and WILKINS, Eithne — *Robert Musil. Eine Einführung in das Werk*, Sprache und Literatur, 4, Stuttgart, 1962.

KARTHAUS, Ulrich — *Der Andere Zustand. Zeitstrukturen im Werke Robert Musils*, Philologische Studien und Quellen, 25, Berlin, 1965.

KERR, Alfred — 'Robert Musil', in: *Der Tag*, 21 December 1906, quoted in: Corino, 'Robert Musil und Alfred Kerr', *Studien 1970*, pp. 236–83.

MAGNOU, Jacqueline — 'Grenzfall und Identitätsproblem (oder Die Rolle der Psychopathologie) in der literarischen Praxis und Theorie Musils anhand der Novellen "Vereinigungen"', in: *Sprachästhetische Sinnvermittlung*, 1982.

MÜLLER, Gerd — *Dichtung und Wissenschaft. Studien zu Robert Musils Romanen "Die Verwirrungen des Zöglings Törless" und "Der Mann ohne Eigenschaften"*, Uppsala, 1971.

NAGANOWSKI, Egon — ' "Vinzenz" oder der Sinn des sinnvollen Unsinns', *Musil-Studien* 4, 1973, pp. 89–122.

OTTEN, Karl — 'Eindrücke von Robert Musil', LWW, pp. 357–63.

RASCH, Wolfdietrich — 'Erinnerung an Robert Musil', LWW, pp. 364–76.

RENIERS, Annie — 'Drei Briefe Robert Musils an Josef Nadler und ihr Hintergrund', *Studien 1970*, pp. 284–93.

—— — 'Törless: Freudsche Verwirrungen?', *Studien 1970*, pp. 26–39.

RENIERS-SERVRANCKX, Annie — *Robert Musil. Konstanz und Entwicklung von Themen, Motiven und Strukturen in den*

	Dichtungen, Abhandlungen zur Kunst- Musik- und Literaturwissenschaft, 110, Bonn, 1972.
ROTH, Marie-Louise	*Robert Musil. Ethik und Ästhetik*, Munich, 1972.
STRUTZ, Josef	*Politik und Literatur in Musils "Mann ohne Eigenschaften". Am Beispiel des Dichters Feuermaul*, Literatur in der Geschichte, Geschichte in der Literatur, 6, Königstein, 1981.
THÖMING, Jürgen C.	'Der optimistische Pessimismus eines passiven Aktivisten', *Studien* 1970, pp. 214–35.
ZELLER, Rosmarie	' "Die Versuchung der stillen Veronika". Eine Untersuchung ihres Bedeutungsaufbaus', in: *Sprachästhetische Sinnvermittlung*, 1982.

(b) *In English*

GOLDGAR, Harry	'The Square Root of Minus One; Freud and Robert Musil's "Törless" ', *Comparative Literature*, XVII, 1965, pp. 117–32.
HAMBURGER, Michael	*From Prophecy to Exorcism*, London, 1965.
JANIK, Allan and TOULMIN, Stephen	*Wittgenstein's Vienna*, London, 1973.
KAISER, Ernst and WILKINS, Eithne	'Empire in Time and Space', *Times Literary Supplement*, no. 2491, 28 October 1949, pp. 689–90.
PASCAL, Roy	*From Naturalism to Expressionism. German Literature and Society 1880–1918*, London, 1973.
STOPP, Elisabeth	'Musil's "Törless": Content and Form', *The Modern Language Review*, January 1968, 63, 1, pp. 94–118.
TURNER, David	'The Evasions of the Aesthete Törless', *Forum for Modern Language Studies*, X, 1 January 1974, pp. 19–44.
WILLIAMS, C. E.	*The Broken Eagle. The Politics of Austrian Literature from Empire to Anschluss*, London, 1974.

Further reading

	*Musil in Focus, Papers from a Centenary Symposium, ed. Lothar Huber and John J. White. Publications of the Institute of Germanic Studies, 28, London, 1982.
FURNESS, Raymond	*The Twentieth Century 1890–1945*, The Literary History of Germany, 8, London and New York, 1978.
LUFT, David S.	**Robert Musil and the Crisis of European Culture 1880–1942*, Berkeley, 1980.
PETERS, Frederick G.	**Robert Musil: Master of the Hovering Life. A Study of the Major Fiction*, New York, 1978.
PRAWER, S. S.	'Robert Musil and the "Uncanny" ', Oxford German Studies, 3, 1968, pp. 163–82.

* It is regretted that these books could not be used for this study, since they only became available at an advanced stage of the work.

(c) *In French*

Anthology

Robert Musil, Cahiers de l'Herne, 41, ed. Marie-Louise Roth and Roberto Olmi, Paris, 1981. (*L'Herne* 1981)

KREISKY, Bruno | 'A l'occasion de la Fondation de la Société Internationale Robert Musil, le 11 juin 1974, Vienne', *L'Herne* 1981, p. 293. Also in *Musil-Forum* 1-1975-1, pp. 67–8 (in German).

MANN, Thomas | 'A propos de l'Homme sans qualités', *L'Herne* 1981, pp. 271–2.

OLMI, Roberto | 'La présence de Nietzsche', *L'Herne* 1981, pp. 153–66,

ROTH, Marie-Louise | *Robert Musil: Les Oeuvres Pré-Posthumes, I Biographie et Écriture, II Genèse et Commentaire*, Paris, 1981.

Musil Research Centres have been established in Vienna and Klagenfurt, Austria, and in Saarbrücken, Federal Republic of Germany. At the University of Reading, the Kaiser/Wilkins collection of Musil papers is kept in the university archives.

Other Works

Translations are listed where available.

ALLESCH, G. J. | *Wege zur Kunstbetrachtung*, Dresden, 1921.

ANONYMOUS | *Everyman and other plays*, London, 1925.

BAHR, Hermann | *Zur Überwindung des Naturalismus*, ed. Gotthart Wunberg, Sprache und Literatur, 46, Stuttgart, 1968. 'Impressionismus', pp. 192–8.

BALÁZS, Béla | *Der sichtbare Mensch*, Vienna-Leipzig, 1924.

BARTÓK, Béla | *Duke Bluebeard's Castle*. First perf. Budapest, 1918.

BERGSON, Henri | *Essai sur les données immédiates de la conscience*, (Time and Free Will), Paris, 1889.

BINET, Alfred | *Les Altérations de la Personnalité*, Paris, 1892.

BISMARCK, Otto von | *Werke in Auswahl*, Centenary edition, 8 vols., ed. Gustav A. Rein *et al.*, 5, Stuttgart, 1973.

BORING, E. G. | *A History of Experimental Psychology*, New York, 1929.

BUBER, Martin (ed.) | *Ekstatische Konfessionen*, Jena, 1909.

BUNYAN, John | *Pilgrim's Progress*, ed. J. M. Hare, London, 1853.

CARLYLE, Thomas | *On Heroes, Hero-Worship, and the Heroic in History*, London, 1904.

— | *The History of Friedrich II of Prussia called Frederick the Great*, 3rd edn., London, 1859.

CARPENTER, Frederick I. | *Emerson Handbook*, New York, 1953.

DARWIN, Charles | *On the origin of species by means of natural selection, or The Preservation of favoured races in the struggle for life*, London, 1859.

DREVER, James | *A Dictionary of Psychology*, Penguin Reference Books, Harmondsworth, 1969.

EMERSON, Ralph Waldo — *Complete Works*, Centenary edition, ed. Edward W. Emerson, Boston, 1903. I *Nature;* II *Essays* I; III *Essays* II; IV *Representative Men*; VI *Conduct of Life*; *Essays I*. Folge, Leipzig, 1902.

— *Lebensführung*, trans. Heinrich Conrad, Leipzig, 1903.

FARRELL, R. B. — *Dictionary of German Synonyms*, Cambridge, 1962.

FECHNER, Gustav T. — *Elemente de Psychophysik*, Leipzig, 1860.

FRENZEL, Ivo — *Friedrich Nietzsche in Selbstzeugnissen und Bilddokumenten*, rowohlts monographien, 115, Reinbek, 1972.

FREUD, Sigmund — *Gesammelte Werke*, London, 1940–52; II–III *Die Traumdeutung* (quoted here from 2nd edn, 1909); V *Drei Abhandlungen zur Sexual-Theorie* (quoted from 1961 edition).

— *Complete Psychological Works,* standard edition, ed. J. Strachey *et al.*, 24 vols., London, 1953–74; IV–V *The Interpretation of Dreams*; VII *Three Essays on Sexuality.*

— and Josef BREUER — *Studies on Hysteria,* Harmondsworth, 1956.

GARTEN, H. F. — *Modern German Drama*, University Paperbacks, 103, London, 1964.

HARTMANN, Eduard von — *Philosophie des Unbewussten*, 6th edn., Berlin, 1874.

HELMHOLTZ, Hermann von — *Philosophische Aufsätze*, Leipzig, 1887.

HOFMANNSTHAL, Hugo von — *Gesammelte Werke*, ed. Herbert Steiner, Stockholm-Frankfurt a/M, 1945–59; *Prosa* II, 1951, 'Ein Brief', pp. 7–22.

— *Selected Prose*, trans. Mary Hottinger *et al.*, Bollingen Series XXXIII, New York, 1952. 'The Letter of Lord Chandos', pp. 129–41.

HOLBORN, Hajo — *A History of Modern Germany*, 3 vols., 3, *1840– 1945*, New York, 1965–9.

HUSSERL, Edmund — *Logische Untersuchungen*, Halle/Saale, 1900–1.

JANET, Pierre — *Les Obsessions et la Psychasthénie*, Paris, 1903.

KAFKA, Franz — *Betrachtung*, Leipzig, 1913.

— *Der Heizer*, Leipzig, 1913.

KANDINSKY, Wassily — *Über das Geistige in der Kunst. Insbesondere in der Malerei*, Munich, 1912.

— *On the Spiritual in Art*, trans. H. Rebay, New York, 1947.

KANT, Immanuel — *Kritik der reinen Vernunft*, Riga, 1781; *Critique of Pure Reason*, trans. Norman Kemp Smith, London, 1973.

KÖHLER, Wolfgang — *Die physischen Gestalten in Ruhe und im stationären Zustand*, Braunschweig, 1920.

KOHN, Hans — *The Mind of Germany*, London, 1961.

KRETSCHMER, Ernst — *Medizinische Psychologie* , Leipzig, 1922.

LÉVY-BRUHL, Lucien — *Les fonctions mentales dans les sociétés inférieures*, Paris, 1910.

MACH, Ernst — *Die Analyse der Empfindungen und das Verhältniss des Physischen zum Psychischen*, 2nd edn., Jena,

MACH, Ernst

1900; *The Analysis of Sensations and the Relation of the Physical to the Psychical*, trans. C. M. Williams, revised S. Waterlow, New York, 1959.

Erkenntnis und Irrtum, Leipzig, 1905; *Knowledge and Error*, trans. T. McCormack and P. Foulkes, Vienna Circle Collection, 3, Dordrecht, 1976.

—

Die Geschichte und die Wurzel des Satzes der Erhaltung der Arbeit, Prague, 1872; *The History and Root of the Principle of Conservation of Energy*, trans. Philip E. B. Jourdain, Chicago-London, 1911.

—

Populärwissenschaftliche Vorlesungen, 3rd edn., Leipzig, 1903.

—

Die Prinzipien der Wärmelehre, 2nd edn., Leipzig, 1900.

—

Die Mechanik in ihrer Entwicklung, 5th edn., Leipzig, 1904; *The Science of Mechanics: A Critical and Historical Account of Its Development*, trans. Thomas J. McCormack, La Salle, Illinois, 1960.

MAETERLINCK, Maurice

Le Trésor des Humbles, Paris, 1896.

—

La Sagesse et la Destinée, Paris, 1898.

MOELLER van den BRUCK, Arthur

Das Dritte Reich, Berlin, 1923.

MOELLER-BRUCK, Arthur

Germany's Third Empire, trans. E. O. Lorimer, London, 1934.

NADLER, Josef

Literaturgeschichte der deutschen Stämme und Landschaften, 3rd edn., Regensburg, 1932.

NIETZSCHE, Friedrich

Werke, ed. Karl Schlechta, 3 vols., Munich, 1965; I *Menschliches, Allzumenschliches*; I *Morgenröte*; II *Zur Genealogie der Moral*; II *Der Fall Wagner*; II *Götzen-Dämmerung*; *Complete Works*, ed. Oscar Levy, New York, 1974; 6 *Human, All-Too-Human* Part I, trans. Helen Zimmern; 8 *The Case of Wagner*, trans. Anthony M. Ludovici; 9 *The Dawn of Day*, trans. J. M. Kennedy; 13 *The Genealogy of Morals*, trans. Horace B. Samuel; *Twilight of the Idols and The Anti-Christ*, trans. R. J. Hollingdale, Penguin Classics L207, Harmondsworth, 1968.

NOVALIS, Friedrich von Hardenberg

Gesammelte Werke, ed. Hildburg and Werner Kohlschmidt, Gütersloh, 1967.

PLOTINUS

Enneaden, ed. and trans. H. F. Müller, Berlin, 1878–80.

RATHENAU, Walter

Zur Mechanik des Geistes, Berlin, 1913.

READ, Herbert

A Concise History of Modern Painting, The World of Art Library, London, 1969.

RICHARDS, Denis

An Illustrated History of Modern Europe, London, 1967.

RILKE, Rainer Maria

Sämtliche Werke, ed. Ernst Zinn *et al.*, Frankfurt a/M; IV, *Frühe Erzählungen und Dramen*, 1961; 'Turnstunde', pp. 601–9.

ROMANES, George J.

Mental Evolution in Animals, London, 1883, *Die geistige Entwicklung im Tierreich*, Leipzig, 1885.

RÖMER, Karl (ed.) — *Facts about Germany*, Gütersloh, 1979.

SCHILPP, Paul A. (ed.) — *Albert Einstein Philosopher-Scientist*, 2 vols., Library of Living Philosophers, New York, 1959.

SCHNITZLER, Arthur — *Gesammelte Werke*, Frankfurt a/M; *Die Dramatischen Werke*, I and II, 1962; I *Anatol*; I *Reigen*; *Anatol*, trans. Granville Barker, London, 1911 and 1933—4; *Merry-go-round* (Reigen), trans. F. and J. Marcus, London, 1953.

SHAW, George Bernard — *Saint Joan*, London, 1937.

— *Pygmalion*, London, 1937.

SOKEL, Walter H. — *The Writer in Extremis*, Stanford, 1959.

SORGE, Reinhard J. — *Der Bettler*, Berlin, 1912.

SPENGLER, Oswald — *Der Untergang des Abendlandes. Umrisse einer Morphologie der Weltgeschichte*, I, Vienna-Leipzig, 1918; *The Decline of the West*, trans. C. F. Atkinson, London, 1971.

— *Preussentum und Sozialismus*, Munich, 1919.

STRINDBERG, August — *The Dream Play*, in: *Plays*, trans. E. Björkman, London, 1912.

— *Till Damaskus (The Road to Damascus)*, A Trilogy, trans. Graham Rawson, London, 1939.

SWALES, Martin — *Arthur Schnitzler. A Critical Study*, Oxford, 1971.

THACKERAY, William M. — *Vanity Fair*, London, 1873.

TREVOR-ROPER, H. R. — *The Last Days of Hitler*, 5th edn., London, 1978.

— 'Thomas Carlyle's historical philosophy', *Times Literary Supplement*, no. 4082, 26 June 1981, pp. 731—4.

VIAU, J. — 'Egyptian Mythology', in: *Larousse Encyclopedia of Mythology*, London, 1962.

WALSER, Robert — *Geschichten*, Leipzig, 1914.

WEDEKIND, Frank — *Gesammelte Werke*, Munich, 1924; II *Frühlings Erwachen*; III *Erdgeist*; III *Die Büchse der Pandora*; *Five Tragedies of Sex (Spring's Awakening, Earth Spirit, Pandora's Box, Death and Devil, Castle Wetterstein)*, trans. B. Fawcett and Stephen Spender, London, 1952.

WEININGER, Otto — *Geschlecht und Charakter*, 18th edn., Vienna-Leipzig, 1919.

WHYTE, Lancelot L. — *The Unconscious before Freud*, Social Science Paperbacks, 19, London, 1967.

WIESE, Leopold von — *Soziologie des Volksbildungswesens*, Munich, 1921.

WITASEK, Stephan — 'Über willkürliche Vorstellungsverbindung', in: *Zeitschrift für Psychologie und Physiologie der Sinnesorgane*, 12, 1896, pp. 185—225.

WITTGENSTEIN, Ludwig — *Tractatus Logico-Philosophicus*, trans. D. F. Pears and B. F. McGuinness, London, 1974.

WORDSWORTH, William — *Poetical Works*, ed. Thomas Hutchinson, revised Ernest de Selincourt, London, 1971.

WUNDT, Wilhelm — *Beiträge zur Theorie des Sinneswahrnehmung*, Leipzig, 1862.

MUSIL INDEX

Robert Musil's Works and Other Writings

NAME INDEX